ENDANGERED

Also by Lamar Giles

Fake ID

ENDANGERED

LAMAR GILES

HARPER TEEN
An Imprint of HarperCollinsPublishers

J

HarperTeen is an imprint of HarperCollins Publishers.

Endangered
For information address HarperCollins Children's Books, a division of HarperCollins
Publishers, 195 Broadway, New York, NY 10007.
www.epicreads.com

Library of Congress Cataloging-in-Publication Data
Giles, L. R. (Lamar R.)
     Endangered / by Lamar Giles. — First edition.
          pages   cm
     Summary: "When Lauren (Panda), a teen photoblogger, gets involved in a deadly
game, she has to protect the classmates she despises"— Provided by publisher.
     ISBN 978-0-06-229756-3 (hardback)
     [1. Mystery and detective stories.   2. Photography—Fiction.   3. High schools—
Fiction.   4. Schools—Fiction.   5. Racially mixed people—Fiction.]   I. Title.
PZ7.G39235En   20152014028439
[Fic]—dc23   CIP
                                                                                         AC

Typography by Megan Stitt
15 16 17 18 19   PC/RRDH   10 9 8 7 6 5 4 3 2 1
❖
First Edition

For Clem and Britney, my original female protagonists

CHAPTER 1

I'VE HAUNTED MY SCHOOL FOR THE last three years.

I'm not a real ghost; this isn't one of *those* stories. At Portside High I'm a Hall Ghost. A person who's there, but isn't.

The front of the class is where I sit because despite ancient slacker lore, teachers pay more attention to the back. Between bells, I keep my head down and my books pressed tight to my chest, brushing by other students a half second before they think to look. If they catch a glimpse of me, it's most likely a blur of dark curls and winter-pale skin flitting in the corner of their eyes. Depending on who they are—or the sins they've committed—they might feel a chill.

Okay. Yes. I *sound* like a real ghost. But I promise I'm alive.

Jocks don't bump into me, and mean girls don't tease me, and teachers don't call on me because I don't want them to. Hiding in plain sight is a skill, one I've honed. My best friend, Ocie, calls me a Jedi ninja, which is maybe a mixed metaphor *and* redundant. But it's also kind of true.

I wasn't always like this. There were days during the first half of fresh-man year when I couldn't make it from the gym to social studies without running a gauntlet of leers and insults.

Time provided new targets to ridicule, fresh scandal—with some help.

Patience let me slip under the radar, then burrow deeper still. From there, it was easy to engineer my Hall Ghost persona. Now, in the midst of junior year, I've perfected it.

My name is Lauren Daniels. On the rare occasion one of my peers addresses me to my face, they tend to call me "Panda." Not always affec-tionately. My most popular alias—likely because no one knows it's *my* alias—is *Gray*, the name under which I provide a valuable, valuable public service. I make myself unnoticed by day because I need to be unsuspected by night.

It's what all the cool vigilantes do.

We're all something we don't know we are.

Take my dad, who doesn't know he's romantic because mostly he's not. Sometimes though, like on a random Wednesday or Thursday, he'll bring home a bunch of *Blachindas*—these German pastries filled with pumpkin; here in the States, we'd fill them with apples and call them turnovers. He tells Mom he really likes the taste. Which is true, he does. He skips the part about how difficult it is to get the foreign delicacy. He has to special order a dozen from this Old World bakery in town every time he wants to surprise her, and the extra effort on the part of the chefs isn't cheap.

What he also doesn't say is that she introduced him to the dessert on their first date eighteen years ago, outside of an army base in Stuttgart,

Germany. Every time she gives her account of that night—with her eyes glassy, like she's reliving the evening, not just talking about it—I feel I'm there, too. A time traveler spying on the prelude to my own conception. I love it, and them, and I gulp *Blachinda* even though I hate pumpkin just so I can hear more. While she talks, Dad's dark fingers and Mom's pale ones intertwine like yin and yang in the flesh. She blushes while he nods and eats. It's an incredible ritual to witness, Dad wooing Mom instinctively.

My parents are my Happy Place Thought as I lie prone in the bushes, pinecones and night-chilled rocks clawing at my stomach despite my layered clothing. A beetle slowly prances up my forearm toward my shooting hand. I brush it away as gently as I can and reestablish my aim. My target is stationary, in a parked car, one hundred yards away. A quick lens adjustment turns her face from fuzzy to sharp despite the darkness. An easy shot. Which I take.

Keachin Myer's head snaps forward, whiplash quick.

I shoot again.

Her head snaps back this time, she's laughing so hard. Odd, I was under the impression the soulless skank had no sense of humor.

I rub my tired eyes, and switch my Nikon D800 to display mode. I scroll through three days' worth of dull photos stored in the camera. Saturday: Keachin using her gold AmEx to treat her friends at Panera Bread. Sunday: Keachin dropping a hundred dollars to get her Lexus detailed. Today: Keachin—rendered in stark monochrome thanks to the night-vision adaptor fitted between my lens and my camera's body—belly-laughing at whatever joke the current guy trying to get in her pants is telling. Basically, Keachin being what everyone in Portside knows she is. Rich, spoiled, and popular. Nothing the world hasn't already gleaned about this girl. Nothing real.

I intend to fix that. If she ever gives me something good.

Keachin Myer is as clueless about what she is as anyone else. And being unfortunately named is not the part she's unaware of. If you let her tell it, her parents strapped her with such an ugly handle because, well, she couldn't be perfect, right? That sort of conceited admission would come off like a dare from most kids, opening them up to a barrage of teasing akin to machine-gun fire. No one challenges Keachin, though. Because she's beautiful.

That she knows, too.

She's girl tall, with a curve above her hips that seems custom-made for football players to grab and lift and spin her while she squeals and fake-pounds their chests. I swear, it happens at least three times a week. Her eyes are *blue* blue. Her hair is long and shines like black glass. She's got boobs that more than a few girls in the school may be describing to a cosmetic surgeon one day. *I need something slightly bigger than a C, but really round and perky, like, well—have you ever seen Keachin Myer?*

Here's the part that Keachin doesn't know about herself: she's a Raging Bitch Monster.

I'm sure she suspects it, but not in the way, say, a meth-head might suspect that smoking chemicals brewed in a dirty bucket isn't the best move, thus triggering thoughts of a lifestyle change. Keachin, as best I can tell, does not have such moments of clarity. To her and her pack, bitchiness seems to be something more altruistic. An act of kindness because, otherwise, peons might not know their place.

I've watched her do it for years. Not the way I watch my dad and his pastries. There's nothing about Keachin's judgy tirades that I like. I'm an observer by nature. I needed to know if she required more of my attention.

For a long time I thought not. Sometimes my peers are douche-nozzles. Period. There aren't enough hours in the day for me to nip that bud. But, there's mean, then there's what happened to Nina Appleton.

My fingers are shaking, and not from the cold. What Keachin did to that girl . . .

Breathe, Panda, breathe.

I suck in frigid air, so cold it feels like ice chips cartwheeling down my throat and into my lungs. I fight the shivers. Something rustles a nearby grove of trees, and I'm no longer breathing or shivering. I'm stuck mid-exhale, listening, or trying to. My suddenly elevated heart rate causes blood to roar in my ears. Of all my senses, unimpeded hearing is the one I want most in this moment because my eyes are useless under the moonless sky. Unlike my namesake, I don't have an enhanced sense of smell. I need my ears to confirm/deny what I fear is true.

That I'm not the only watcher in the dark tonight.

A twig snaps and I choke down a yelp. Screw this. I point my camera in the general direction of the commotion. The whole forest flares neon white and gray in the LCD display. I pan left to right over X-ray-like images of inanimate trees, and brush, and long dead leaves. Nothing capable of making any noise without assistance from the wind, or, um, an ax murderer.

My heart keeps pounding, I keep panning, and when I detect movement to my extreme left, I freeze.

There. Staring at me. A raccoon.

It scopes me like the trespasser I am, a silver animal shine in his eyes. I toss one of the pebbles that's been making my evening uncomfortable in his general direction. He jerks a foot to his right, though he was never in danger of being hit, then slinks off into the night, rustling more forest debris on his way.

I reposition, adjusting my lens for another clear view of Keachin in the car. The scene change is apparent.

She's no longer laughing her head off, or facing the proper direction. She's turned toward the rear of the car, propped on her knees and hunched, her head lightly bumping the vehicle's ceiling. The passenger seat she occupied is reclined so it hovers inches over the backseat. Also, the guy who drove Keachin to this secluded spot, his face in shadow, is in the seat with her. *Under* her. Directing her slow up and down motion with hands on hips, which has the car rocking to their rhythm, the geeky *My Other Car Is an X-wing* bumper sticker rising and falling by degrees. . . .

As a reflex, I reach for my shutter release to take the picture. My finger jabs the button with half the pressure required to trigger a shot. I pause, waiting for the perfect moment.

The guy's having a good time, he's thrashing his head in ecstasy, first to his left, toward the steering wheel. Then right, toward me. His face is visible in my display now.

Oh. My. God.

I recognize him. Anyone who goes to Portside High would.

He's been teaching there for years.

CHAPTER 2

NINA APPLETON, THE GIRL KEACHIN HUMILIATED, is not my friend. I don't have many of those.

I like her, though. Before last week, I would've said everyone in school liked her, too.

Nina has cerebral palsy and walks with the aid of forearm crutches. That's not what's most memorable about her or the reason she's so well liked. She's not the school's pity mascot for disabilities or anything like that. People like Nina because she's funny as hell.

We had algebra together once, and Mr. Ambrose worked this problem on the whiteboard. It was all this exponential, carry the such and such, divide it by whatever stuff. In the end, the answer was "69," and you could just about hear him curse under his breath as he finished writing it.

He spun around, saw the grins on all our faces, then stared Nina down.

"Go ahead," he said, anticipating the dirty joke he'd set up, "I walked right into it."

Nina's eyes bounced over the room—her audience—then she threw her hands up, exasperated. "I got nothing."

It was enough. Perfect timing. Expert inflection. Playing against the tension and buildup. The class roared. Even Ambrose smiled, appreciating how classy she'd been in the moment.

Class Clown three times running, she was quoted in the last yearbook as wanting to be the first disabled regular on *Saturday Night Live*. Personally, I think it's foolish to bet against her. As long as her spirit's not broken. An atrocity Keachin may have already committed.

That atrocity must be repaid.

Funny kids have a way of pissing off humorless people. When Nina, perhaps thinking herself brave, interrupted Keachin's reaming of a lowly freshman girl to say she saw Keachin's new red leather jacket on sale at Goodwill as part of a Santa outfit, it put her on the Fashion Tyrant's radar in the worst way.

I didn't see what happened in the bathroom after that, but I heard. Everyone heard.

Nina's crutches got "misplaced," and she was forced to crawl across the filthy floor, crying for help. No one heard her until class change, over an hour later. The vice principal had to carry her to the nurse's office while everyone watched.

When the administration questioned Nina about the assault (make no mistake, that's what it was—not a joke, or some "kids being kids" BS), Nina kept quiet in some misguided attempt to honor the code of the streets. Snitches end up in ditches, or something.

I don't blame her for that. I've been there.

But now I'm *here*, doing what Nina can't do for herself. I depress the shutter release, capturing Keachin's tryst with Coach Eric Bottin, gym teacher and fearless leader of our district champion football team.

I take more photos, fighting the unease of watching such a personal, and possibly illegal, *performance*. Of all the times I've done this—of all the secrets I've exposed—this is easily the most mind-blowing.

Get every detail, Panda.

Increasing my aperture, ramping down my shutter speed, and a bunch of other tiny in-the-moment adjustments are the difference between crisp images and blurry abstractions in such low light. I make all these changes across the mission control–style menus in my camera without looking. Like Petra Dobrev—a celebrity in the wildlife photography community and my idol—says you should.

"When you're shooting a pride in Africa," Petra says in her instructional photography DVD, *Lensing Wild Things*, "you want your eyes on those hungry lionesses, not your switches and buttons."

Then again, Petra also says, "If you're determined to shoot hungry lionesses, I recommend a camera trap. The plastic and metal are much less appetizing than flesh and bone."

A camera trap shoots without a photographer being in the vicinity. Great if you know where your prey will be ahead of time. My work rarely has that sort of predictability, so I have to know my camera the way a blind man knows Braille. I use it the same way I use my lungs. Inhale, adjust exposure. Exhale, shoot.

The car's bouncing motion increases with such verve, I hear the suspension squeaking. There's a final groan from the shock absorbers, and it's done; a panting Keachin hurls her sweaty self into the driver's seat as if Coach Bottin is suddenly too hot to touch. He twists and shifts oddly. After a second, I realize it's the motion I use when I tug on my jeans lying down.

Maybe they're too tired to perform whatever limber maneuver got them into opposite seats, because they open their respective doors and circle to the rear of the car, where Keachin adjusts her skirt and gives him a brief peck on the lips before reentering the vehicle for Coach Bottin to drive her home. I've got shots of it all. The hungry lioness never knows I'm there.

There's another piece to Petra's advice, though. A piece I forget. Or ignore because I'm giddy over the debauchery gold that's now stored on my SD card.

"When you're watching a beast, ensure no other beast is watching you. Lest you're caught unaware. The roles of 'hunter' and 'prey' can reverse with a breath and a pounce."

Coach Bottin and Keachin drive away, and I gather my equipment to make the hike back to my own car. Never realizing that I'm not alone, and I'm not talking about a raccoon.

We're all something we don't know we are. In that moment, I have no idea that I've gone from watcher . . . to watched.

CHAPTER 3

IT'S 10:37 P.M. WHEN I GET home, nearly an hour past my weekday curfew, and there's mud on my steering wheel.

I'm in my beat-up Chevy, parked in the driveway behind Mom's Honda and Dad's truck. I have four missed calls from my parents, and every light is on in our house, like they're looking for me behind the furniture. I peel off my dirty gloves, shimmy free of my dark zippered hoodie. Hitting the switch on the dome light, I check my face in my visor mirror for smudges, sweat, and/or blood. When you're sneaking through the woods, hopped up on adrenaline, you might not feel a stray branch or briar scrape you. With my complexion, the slightest scratch looks like I've been mauled.

I'm claw-mark free, so I take the time to mentally rehearse my story while I pop my trunk to stow some of my more nefarious tools. My rolled-up shooter's blanket goes into the duffel bag with my climbing gloves, grappling hook, night-vision goggles, lock picks, a couple of wigs, and a few other knickknacks relating to my, er, hobby.

I push all that to the corner of the trunk and gently dress the bag in a bunch of car junk—jumper cables, a rusty jack, half-full bottles of tire cleaner.

I slip my Nikon case into my school backpack. That goes inside with me. Always. Before I start the show, I remove the battery from my cell, drop it in my hip pocket.

When I enter the house, hobbled by my heavy bag, they descend on me immediately. Parental hyenas.

"*Wo warst du, Lauren?*" Mom says. I can tell she's irritated because she's speaking German. *Lauren, where have you been?*

"*Bei Ocie, lernen.*" *At Ocie's, studying.* I answer back in German because it seems to calm her. She likes the bond.

"Try again," Dad says. "Ocie's mom said you finished studying over three hours ago." He sounds every bit the army drill sergeant he used to be. Sometimes I let him believe his intimidation voice still works on me. Like now.

"Yes, that's true." I reach into my bag and produce a kettlebell-heavy copy of *The Complete Shakespeare*, purchased yesterday. "We're doing *Macbeth* in Lit Studies, but the school's copies are all scuzzy. I went to the bookstore to grab my own. When I got there, pumpkin spice lattes got the best of me and I lost track of time in the photography section. Sorry."

Mom switches to English, but her accent comes through, she's still half-irritated. "There is no point for you to have a phone if you do not intend to answer."

"Battery died and I forgot my charger." I hold up my dark, dead cell. "See?"

My parents maintain their wide-legged, crossed-arm stances, and exchange looks. Mom softens first, relieved I'm home and not stuck in some serial killer's basement. Dad maintains the attitude, but I know how to soothe him. I produce another book, also purchased yesterday. "Saw it in the bio section and thought of you."

One corner of his mouth ticks, though he recovers quickly. He suppresses his grin as I hand over the biography on the late, great Sam Cooke. Dad's got a whole playlist dedicated to Cooke's songs, having proclaimed the singer/songwriter a genius many times. I suspect Mr. Cooke's music has some significance to my parents grand back-in-the-day romance. Unlike the *Blachindas*, I haven't heard any backstory here and I don't want to.

Mom glances at the book and they exchange looks again, this time with the *ewwww* factor cranked up. If I have a new sibling nine months from today, it will only be a mild shock. I sneak upstairs to my room while they're distracted. To finish my work.

Nudging the door shut severs a column of hallway light, leaving me in darkness, where I'm most comfortable. I unpack my camera and power it up. The hi-def display flares, casting me in blue light before tonight's photos appear. Cycling through them, mentally flagging the best shots, I'm short of breath.

"This is real," I say, the depravity stuttering before me like a flip book.

Pushing a button on my desk lamp illuminates the soft marble eyes of two dozen panda bears. Or rather their glossy photos, plastered on the wall over my desk in a neat grid. I take my chair, plug my camera into my MacBook, and view the images in a larger aspect, each mouse click causing my pulse to snap. I've got more than forty usable shots, but I only need a few to tell the story. The imaginations of my many loyal followers will fill in any blanks.

Minimal touch-ups are needed. A slight hue adjustment makes the skin tones more natural—wouldn't want Keachin's flawless makeup to go unnoticed. Then, some shifts in the levels to decrease the shadows. Almost done. One final touch, a caption.

Keachin Myer takes phys ed way too seriously.

I publish the pictures to *Gray Scales*, my anonymous photoblog. The site's done up in all the shades of gray, except for the photos I reveal. I even have the blindfolded justice lady with the sword and the scales as my logo. When I post the Keachin/Coach photos, it triggers an alert on the cell phones, tablets, laptops, and PCs of my subscribers. The whole school.

All my various social media are arranged in separate windows on my desktop. Twitter, Facebook, Tumblr, and, of course, the comments on *Gray Scales*. I watch them refresh for the next hour as the scandal goes wide and the world sees what Keachin Myer really is.

When I pop the battery back into my cell, it immediately buzzes with an incoming text. I already know who it's from.

> **Ocie**: Oh Sugar Honey Iced Tea. Gray strikes again. Have u seen?
>
> **Me**: I don't pay attention to that trash. It's like high school soaps.
>
> **Ocie**: Today's episode is TV-MA. You've got 2 check the site. Keachin Myer and Coach Bottin. Emphs on AND
>
> **Me**: No way. I don't believe it.
>
> **Ocie**: Totes. It's like porn. Or prom.

The texts go on, Ocie having a gossip aneurism, me playing dumb. I'm still watching my monitor so I see the email the moment it comes in.

The sender's address is unfamiliar, **SecretAdm1r3r**. I might've written it off as penis-growth spam and doomed it to my junk folder if not for the subject.

A PANDA in her natural habitat.

I want to believe it's innocent, some marketing thing triggered by all the wildlife sites I visit. But the caps lock on "PANDA" makes me uneasy before I open my in-box. Part of me knows.

I preview the message, dropping my phone when I see the embedded photo.

It's me, skulking through the woods at the scene of Keachin's tryst. Another message arrives, same subject, but this one is a wide shot of me taking pictures of Coach Bottin's car. A third message/photo comes through, this one of me by my car as I lose my footing and plant both gloved hands in a huge mud puddle to keep from falling on my camera.

Me. Me. Me.

The pictures even come with a caption: *How do you get the color Gray? Throw a Panda in the blender and turn it on.*

Even though the sender's grasp of color theory is suspect, I get the point.

I'm busted.

CHAPTER 4

WHEN I STARTED THIS WHOLE GRAY business, the second person I exposed was Darius Ranson, a Portside baseball star who'd developed a pregame ritual known as "Target Practice." It went like this: Darius and his storm troopers snatch some frail/shy/defenseless underclassman and drive him to Kart Krazy, a run-down arcade and go-kart track. Also on the premises, batting cages.

The owner was a huge baseball fan who gives—*gave*—any Portside Pirate player the run of the place, which was all but deserted on weekdays. Darius and his teammates used one batting cage exclusively, having removed most of the safety netting to meet their needs. In that cage, they tied up their victim somewhere *behind* the pitching machine. If Portside's next-day opponent had a weak left fielder, the underclassman got positioned to the left. If the right field was vulnerable, he was placed to the right. Then, Darius and the rest would take turns popping line drives over the kid's head. If he was lucky.

Stupid. Illegal. Dangerous. All words applied. Inevitably, something went wrong. A concussion-and-broken-nose wrong. Claiming the injury happened innocently—intimidating the battered kid to back up a ridiculous story—Darius snaked out of any consequences and resumed Target Practice with updated safety regulations. New targets got an umpire's mask.

I did my thing, taking pictures of a Target Practice session from two hundred yards away with a telephoto lens. Had to climb a tree for those shots. Among my pictures were a few of Darius making a shady exchange with Kart Krazy's owner. Cash for a crumpled paper bag. It got me thinking about our star shortstop, and how he excelled beyond so much of the competition in the district. A couple of days later, I snuck into the team's locker room during a Saturday practice and picked Darius's lock. That's how I discovered his steroid stash.

A few quick snaps with my cell phone and I had a complete collage. *Gray Scales* was new then, so it took days instead of hours, but word spread.

Kart Krazy was shut down, the owner arrested for dealing dope and endangering minors. Strict drug-testing rules were implemented for all Portside High athletes. Darius got kicked off the team, then expelled thanks to zero tolerance. Harsh, maybe. But so was bouncing baseballs off other humans for fun.

Busting him was a flagship moment for my crusade. What I did made a difference.

I think of Darius as I click through the candid photos of me spying on Keachin and Coach Bottin. On to the next I go, not seeing myself, but the unsuspecting faces I've dragged into the light of day over the last three years, exposing their twisted moments.

Darius threatened to kill "the guy" who outed him. Surely the dozen others who've suffered his fate have similar vendettas. This is so, so bad.

There's always been a buzz around the school. Who is Gray? Whenever a new scandal debuts on the site, along come new theories. An angry friend or jilted ex. It *has* to be someone close to the exposed. Everyone watches too many cop shows.

It's never personal. Not after that first time. That's how I don't get caught.

Until now.

How could I *not* notice someone else with a camera out there? How many of *my* targets think the same thing?

I hit REPLY on the first email, type, and send a single-line message: *Who are you? What do you want?*

The mystery photographer won't reply. That's what I expect. But I'm wrong. I get a response almost immediately.

;)

That's all. An emoticon. I resist the urge to demand answers, realizing the stranger's response is an accurate one. He's enjoying my anxiety. Winky face.

Ocie keeps texting past midnight, but I don't have it in me to respond. I sit up all night, scared, barely noticing the Sam Cooke music coming through the walls from my parents' room. I wait for the secret photographer's pictures to go live somewhere, outing me as I've done to so many others. At dawn I'm still waiting. It never happens.

And that scares me more.

CHAPTER 5

BY 6:00 A.M. I ACCEPT THAT there will be no more messages from whoever-the-hell. I'm exhausted in the worst way possible. It's a tense sort of tired where the fatigue settles into my shoulders and lower back, knotting the muscles into borderline cramps. Staying in bed *sounds* great, except my mind won't switch off. I try to sleep with the same results as trying to fly. As my mom says, in her least attractive adaptations of English colloquialisms, it's "all retch and no vomit."

So, no sleep. I could play sick and stay home from school. But why? To spend the rest of the day doing exactly what I've done for the last seven hours, clicking refresh on my web browser, waiting to be exposed? No way. I've never missed school the day after a *Gray Scales* reveal. I'm not about to let some sneaky degenerate make me break tradition.

School it is. First, I need to put on my face.

Or pull it off. Depending on how you look at it.

Part of the reason I can do what I do as Gray is because I'm a Hall Ghost. It's a talent that I'm super proud of because at one time, I was the most infamous person in my grade.

Pulling off a complete notoriety reversal like that was difficult, but you'd be surprised how many books and websites there are that tell a person exactly how to disappear in a crowd. A combination of social engineering—which is like psychological manipulation, or "people hacking"—stealth, and misdirection goes a long way.

My dad's sister, Victoria, who comes around annually to semi-ruin Thanksgiving and Christmas, has this saying: "Pretty is natural, but real beauty takes work."

Usually, it's said directly to me, preceded by a frown, and followed up with a gleaming, optimistic smile. Like she's a doctor who's given me a scary diagnosis, but has high hopes about my treatment options: Shiseido skincare products and gift subscriptions to *Seventeen* magazine.

"You could look like a young Alicia Keys," she'll mention at some point in the evening, like I missed it the first few years she said it, "with some effort."

It's clear that Vicky thinks my actual look—an age-appropriate Lauren Daniels—is the epitome of disinterest and laziness. I don't doubt that her standard of beauty takes work. So does invisibility. Her disapproving, squinty-eyed glances are the best compliment she can give.

After a quick shower that does nothing to make me feel more alert, I put on the day's Jedi ninja uniform. Dark-blue cowl-necked sweater that falls to midthigh, some fitted Old Navy jeans, and crisp, clean Skechers (oddly, people tend to notice dirty shoes). In front of my lighted makeup mirror—last year's not-so-subtle gift from Victoria—I add final touches. Plain ChapStick instead of the unopened lip glosses Victoria included with the mirror. A bit of foundation to conceal the sleep luggage under my eyes and a patch of pimples on my forehead. And I pin my curls back, wrapping the excess in a bun. Finally, the tried-and-true classic that has served the world's greatest superhero for over seventy years, a pair of black-framed glasses to draw some attention from my unusual eye color (gray, ha!).

By themselves, these little tricks and cover-ups don't make me the chameleon I've become. There's much more technique to it than that, but it's the base. I'm proud of how good I've gotten at it.

Until I remember a certain set of photos could undo all my good work, and a corkscrew plants in the bottom of my stomach, turning and turning.

I grab my keys and bag, trod downstairs past the kitchen, grunting a good-bye to Mom and Dad, who are busy making sexy eyes at each other over orange juice.

"Hey there!" Mom calls.

I stop in the foyer, my hand resting on the doorknob. She rounds the corner, tugging her robe tighter, only I still get a glimpse of some black lacy thing before it disappears under her lapel. In spite of myself, my mood warms by a degree or two.

"Are you feeling all right this morning?" she asks.

"You're moving kinda slow, kiddo," Dad calls, joining Mom, his hand on the small of her back. "You catch a flu bug?"

Mom presses the back of her hand to my forehead. "She is not warm."

"I'm not sick," I say, not in the way they think. "I was just up late finishing a project that's due today."

Mom says, "You should not worry yourself over grades the way you do. You work hard. You will get what you deserve."

The corkscrew in my belly twists a half turn. "Gotta go."

I'm more like a Car Zombie than a Hall Ghost as I drive, every stoplight tempting a nap. I probably shouldn't be behind the wheel at all.

I pull up to the curb outside of Ocie's house. Drivers motor past so fast my car shakes. She lives on Claremont, a busy four lanes that are so noisy she can't always hear my signal. I wait for a traffic gap before I beep, nearly missing my window because the warm air blowing from my heater and a super-mellow song (thanks, iPod shuffle) have me dozing by the time the road sounds ebb. I jerk from the edge of slumber and quadruple tap my horn, a tone I imagine as *"Come, Ocie, come"* but probably sounds like *Honnk-Onk-Onk-Honnk* to everyone else.

While I wait, I turn off the heat and scroll to something random on my hip-hop playlist. The erratic bass line is sonic caffeine.

Then Ocie's there, hopping into the passenger seat dressed in a green sweater, matching knit cap with her hair flipped up on the sides, dark denim, and black/green high-tops. She's short, so the outfit makes her look like a trendy elf.

She says, "What up with you going off the grid last night? I texted fifty times."

"What normally happens to people at night? I fell asleep."

"Oh."

She's looking at her front door like she wants to escape my carriage of bitchiness. Okay, I was somewhat harsh. All-night anxiety will do that to you.

I change the subject. "Why are you all *Leprechaun in the Hood* this morning? Are you having an episode?"

A sidelong glance tells me this green-on-green thing isn't one of her quirky fixations where stuff has to be in a certain order, arranged in the most precise way ever. "Ocie" is short for OCD. Her real name is Mei Horton.

"No, Panda-Boo." She pulls her knee to her chest, displaying the emerald sole and swoosh on her shoes. "These Nikes I ordered came yesterday, so I put something together."

"Explain to me again how your freaky sneaker fetish and the resulting color coordination don't classify as obsessive or compulsive."

She pokes her lip out. "You and my dad are making me feel really bad."

"What did he say?"

"He called me 'Frogger' and told me to be careful crossing the street."

"Huh?"

"I don't know, the man speaks in riddles. For reals, what do you think? Be honest." She strikes poses in my periphery.

It's too flamboyant for my Hall Ghost tastes and may be better suited for St. Patrick's Day, but she's working it. "Kinda hot."

"I know. It's our black."

She's referring, of course, to our shared lineage. We are both mixed race, half African American, half something else. My mom is German. Her mom is Chinese. Whenever we agree on anything, "it's our black." Disagreements are "so other." For a moment, I'm energized by our familiar routine. I shift to drive and start into traffic.

Ocie says, "I hear Coach Bottin got fired last night."

"What?!" I hit the brakes so hard a car nearly rear-ends us. The driver slingshots around, laying on the horn. Everything I'd managed to forget in the twenty seconds of friend banter comes crashing back.

Driving again, I say, "No way. Too soon."

You knew there would be consequences, Panda. Not that fast, though.

"Now who cares about high school soaps? It's unconfirmed," Ocie says, like she's a reporter. "I've seen Facebook statuses about him losing his job. We know how accurate those can be. It could happen, though. Right?"

"Probably will."

"He might go to jail. What if we, like, see him on the news doing a perp walk or something?"

My mind's drifting back to the email I got last night. I only half hear Ocie, and the best image I can come up with is *me* doing the perp walk. In front of all my classmates as they hiss and boo like angry villagers sans torches and pitchforks. Headline: *Secret Teen Paparazzo's Identity Revealed.*

"Too awesome," Ocie gushes, obviously having no trouble conjuring a visual. "Don't you think?"

I want to agree, but all things considered, that crap is so other.

Paranoia ramps up as we near our destination. Sleep deprivation and the power of Ocie's suggestions make me superimpose phantom news vans in front of the school. Channel 9. And channel 13. And channel 20. The reporters forming a loose semicircle, each with their network's camera pointed at them, recording lead-in spots with the brick Portside High School marquee in the background. I turn into the student lot with my neck craned, eyes on the imagined commotion.

"Panda!"

I slam the brakes with both feet. My seat belt snaps tight against my chest, and Ocie plants her palms on the dash as if afraid hers will fail. Our momentum settles and we rock back into our seats. I make eye contact with the person I nearly pancaked.

Taylor Durham.

He's a foot from my bumper, tall and slim. His backpack's cinched tight over the shoulders of his denim jacket. His baseball cap is canted at an angle, the brim curved like a duck's beak. He thinks it looks cool, but he's twisted partially toward me and partially toward the sun so the hat creates this weird dark shadow that falls over his darker face. The effect makes him look almost as shady as he actually is.

Neither his skin nor the shadow is as dark as the look he gives me. I almost hit him with my car and he's angry. If he were anyone else, I'd say rightfully so.

Taylor slaps my hood with both hands. "Jesus, Lauren!" He points at himself: "Pedestrian," then points at the white lines bordering the cross-walk, "right of way."

I glare back. If he's waiting for an apology before he moves, then we're both going to be late for homeroom.

Someone behind me sounds a horn, a short belch. Taylor and I continue our stare down. The belch becomes an extended groan. I ease off my brake so my car lurches at him, like I mean to finish the job of turning him into roadkill.

Taylor sneers, continues across the asphalt shaking his head.

With the road clear, I drive into the student lot, all too aware of Ocie eyeballing me with a *Was that really called for?* expression she must have borrowed from my mom.

"Don't say a word," I warn.

"Wasn't even considering it."

I grab a parking space and say, "Thank you for not letting me hit him, though."

"You're welcome. Nice to know you're not completely merciless when it comes to Taylor Durham. It was a long time ago. I'm sure—"

"No, no, no," I cut her off, "I only mean my car's beat up enough. I don't need an extra dent."

But as I kill the engine, I'm thinking, for Taylor Durham, another dent would've been worth it.

Taylor was my first. But not like *that*.

I mean, it *could've* been that way between us. We almost went there.

I thought I loved him.

It was stupidity. When I say he was my first, I mean my first exposé. The one time it was personal. He's the reason I started *Gray Scales*.

What I caught him doing wasn't earth-shattering. More opportune than anything. We were still freshmen. I was on the indoor track team because I'd joined before he made school horrible for me, and I didn't want to quit after because I don't do quit. Taylor was a junior varsity basketball player suffering from a knee injury that kept him sidelined. As a member of the team, he still tried to contribute (which makes him sound more honorable than he is). He got consigned to a manager role, racking the balls at the end of practice, washing the uniforms.

Track practice wrapped up shortly after basketball practice, and I passed by the gym doors as Taylor, alone in his managerial duties, wheeled a big rolling laundry basket of sweaty team gear to the washroom. When I saw him, I said a silent prayer for something horrible to happen—athlete's foot on his face, maybe.

Taylor tripped.

Maybe it was his injured knee giving way. Maybe there was sweat on the floor. Maybe it was an angel answering my prayer. He went down, taking the basket with him, spilling soiled gear everywhere.

He did what everyone does when they fall: his head jerked around, scanning for witnesses. Reflex made me duck away from the porthole windows in the gym doors. A different reflex made me reach for the cell phone in my pocket. I peeked through the windows and saw him grabbing handfuls of clothing, stuffing it all back into the basket. With my phone, I snapped photo after photo.

To this day, I still don't know what made me do it. I just know that when I got home and uploaded the pics to my MacBook, the seed of revenge was already growing, sprouting fruit.

Most of the shots were mundane—a guy grabbing clothes off the floor. But there were a couple of shots where the clothing was very specific (jockstraps) and the expression on his face could be left up to interpretation. Most likely, he was disgusted, right? I mean, dirty jockstraps.

But a bit of added commentary, say a caption, could suggest something different. Something deviant.

Something special.

I waited until his knee healed and he was back in the starting lineup before I launched the site with that deceptive picture that looked like Taylor grabbing bunches of his teammates' nasty undergarments and sniffing them the way a perfume maker sniffs beakers in a lab.

The caption I settled on: *Most people prefer roses.*

Life at Portside got bad for Taylor after that. Almost as bad as he made things for me.

The difference was, he deserved it.

Him and everyone after.

CHAPTER 6

RUMORS ABOUT COACH BOTTIN'S JOB SPREAD. Everything from him being suspended (which is the most prevalent and likely rumor) to him hiring some underworld cleaner to change his identity so Keachin's father can't find him. Either way, the Keachin-Coach thing is all anyone talks about. Even the teachers seem distracted.

Of the parties involved in the scandal, I'm the only one who shows my face on school grounds. I'm okay during homeroom and Spanish 2, but by ten o'clock, I'm regretting it, barely able to keep my eyes open. All my teachers sound like the adults from Charlie Brown cartoons, *Whanh-whanh-wawwing* me into a near coma.

The good news: I'm so tired I stop feeling anxious about the elevated level of attention this story is getting or the person who stalked me while I exposed Keachin. In the midst of my sleep deprivation I think of how it's just my luck to get a "Secret Adm1r3r" who woos me with incriminating evidence. It makes me chuckle.

"Lauren," says Mr. Thompson, "is there something amusing about Reconstruction?"

I blink myself back into the moment, and see the kids in my history class stare-giggling. It's the first time they've noticed me this year. *You're slipping, Panda.*

"No, sir," I say. "There is *nothing* amusing about this lecture. At all."

The class cracks up. Inwardly, I groan, knowing they're taking it the wrong way. Them and Mr. Thompson.

He narrows his eyes. "Watch the sass, Miss Daniels."

I trudge through biology and lunch—where Ocie regales me with new rumors of Coach Bottin's whereabouts (he's seeking asylum in Cuba)—before I catch a second wind in my afternoon elective, Digital Photography.

I know, I know. Me being in this class when I do the things I do may *seem* counterintuitive, but it's another level of Hall Ghostiness. Obviously, Gray would be a student at Portside, likely enrolled in DP at some point. That's why it's perfect.

Everyone who's *ever* taken DP has been suspected as Gray, me included. The accusations are quickly debunked when comparing our DP classwork to Gray's portfolio.

Gray is a skilled photographer with superior equipment. The DP class takes pictures with cheap point-and-shoot loaner cameras. Quality photos are the exception, not the rule, in here. My technical know-how is enough to squeeze some decent snaps from the raggedy class equipment, but I make sure to turn in mediocre assignments, so as never to raise any eyebrows.

There's a sucky element to this charade, though. I don't like seeming less talented than I really am. I could be the class star, but my night work is more important than personal glory in a class where we're all getting As for effort. I've learned to live with the tiny bit of honesty DP allows me.

My parents and Ocie know I want to shoot wildlife for *Nat Geo* one day, and they're used to seeing some DSLR magazines or used Craigslist lenses lying around my room. Any questions that arise, I blame on the class. Hiding in plain sight, remember.

Digital Photography is a good mix of sophomores, juniors, and one senior. Some are here because it's a better deal than losing a finger in wood shop, others show passing interest and may someday use the skills they pick up to make the best family vacation albums ever.

Then there's Marcos Dahmer, who often smells of deep-fried hush puppies thanks to his part-time gig at the über-gross fast-food chain Count of Monte FISHto. There's a joke around the school: *Man's gotta eat. But not there.*

He brings his own equipment to class, an old Olympus, and pulls some great shots from it, mostly for the yearbook, which he's editing this year. If I took this class serious enough to be competitive, he'd be the kid to beat.

When I arrive, the room is buzzing over today's fresh scandal. A small huddle forms around one of the three communal computers. There are nine of us in DP, but I notice two extra faces in the room and know the kids hoping to access *Gray Scales* are going to be sorely disappointed.

I'm disappointed, too. Through my extracurricular activities it seems I've inadvertently engineered another run-in with Taylor.

He's hunched over a computer in the far corner of the room, typing and talking to a girl I've seen around. Rozlynn Petrie, beanpole tall and freshman awkward. Together they are part of the student tech support team, here to ruin everyone's fun.

I join my classmates around computer station #1. As I expect, frustrated sighs fill the air when they discover access to *Gray Scales* has been blocked.

Marcos Dahmer makes it into the room as the bell rings. The crowd moves to the second computer station, fighting the inevitable. But Marcos rolls his pink-tinted eyes, drops his bags, book, and camera on the floor next to his chair before laying his head on the desktop. He curls an arm around his face to block the light.

Alyssa Burrell, one of Marcos's fellow yearbook staffers (but not nearly as talented a photographer), calls to him, "Hey, Marcos, you wanna check *Gray Scales* with us?"

"Screw Gray," he says in a foghorn groan, sounding as worn as I feel. Apparently, I'm not the only one who had a late night.

His disgust/dismissal of Gray is nothing new. *Everyone* who's taken DP has been suspected of being Gray. That type of scrutiny has gone better for some than others. Marcos falls into the "other" category.

Alyssa shrugs off Marcos's dismissal and joins us at the #2 station. "Can you believe it?" she says to me. "I just shot Coach Pedophile and the football team for the yearbook. Thank God I wasn't alone with him. Who knows what might've happened."

A yawn scales my throat. Fatigue makes me cranky, and I think, *I know. He'd ignore you, like most boys do.*

Fact: Alyssa's frizzy blond curls, mud-brown eyes, and freckles don't exactly have the same draw as Keachin's almost-a-model looks. Sorry.

Ms. Marcella, our teacher, reclines in her chair, amused by sighs and teeth-sucking when it's discovered *Gray Scales* is blocked on this station, too.

I glance toward Taylor, who offers his seat to Rozlynn. She takes his place at the station, her spindly elbows protruding from the rolled-up sleeves of multiple baggy shirts like curtain rods from a mound of discarded drapes. She types commands on computer #3, completing the lockout, ensuring my classmates' thirst for sordid visuals goes unsated.

"It's done," she says, pushing away from the desk and unfolding herself from her chair. She stops just shy of her full height, as if the self-conscious slouch somehow makes her less noticeable than the additional inch a straightened spine provides. What if it does? Perhaps I'll work it into my Hall Ghost act.

Taylor checks her work, nods, and says, "Good job."

She half grins, a glint of a retainer visible between her parted lips. For a moment our gazes meet, her eyes as blue as tropical water when she's not casting them down, and I smile at her. She looks away, embarrassed. The term "painfully shy" doesn't seem strong enough for this girl. "Agonizingly shy" maybe? "Torturously shy"?

Ms. Marcella approaches Taylor and bashful Rozlynn with signed hall passes. "That will be all," Ms. Marcella says. "You can get back to your computer science class now, and thank Mr. Bradford for me."

Rozlynn flits from the room, but not before giving me a warm smile and a wave. Being a Hall Ghost doesn't mean I'm a complete unknown. I play shy, and the real shy kids tend to acknowledge each other, if only in passing. I wave back and she's gone.

Around me, my classmates remain in a mild uproar over being denied a dose of scandal. A white, cornea-staining explosion toward the front of the room quiets them.

Ms. Marcella fired a large flash unit—-a device that houses a 250-watt lamp bulb and looks something like a laser gun from a science-fiction movie—toward the underside of a white light reflector shaped like an umbrella. Combined with a tripod and light meter, the entire apparatus makes up the standard flash kit, used the world over by everyone from high-fashion photographers to the cheesy family portrait shooter at Sears.

It's wondrous to the noobs, who've never seen this kind of setup before. My eyes droop and I stifle another yawn. I've got this gear in the trunk of my car.

"Now," Ms. Marcella says, "if you all can manage to focus, let's talk studio lighting and using a flash to your advantage."

Taylor is still in the doorway, momentarily stunned by Ms. Marcella's flash trick like everybody else. He blinks my way, catching the remnants of the smile meant for Rozlynn, and he returns it. By the time my tired mind remembers I should be frowning/scowling/hissing at all things related to him, he turns the corner.

You really are slipping, Panda.

After DP the hallway crowds part and I see a face I've been looking for all day. Nina Appleton.

She navigates the rush with a gazelle-like bounce that's partially due to her crutches and partially due to her usual manic energy. The girl vibrates.

Today there's an extra bit of buzz to her, something that wasn't there the last few times I've seen her. Also present after a long hiatus, a smile on her face.

"Hey, Nina," I say as she passes.

She glances back over her shoulder, skids to a stop. "Hey, Panda!"

"How are you?"

"Stupendous!" she says, stretching the word. *STUUU-pendous!*

To pry further is risky. I already know why her day's so good. Justice has been served. Her wrong righted. I'm one of the Avengers.

"Uh, Panda?" Nina's staring at me. When did she start staring?

I shake off my exhaustion daze. "Sorry. I spaced."

"Don't be. I may need some of whatever you're smoking one day. It's nice to know you've got the hookup."

I snort a laugh. Good one, Nina.

She says, "Well, I gotta"—dramatic pause as she looks down, her face suddenly serious—"I was going to say 'run,' but we both know that ain't happening. How about 'crutch'? 'Gotta, crutch' sounds about right."

"Um. I don't—"

Her grin resurfaces, and she speaks with an exaggerated cowgirl accent. "Caught'cha off guard with the Old-Time Appleton Humor. Common affliction 'round these parts. Later, Panda!"

She's gone, but that Old-Time Appleton Humor gives me a surge that I coast on for the rest of the day.

By the time the final bell rings, I'm halfway to thinking the fifteen minutes of fame Keachin got from screwing a teacher is winding down, as all *Gray Scales* scandals eventually do. Ocie's got band practice, so I drive home alone.

In my room I open my MacBook and the messages from my Admirer are still on my screen. *How do you get the color Gray? Throw a Panda in the blender and turn it on.*

That corkscrew twists, but I will it still. I'm too tired to be stressed over someone playing stupid, childish games. I helped Keachin get what she deserves, and the glow on Nina's face proves that it was worth it. The pictures my Admirer sent don't show me screwing a teacher, or using drugs, or breaking into my neighbors' houses, or sniffing jockstraps, or any number of twisted things I've caught on camera. He caught me being exactly what I am: karma personified.

There's nothing I can do to change that, at least not while I can barely keep my eyes open. I collapse into what should be a peaceful slumber but isn't. I have a single protracted dream.

About a blender.

CHAPTER 7

THERE'S A PRESENCE IN MY ROOM.

A weight that can only be Dad's bulk presses on my mattress. "Lauren, wake up."

I grumble something about it not being morning yet, but he gets stern.

"I got some troubling news. We need to talk about you and Coach Bottin. Now."

Me and Coach Bottin?

I sit up, fully awake, knowing my Admirer's exposed me. Along with the horror comes a sense of relief. It's over. No more surprises.

Turning on my bedside lamp, I see something different from the parental fury I'm expecting. Dad's jaw is set, and he's having a hard time looking me in the eye. Mom's in the doorway, hugging herself like she's scared to come closer.

"Dad?"

He says, "We got a call about a thing involving your old gym teacher."

"A call from who?"

"Don Zeller gave me a buzz."

Okay. He and Dad work out at the same gym. His son, Zach, is in trig with me. So far, so blah. Please stay blah.

Dad asks, "The rumor is he's had some sort of inappropriate relationship with a senior girl. Do you know anything about it?"

Carefully I say, "Everyone knows. It's all over the school."

Dad's nodding before I finish. "Don said the teacher's been suspended. The cops are looking into it."

Zach Zeller's dad *is* a cop. This is not as blah as I'd like.

An unexpected twinge of guilt shoots through me. "Is Coach Bottin going to get locked up?"

"*Er sollte*," Mom says. *He should.*

Dad says, "I don't know. Don couldn't tell me much, but it seems the girl's been eighteen for a while now. I guess what happens to that sicko depends on when it all started. Or if there are others."

He lets the last part hang and finds sudden interest in my closet door, fixing his eyes there.

Mildly grossed out, I say, "You don't think me and him . . ."

"No, baby," says Mom, "we do not. But, we know he was your gym teacher last year, and we only want to know if you were ever approached, or if you saw him with any other girls?"

"No way. This is as much of a surprise to me as everyone else." Well, not *as* much.

My parents exchange looks that suggest a shared relief, an indication they won't press this awkward conversation further. My computer chimes. A new email.

Cutting my eyes to the screen, I see the subject, and nearly double over from the resulting stomach cramp. The message title: *PANDA's next shoot.*

Mom and Dad don't notice, too into the asking-our-daughter-if-she-got-molested-by-the-PE-teacher moment. I need them to leave. Now.

I play on my nervous stomach, rubbing it and saying, "Guys, I'm having some, um, woman issues. Do you mind if I lie down a little longer?"

Dad springs to his feet like I said I had some Ebola issues. "Right, yeah. Sorry to wake you."

"Do you need medicine?" Mom asks.

"No, some rest will be fine. Could you close the door when you leave?"

They comply, and I'm at my desk as soon as their footsteps recede down the hall. I open the message and there's an attachment. I click the JPG before I read, and stare at the image a moment. More than a moment. "What the hell?"

Considering the picture, a more appropriate question might have been "Is this hell?"

There are a couple of couches, and a coffee table, and a framed painting on the wall. It doesn't look much different from my family's living room. Except it's all on fire.

The floor, the seats, not just the painting, but the entire wall, consumed by flames wicking air from the top of the frame. It's like the fire is liquid poured into the room from a giant molten cup, and the photo's capturing the splash. How's that even possible?

I drag the photo to the side of my monitor, so I can read the message underneath.

Panda, I can imagine you had a rough day. Your world and passions threatened; you powerless to do anything about it. I hate feeling that way so I will end your agony. I'm not blowing the whistle. I've followed your work for some time and don't want to see you retire. Nice job on your most recent

*character assassination, by the way. Decent photos. Eric would probably call
them life changing.*

I should feel relief that he's a fan and doesn't plan to blow my cover, but
I'm stuck on two words.

Decent photos.

I did top-tier work, considering the conditions.

My eyes shift to that amazing fire photo, unable to fathom pulling off
such a shot, and immediately doubt my conviction. I read the rest.

How do you like MY work? I call the piece I sent you Dante. *Get it? It's
part of a series, one I want you to help me complete. Or maybe you prefer
skulking in the shadows. If you're ready to do something on the next level,
the assignment is simple. Top my photo. I understand if you're not into it. Or
just can't. Either way, think it over. I'll give you a week until I reconsider my
position on sharing your trade secrets. Happy shooting.*

There's no signature. Of course there's no signature.

Blackmailers don't sign their demands.

I click between that fiery photo and his message at least a dozen times.
With each iteration, my angry index finger threatens to crack the pearly
white surface of my Magic Mouse.

If I'm being honest, though, being blackmailed isn't what bothers me
most.

Top my photo. I understand if you're not into it. Or just can't.

I can write back, but I don't want to toss email taunts. Trading words is
a waste of my time. Besides, when it comes to words, you know how much
a picture's worth.

Game on.

CHAPTER 8

GAME . . . NOT SO ON.

It's been two days since my admirer dropped the gauntlet and I'm dry. I mean, I'm never short on things I can shoot. As Petra Dobrev says, "Life's the photo!" But I've got nothing that trumps that so-incredible-I-hate-it fire portrait. I wasted a bunch of time trying to figure the logistics of *that* shoot. Or, rather, debunk it.

At first I was all "This has to be Photoshopped," like those fuzzy pictures of Bigfoot or the super-obvious UFO fakers. I looked for telltale signs of overlays, and duplications, and masking. Like out-of-place shadows, odd blurring around the couch suggesting it was cut from some other image and blended into this one. Or a lack of charring on flaming items, which could mean he used a digital paintbrush styled to *look like* flames instead of *actual* flames. Anything that showed I was dealing with a *great digital artist* instead of a photographer with an envy-inducing eye for the most dramatic amateur shot I've ever seen. I found nothing.

Doesn't mean I'm wrong. He could be a *pro-level* digital artist. The kind who's so good he leaves zero clues.

Yeah, right.

The fire is real. So real I expect it to flicker and crackle every time I look at it. Never mind that the temperature had to be like a thousand degrees in the room where the picture was taken, maybe hot enough to melt the camera. How did he get that shot?! *Grrrr.*

"Why are you growling?"

I look across the lunch table. "What?"

Ocie's giving me her WTF squint, curling her lip for extra emphasis. "You were quiet and I thought we were doing the oh-my-God-it's-Thursday-why-can't-it-be-Friday silent dread thing. Then you went all feral and growled."

"Just clearing my throat."

"Like a dog?"

Her blue-on-blue ensemble becomes a tempting target for changing the subject. A Smurf joke is too easy. Besides, being a Hall Ghost works in crowds, not at our private, two-(wo)man table in the corner of the cafeteria. Really, I'm never invisible to her.

I make up something while molding my gross mashed potatoes into animal shapes with my fork. "There's this online photo competition. I need to come up with something to win it, and soon. The, uh, organizer's being a jerk about the whole thing. He's won it in the past, and thinks he's God's gift to eyeballs. He—he just irritates me. You know?"

After finishing my horrible version of a potato cheetah, I glance up, expecting Ocie to be infected with my indignation, even more squinty. Instead, she's giving me a portrait-perfect smile that I can never get her to duplicate when I catch her on camera. "What?"

She says, "Is he cute?"

Mind. Blown. "Really? Is that all you think about?"

"Yes. When I don't have to think about World War II and statistics and *Jane Eyre*. What else do we have to think about but school and boys?"

I slaughter the spud cheetah with a fork jab to the gut. "Maybe you should rethink that outfit. You look like the Blue Man Group."

Her curious grin falls away. Quietly, she says, "You're being so other right now."

Maybe I am. But, jeez, her questions.

An apology may be in order, but the thought is lost when we're suddenly a party of three. Taylor Durham stands in my periphery. It's like he just appeared. All that's missing is a puff of red smoke and the scent of sulfur.

What's this about? Has he built up some steam to confront me about nearly running him over the other day? He doesn't even look my way.

"Mei, hey," he says, eyes on Ocie, "thanks for the chem notes." He passes a binder covered in Ocie's doodles to her.

She hesitates, then accepts her returned property, eyes flicking from him to me. My nostrils flare, like I can smell her fear.

She says, "Uh, thanks."

"We still on for tomorrow night?" he asks.

Ocie shifts in her seat, visibly uncomfortable. "Sure. Text me when you're on your way."

She wants this exchange to end, as do I. Now, I have questions—a lot of questions—for her. Only, Taylor's still here. Why?

He says, "Did you two get the Letter?"

Ocie brightens, unable to resist the gossip despite the source. "Oh, God. Yes."

The Letter. I knew the moment Mom ripped open the envelope that, presumably, the school sent it to every student and parent. A Cover Your Ass mail campaign, if you will. Mom called me downstairs and read it aloud like it was some executive order from the president. For all the drama, it was vague, referring to an "incident of an inappropriate nature," while reassuring everyone that Portside High was a safe, educational environment where the faculty upholds the highest moral standards. No names were mentioned.

Taylor asks me, "Did you get one?"

He's so casual, like I didn't almost kill him with my car. His nice-guy ruse. I nod simply to hurry this along.

Redirecting his attention to Ocie, he says, "Has anyone seen Keachin since this blew up? Seems like it's getting serious."

"I heard she's in Alabama," Ocie says. "She's got an aunt there, the only person who'll take her in because she's shamed her family."

That's BS. I saw the light glowing in Keachin's bedroom when I rode past her house last night. "Where do you get this stuff?"

"The band," Ocie says. "Nothing happens in this school that we don't know about."

Her cluelessness makes me laugh; it's one of my favorite things in the world.

My giggles are the only sound now. Taylor shuffles foot to foot before saying, "Mei, tomorrow then."

"Yeah, sure."

I rise and take my tray to the dishwasher window. They can finish this nonsense on their own. When I return to the table, he's gone and Ocie's twisted in her seat, tracking me with her eyes. Anxious.

"Panda, about that—"

"Sorry," I say. I grab my bag off the back of my chair. "Lunch is over. Gotta get to class."

There's a full five minutes left in the period, but Ocie doesn't argue. I'm sure she knows there will be plenty of time for that later.

We're all something we don't know we are.

Let me tell you about a girl who didn't know she was a freaking idiot.

It's not a long story; take out the specifics and it probably isn't even uncommon. A gorgeous boy came to her school. A military brat, like she used to be. Even spent time in her mother's birthplace. Long enough to learn the language. They bonded over similarities until they started creating shared moments.

Movies and pizza and birthday parties. His parents dropping him off for dinner with her family. Her sneaking kisses on the couch between her dad's chaperone patrols.

She told him about the camera she wanted for her birthday, and her subscription to *National Geographic*, and how she knew who took the picture of each and every panda on her wall. He told her private things, too, but even now she doesn't share them, because she still can't destroy their old trust the way he did.

Things between them were good. Until they weren't.

One weekend she was home alone. His older basketball buddies brought him by well after dark. They took a trip to her room where it didn't go all the way, but got close enough to frighten her and irritate him.

She got it. She really did. She wanted him. *Bad.* But she was scared. Scared that something would go wrong, something that would last a lifetime, and chase away all the dreams they talked about so much.

He said he understood, said he wasn't mad. When his friends picked him up, he must've said different things.

By Monday morning, the school was saying them, too.

Things like how she was obsessed with pandas, but not in a real way. Like a freak show.

They called her "Panda Fucker."

Because she trusted the wrong boy.

That girl is something different now. She won't make that mistake again.

Though she may need to consider which girls she trusts, if they can't recognize the wrong boys either.

CHAPTER 9

OCIE'S TEXTS BLOW UP MY CELL as I eat dinner with my parents.

Dad's complaining to Mom, for like the thousandth time, about how frightened Virginians get over "a little wind and rain." There's a bad storm forecast for tomorrow night, and whenever that happens, there's a run on bread and water at all the local stores because folks around here are afraid of flooding and lengthy power outages. Dad drew the short straw tonight and had to brave the crowds for milk and cheese on his way home. Thus, the tirade.

"You'd think they're expecting a category five hurricane," he says.

Mom smiles. "They? We have been here for ten years. We are Virginians, too."

"Maybe. We're not the kind that overreact, though."

Mom glances toward the pantry. "So you suddenly felt we needed three cases of water because . . ."

"I was thirsty. Most Americans are chronically dehydrated."

I can't help but giggle, even as I'm palming my phone under the table because dinner's supposed to be tech-free. Ocie's messages are all *I know UR mad, but . . .* and *I need 2 explain about T . . .*

What's to explain?

My best friend is consorting with the enemy.

"Lauren," Dad says, diverting talk of storm paranoia away from himself and peering over the tines of his fork with SternFace, "something pressing on your phone?"

"Nope. Not at all."

I put it away though it purrs against my thigh. Ocie gets the hint shortly after dinner and stops the thumb groveling. Good. She should take some time to reflect on what she's done. We'll settle up soon.

Tonight, my Admirer problem.

I'm not down for the invisible puppet master act and I'm in just the right mood to make a thing of it. Even if I did have a concept to top his photo, why should I have to prove anything to some anonymous creep? I compose a quick message expressing my dissatisfaction.

Who are you? Tell me or I'm not shooting anything.

When I send the email I'm sweating. It's a big bluff. The last thing I want is for him to expose me, not while the Keachin-Coach stuff is getting hotter by the day. I mean, I *never* want to be exposed, but especially not now.

Coach Bottin's sure to lose his job soon, and talk of jail if Keachin was underage when they started is still circulating. Here's the thing: if Coach Bottin broke laws, he should go to jail. Me and Mom are in 100 percent agreement on that. But . . .

Jail is full of thieves, and murderers, and child molesters. People are lumping Coach into that last category. When I hear *molester*, I think of creepy guys in nondescript vans scoping out playgrounds. I had Coach Bottin when I was a sophomore, and he was one of my favorite teachers. He never freaked if you really didn't understand how a three-man weave goes, or couldn't get a softball all the way from the mound to home plate. I never got the vibe he was ogling us like some porn scout. And trust me, the uniforms us girls get duped into wearing—little booty shorts and tight shirts, like the school orders them from a Vegas burlesque emporium— probably would've drawn him out. It sure did for other teachers.

I'm thinking about you, Mr. Mitchell, aka *GawkEye*. Really, what possible reason does the Automotive Arts teacher have to walk through the gym two to three times a week?

My point: Coach Bottin was not the one I was after. He shouldn't have done what he did, and maybe I somehow *saved* Keachin from a monster who manipulated and took advantage of her. But when I think about Coach's life in shambles, why don't I feel like a Panda the Vampire Slayer badass?

My computer makes this weird, unfamiliar *ding*ing noise. A window I've never seen before flashes in the center of the screen.

SecretAdm1r3r wants to chat. Do you accept?

Oh, fu—

I snatch my hands from my MacBook like it's grown teeth. A quick glance over my shoulder confirms my door is closed. I cross the room on gummy legs to make sure it's locked, and my palm is slick when I jiggle the knob.

I'm slow returning to the machine. My bluff's been called.

Forcing myself into the seat, I reread the message flashing.

SecretAdm1r3r wants to chat. Do you accept?

I do.

I click the YES button and a new window opens.

It's the messenger program that came with my computer. I never use it, had forgotten it existed. My default username, *PandaD*, occupies the chat window next to an impatient flashing cursor. My parents' caution voices whisper across time, warning my eleven-year-old self never to chat with strangers, in person or on the internet. I won't let this go anywhere skeevy.

PandaD: Hello?

SecretAdm1r3r: Hi.

PandaD: Hi? That's it?

SecretAdm1r3r: Sorry, I'm a little starstruck. I'm talking to *GRAY*

PandaD: Who are you?

SecretAdm1r3r: You know I can't tell you that, Panda. If I did, I'd be in the same predicament you're in.

PandaD: What you're doing is creepy.

SecretAdm1r3r: Says the girl who follows people, takes picture of their most private moments, then pimps them for retweets.

PandaD: That's not the way it is! If you knew what they did you wouldn't come at me like this.

SecretAdm1r3r: Oh, I know. Joshua Amell, number 5 on Gray's Hit List. He switched little Larry Marsh's chocolate milk with something that was almost totally ex-lax. That kid only drank half, but the explosive diarrhea—which hit during, and ended, a school assembly— still put him in the hospital for two days. And earned him the nickname "Shittermission." You posted pictures of Joshua stealing from the Salvation Army's overnight drop box. How low is that guy?

Joshua is a sleaze. That bit of petty larceny got him a few hundred hours of community service, which included him apologizing to a bunch of underprivileged kids. Nowhere near Keachin-gate level, but good enough.

SecretAdmlr3r: Simone Presley, number 9. She befriended a lonely, unattractive transfer student on a dare, then invited the girl to her birthday party where all the other pretty people brought unattractive guests as part of some narcissistic competition where the climax of the night is embarrassing all the clueless victims. A "Pig Party," I hear they're called. You got a picture of Simone scoring some Molly downtown, right?

PandaD: Actually, it was coke. She's old school. That photo got her a stint in rehab.

SecretAdmlr3r: Forgive me. I might be fuzzy on the specifics, but I see the theme of your work.

PandaD: Do you go to Portside?

SecretAdmlr3r: I'm not judging, Panda. I want you to know that.

PandaD: You're just dodging my questions.

SecretAdmlr3r: Those I don't want to answer. Ask better ones.

PandaD: Okay. Why aren't you busting me?

SecretAdmlr3r: I understand you. Better than all your little website followers, better than the people you're avenging. Better than anyone.

PandaD: How do you figure that?

SecretAdmlr3r: I've got a camera, too.

PandaD: Old people on dinner cruises have cameras. What gear were you using that night?

SecretAdmlr3r: Canon 20D with a EF50mm lens. Gives me great shots in low light.

PandaD: Interesting. I used something similar when I first started. That's a good beginner's rig.

SecretAdmlr3r: It's a lot less bulk than what you're shooting. Was it a Nikon? Hard to tell because your massive lens distracts me so.

PandaD: Oh, whatever! It takes a lot of skill to handle high-quality zoom lenses, thank you very much. One day, if you're ever comfortable with pro gear, you might see.

SecretAdmlr3r: Pick the right spots and you don't need zoom. Case in point, me shooting you. But, you know, I'm not a pro or anything.

PandaD: Okay, okay. Truce. Tell me about that room you shot. *Dante.*

SecretAdmlr3r: Awesome, right?

PandaD: How did you get that fire?

SecretAdm1r3r: What?

PandaD: Was it a set? Did you need a crew? What sort of prep did you do to stage it?

SecretAdm1r3r: I lit a match.

PandaD: Oh, come on!

SecretAdm1r3r: I answered your question. Now, I have one for you. Why "Panda"?

On this, I'm slow to respond. When the pause lingers, another message comes through.

SecretAdm1r3r: I know why others began calling you that—I don't believe a word of that nasty tale, by the way. I want to know why YOU keep the name . . . considering the connotations. Come on. Fair is fair.

It's still hard to type. The last time I told the story—the *real* story—I pretty much dropped a nuke on my life.

SecretAdm1r3r: I know so many truths about you already. What's one more thing?

PandaD: Fine. It came from my mom. When I was a kid, mean girls teased me because I'm mixed race. They said I had weird skin, and hair, and eyes. I came home crying one day, and Mom sat me down with this book we got from the San Diego Zoo. She flipped to the pandas and told me, "They're black and white, just like you. They're beautiful, just like you." It stuck, and it helped.

SecretAdm1r3r: Until it didn't.

Until it didn't.

PandaD: What's the deal with this photo challenge you dropped? If I don't do it, you're going to expose me? WTF, dude? If we're in the same gang, why blackmail me?

SecretAdm1r3r: I sense hostility. Calm down. I don't like the B-word. What I'm proposing is a friendly competition. A way to sharpen our focus. Pun intended.

PandaD: I don't need my focus sharpened. I don't even know what that means.

SecretAdm1r3r: I'll tell you sometime. But you'll have to participate in my project if we're going to get to know each other better.

PandaD: I get you're not going to tell me who you are. But, are you someone I helped? Did one of the people I exposed hurt you in some way?

SecretAdm1r3r: You've helped me. And I'm going to help you. I'm going to help you see what it is you're really doing. Clearer than your best lens.

PandaD: I don't need to SEE what I do. I KNOW what I do. I do good.

SecretAdm1r3r: Yes, but there's always room for improvement.

I start to type something snarky, but epic. The ultimate comeback. Only, before I get a word down, my computer sounds an angry buzz.

SecretAdm1r3r has left the chat.

The hell?

I wander downstairs, dazed. A million thoughts and questions remain in the aftermath of my abruptly ended chat with my Admirer.

How is it possible for someone to seem so creepy and cool at the same time?

Dad's upright on the couch and Mom's stretched sideways like a lazy cat, her feet on the cushions and her head wedged in the crook of his shoulder. On the TV, a grayish-green blob swirls in from the Atlantic Ocean over a zoomed-in map of Virginia and North Carolina. The weatherman points excitedly at the storm spiral.

"—we can expect upward of three inches of rain with wind gusts as high as fifty miles per hour tomorrow afternoon—"

Drifting into the kitchen for a snack, my confusion persists.

Who IS this guy? How do I show him I'm the superior shooter?

My phone buzzes again. Ocie's doubling down on the apologies, insisting I respond. In the same moment, the weatherman's voice turns all doom and gloom ("—expect dangerous lightning strikes near the coast—"), and I'm thinking about beating my admirer's *Dante*. Talk about the perfect storm.

Pun intended.

I nearly drop the milk when the idea hits.

It's so exciting—so awesome—that I'm trembling when I text Ocie back.

> **Me:** R U really sorry?
>
> **Ocie:** Totes
>
> **Me:** Wanna make it up 2 me?
>
> **Ocie:** Ok?
>
> **Me:** Free up ur evening tomorrow. I'm going to need ur help.

I think on it a moment, then send a follow-up text.

> **Me:** U might want 2 bring an umbrella.

CHAPTER 10

WE'RE ON THE HIGHWAY, CREEPING THROUGH rush-hour traffic.

Ocie's tapping on her thigh in a rhythm I still hear in my head even though I've cranked the radio to drown it. *Tap-tap-tap*, stop, *Tap-tap-tap*, stop, *Tap-tap* . . .

I lower the music and say, "If you're nervous, we could talk about it."

Her tapping increases. "You should concentrate on the road."

By "road" she means the thirty feet of visible asphalt fading into a torrential downpour that's so bad some drivers angle their cars toward the shoulder, deciding to wait instead of persevere. Looking through my windshield is like looking into a pool, and my wipers fight the water like bad swimmers, breaking the surface long enough to gasp before going under again. One of those fifty-miles-per-hour wind gusts the weatherman warned about swats my car, and I grip the steering wheel with both hands so I don't swerve.

Lightning flashes. The bolt is a crooked electric finger pointing toward the worst of the storm. I don't need the directions, though. Already going that way.

"When you said you needed my help," Ocie says, "I didn't think you meant with committing suicide."

"We aren't going to die." I hope.

Another gust bounces us in the lane.

"I'm glad you're so confident. What are we doing here?"

"Remember that contest I told you about? The one I need a killer photo for?"

I glance over for a reaction. Ocie's jaw is slack. She stares at the roof of my car; I know this look. Really, she's looking to God for a more satisfactory explanation.

"You're effing crazy, Panda. Driving in this? For a photo? Of what?"

I hesitate. She's not going to take this well. "I'm—I'm not sure yet."

"Jesus take the wheel. Like, seriously."

It's true. I have some ideas—what I'd *like* to see when I'm looking through my viewfinder. You never know for sure, not until you're in the moment.

Rain patter and the *thunk-squee, thunk-squee* of my wipers are the only sounds. I need to say something, something that will sell Ocie on today's mission. Something affirming.

"I overreacted about you tutoring Taylor. I'm sorry."

"You might want to apologize to him, since you made me cancel his session to go storm chasing."

That will never happen. "This is about us. I shouldn't have been all bitchy about it."

"Really?"

Maybe. A little. I shrug. "So, you and him are, like, real friends?"

"Not like we are."

Thunk-squee, thunk-squee

Ocie says, "There's nothing going on between us or anything. If that's what you're thinking."

"It never even crossed my mind."

She flinches.

"I just mean you'd have to be pretty stupid to go there with him, O. You know what he's like."

"Are you sure you do?"

Gripping the wheel tight enough to make my hands ache, I say, "What's that supposed to mean?"

"It means—" But Ocie's phone spasms in her lap, emitting a long, aggravated groan that startles us both. She reads the screen. "Emergency alert! You know this mess is a Hurricane Watch now? Are you listening? Don't you have anything to say?"

I gasp, and catch the word rocketing up my throat before it passes my lips. I almost say, "Perfect."

If photographers were soldiers, storm photographers would be our Navy SEALs. The elite shooters who do the things most can't, things most of us shouldn't even try. Storm photography is dangerous for all sorts of reasons. Lightning strikes, flying debris, flash flooding. That stuff kills people who are trying to get *away* from storms; imagine the mortality rate for those going *into* them. Like we're doing now.

We make it to Atlantic Avenue in one piece, a tenuous state. Rain pelts us with greater frequency, peppering so hard I expect a thousand raindrop dents in my ride when this thing is over. I pull into the empty lot of the Oceanview Inn, a dwarf building wedged between two newer, taller luxury hotels.

Ocie hasn't said much since announcing the Hurricane Watch, but her thigh-tapping has morphed into hand-wringing that makes the skin on her palms and knuckles bright red. I catch the flash of nearby lightning from the corner of my eye, and thunder grumbles overhead, a sound like a dozen boulders rolling in to crush us.

I say, "I don't think we'll need to be here for long."

"We shouldn't be here at all," Ocie says, but quietly, like she is talking to herself.

I undo my seat belt, twist into the space between us, and slither into the backseat. My camera bag is there. There's other equipment in the trunk, but I'm losing my nerve the more the crosswinds swipe at my car like a giant cat pawing a ball of yarn.

"Ocie, I need you to drive us onto the boardwalk, just like we do at Christmas, when they have all those lights on the beach."

She twists in her seat. "I'm pretty sure that's illegal any time other than Christmas."

"It'll be fine. There aren't any cops out here."

Two lightning bolts crackle in quick succession.

"I wonder why." She's already climbing behind the wheel and adjusting the seat to accommodate her short legs. "I should drive us home."

I crank up the syrup in my sweet voice. "You won't, though, because you're my bestie. I really think the photos I'm going for will win me this contest. I think they're the *only* way I'll win this contest."

"I don't understand why this contest is such a big deal. Is it for scholarship money or something?"

Ocie does these formulas in her head where she calculates the value of difficult tasks relative to the speed and distance they can propel her beyond the Portside city limits after graduation. Scholarship money means bigger, better schools. Possibly out-of-state schools. If that justifies risking life and limb for her, well: "Yes, there's a couple of thousand dollars of scholarship money in the prize pool."

She sighs, still looks skeptical. I sweeten the pot. "Do this, and lattes are on me all weekend."

"Two weeks' worth of lattes, and I'm talking venti. None of that tall crap. If you don't get your picture in fifteen minutes, it wasn't meant to be and we're going home. Deal?"

"Deal."

Ocie gets us moving, maneuvering toward a gap next to the Oceanview Inn meant for maintenance vehicles. When she turns on the brick-and-concrete boardwalk, I'm transfixed by the view beyond the steel guardrails and the shore, which is half its normal sandy width thanks to the storm stretching high tide into higher tide.

It's almost sunset. What my tribe calls the Golden Hour—the hour after sunrise and before sunset. There's no studio or digital substitute for the beautiful lighting you get during those very narrow windows at dawn and dusk, a time when the best outdoor photos in the world are shot.

What's happening around us isn't that. Not exactly.

There is a gilded spear piercing the angry cloud cover twenty miles off-shore. A solitary tower of sunlight, flanked by arcing lightning, is the only evidence there is still a star to warm us. Everything else is forced night, and the contrast where the two meet is astonishing.

This is the shot. "Ocie, stop driving."

The car halts. I stretch myself across the seat until my back presses against the door farthest from the ocean. I zoom, trying to crop out visible car parts in-camera, but I'm still getting automotive evidence in my viewfinder. I shoot fast, at least sixty shots. And I know—*KNOW*—none of them is right.

Even with the zoom, it all feels closed in. The pictures aren't *in* the storm. If I were shooting fire, I wouldn't be able to feel the heat.

"Can we go now?" Ocie half yells to be heard over the banshee wind.

No. We can't.

I pull the knob-lever thingy that lowers half of my backseat so I can access more gear in the trunk.

"Panda?"

I grab a tripod and a rain hood for the camera. Then I rip the plastic seal on a disposable poncho and slip it over my head.

"No. No way," Ocie says. Pleads.

She's not going anywhere without me, though. I'm her anchor.

When I pop the latch and push my door against air that's pushing back, I think maybe she's not the one who needs an anchor. Once I'm on the boardwalk, the door closes on its own, like my car's telling me never come back. I walk in a hunch, shielding my eyes from the moist sand blasting me. More thunder. More lightning. Sounds and signs like final warnings, which I ignore.

The light piercing the cloud diminishes as the storm shifts and the sun continues its westward trajectory. There's no time to set up the tripod, so I shoot without it and pray I get something decent despite the forceful wind. I zoom in, out, forgetting the elemental chaos around me. God, the colors alone. Streaking reds, purples, blues, and golds.

Behind me, chairs held down by rope and bungee ties rattle against the short fence that boxes in a hotel restaurant's outdoor area. On warm and pretty days, the patio is filled with hungry tourists enjoying their view of the Atlantic. Now it's a storage area for poorly secured storm projectiles. A plastic chair somehow slips its rope, jumps the fence, and skips past me until it collides with the steel rail standing between the boardwalk and the sand. It hits so hard, the chair cracks.

The splintering plastic shakes me. I look to my car and see a scared Ocie twisted in the driver's seat, looking like she's watching my impending doom.

Fine, fine. I check my camera display, I've taken nearly a hundred shots. They'll have to do.

I run to the passenger side of my vehicle and climb in. Ocie's driving before I get my door closed. She takes us a quarter mile up the boardwalk, then swings a left at the giant King Neptune statue to put us back on Atlantic Avenue. The ocean god, flanked by his army of sea turtles and crabs, stares after us. More lightning illuminates the furious gaze some sculptor etched onto the deity's green stone face.

"You ever wonder why he's so mad?" I ask.

Ocie says, "What?"

"Neptune. They made him angry. But why? Is it because the people who come to him always leave, or because he can't?"

"Panda," Ocie says. "Shut. Up."

CHAPTER 11

THE STORM PASSES AND WE DRIVE home on a deserted highway. When we get to the surface streets, my tires bump over broken tree limbs and loose shingles left behind by the wind. We make one stop at Starbucks, where we switch seats and I make the first payment on my latte debt. At Ocie's house, I say, "What do you want to do this weekend?"

Usually this question results in a number of options—mall/movies/whatever—but all she says is "Don't know. I'll text you."

Meaning she won't. At least not for a day or so while she gets into a space where she can accept any apology I'm willing to give. "Ocie."

"Yes?"

"You kicked ass tonight."

She sighs, shakes her head. "White chocolate mocha, nonfat, no whip, delivered to my cranky, un-caffeinated hand on Monday morning."

I smile. "Done. We cool?"

"You're being kind of *other* right now, but we will be." She leaves the car, taking her coffee with her. "I hope you win your contest, since we almost died for it and all."

"You're exaggerating."

"You're crazy," she counters. "But what else is new?"

With that she's gone, and her annoyance with me is a secondary concern. I'm racing home to show my Admirer what a real photographer can do.

Examining the shots on my MacBook's Retina display, my stomach sinks. I'm halfway through the batch and most of it's blurry, poorly composed garbage. There are a few decent shots, but decent isn't good enough.

Worse, these are the pictures taken from the backseat. I knew they wouldn't be exactly what I wanted, but if the pictures I took from a relatively stable position look this bad, what are the ones I took while fighting the storm going to be like?

I speed up my review, moving to the batch taken outdoors. Right away I see they're terrible. Not even good enough to get a decent grade in Digital Photography class. I'm not used to shooting in weather, and in a couple of shots I managed to capture the edges of the camera's rain hood in frame, obscuring what might have been an okay photo otherwise. I could crop . . . but . . . damn it! I'm better than this!

The number of remaining shots is dwindling, and I'm ready to scream from frustration.

Until . . .

My third-to-last shot catches two bolts of forked lightning flanking the sun column, center frame. High waves crash in the foreground, while the water smooths to black glass at the horizon. It's. Freaking. Gorgeous.

I check my last two shots, and they're great, too. Not as dramatic. But still . . .

"Yes! Yes! YES!"

I drop them into Photoshop and do a bit of cleanup. No cheating, though. I simply highlight the best parts of these stills so my Admirer doesn't miss a thing.

I'm nearly vibrating with excitement when I attach the JPGs to an email titled: *TOPPED*

In the body, I write:

> *Dear SecretAdm1r3r, these photos are BOSS. So, consider the terms of your challenge met. No more blackmail, or lessons, or whatever you call this. If you want to talk shop, that's okay, but I'm not playing games with you anymore. Deal with it.*
>
> *Panda*
>
> *P.S.—I call them Neptune's Fury.*

I click SEND. Hear the swooshing "message sent" sound and sit back, satisfied.

Anything less than congratulations and envy means he's just a hater. I can't wait to hear what he's got to say about such awesome work.

Actually, I end up waiting quite a while.

He doesn't respond at all.

I don't like being ignored. I mean, unless I'm trying to be ignored. Which is most days, yes. Not when I kind of risked my life (and Ocie's . . . she wasn't exaggerating, I guess) to get a damned incredible photo for some jerk who doesn't even acknowledge how freakin' incredible I am!

The weekend slogs. My parents stop by my room frequently—sometimes solo, sometimes as a team—to make sure I'm "all right." I'm not, of course, despite my insistence to the contrary. Saturday evening, they suggest dinner at Yard House, my favorite restaurant out in Pembroke. I ask them to bring me a to-go order of kung pao calamari without ever looking away from my laptop. Dad's truck purrs as they leave the driveway, and I keep glancing at the tiny window in the corner of my monitor, my chat friends list.

SecretAdm1r3r never comes online.

Sunday. Still no word from him.

I do go for frozen yogurt. Guess that's something.

The weather's cool in the aftermath of Friday's storm, so the Sweet Frog yogurt shop is a lonely, pastel-colored cave. Plenty of solitude for brooding over a leaning mountain of creamy goodness covered in chips, and nuts, and candy pieces.

Who the hell does he think he is to just go radio silent on me like that?

Who do *I* think he is?

It's been on my mind since this cat-and-mouse nonsense started. More so now that he's giving me the cold shoulder.

He goes to Portside. I'm certain of it.

And he's got skills with a lens.

There's really only one person I might consider good enough to pull off a photo like *Dante*. The same person who openly despises Gray (over total misunderstandings, mind you) and might be up to screwing with me if he found out we were one and the same.

My Digital Photography rival. Marcos Dahmer.

With the edge of my spoon I shave layers off a swirling cake-batter-flavored peak, cause a chocolate-chip avalanche, and imagine the poor people at the melted base of Mount Yogurt screaming in terror at the wrath of their god.

She is displeased.

CHAPTER 12

I SLEEP THROUGH MY ALARM ON Monday. I'm late, but not really.

My clock's set a half hour earlier than necessary. I need the extra time to get into my camouflage, to "ghost up." Dad wakes me when the chime has gone on long enough to drive him a little crazy.

"What's with you?" he asks, his patience for his sullen daughter thin on this Monday morning.

"Up late," I groan.

"No one told you to stay up all night surfing the web."

"That's not what I was doing." Not exactly. I was combing through Marcos Dahmer's Facebook page looking for Admirer clues.

His best photos—landscapes, portraits—were collected in an album labeled *Portfolio*. Nothing like *Dante*, but impressive.

"You're not staying home," Dad says, reminding me the time for rest has passed, even though my body aches from fatigue.

Somehow my feet are on the floor, betraying me. "I'm up."

A shower helps, though grogginess has me forgetting my shower cap. My hair's soaked before I'm alert enough to realize my mistake, and there's no time to dry or wrangle it. Playing sick comes to mind; Mom would buy it even if Dad didn't, but I think about Ocie. I'm her ride, and I need to regain some goodwill (though I won't be grabbing the venti white chocolate mocha, not if we plan to make first bell).

Bye, Mom. Bye, Dad. Drive. Park. *Honnk-Onk-Onk-Honnk (Come, Ocie, come).*

"Where's my coffee?" Ocie says.

Really?

She doesn't bring up our storm chase, or anything. Maybe because she's caffeine cranky, and that's okay. I know I messed up, but I'm in no mood to beg forgiveness, so silence is best. I don't want to fight, because I won't back down today. I'm that pissed. Until I see the circus in front of the school.

What I imagined a week ago is real. News vans from all the local stations are parked at the curb. Every reporter has one of my schoolmates before their cameras, a bulbous mic shoved toward their faces like strangers offering candy.

"Whoa," Ocie says, perky now. "This thing's getting major pub now. Wanna try to get on camera?"

I don't respond. I drive into the student lot and grab a spot far away from the drama. Unfortunately, the parking space is still in the state of Virginia, so it's not quite far enough.

On my way to homeroom, I scan the hall crowd for a glimpse of Marcos. It's not like I'm expecting him to be wearing an I'm Your Admirer T-shirt, but now that I suspect what I suspect, I want to see him from a distance. I want to look at him as Gray would.

"Hey! Lauren!"

I turn toward the aggravated call—me and several others. Taylor Durham fast walks my way, his face tense and creased. My eyes stretch wide. Seriously?

He forces his voice down an octave. "We need to talk."

I'm walking, shaking my head. "No, we don't."

He's on my heels. "What did you say to Mei?"

"I say lots of things to her on a daily basis. She's my best friend."

"She won't tutor me anymore."

I stop cold and he walks into me, knocking my bag off my shoulder, spilling books. Some jackass laughs, and now I've gotten more unwanted attention.

Crouching, I scramble to gather my things and get away from the angry chem man. The jackass is still *ha-haw*ing, and I remember the laugh from the times when it used to chase me down the hall.

Could this morning get any worse?

The laughter stops abruptly, and Brock Parham says, "Hey, sexy, you new here?"

We've been classmates since the third grade. His memory isn't bad, and he's not half as clever as he thinks. This is what happens when a Hall Ghost suddenly returns to the land of the living. A turf war.

With my books gathered, I try to slide by him and Taylor, but Brock grabs me by the elbow in a way that might've seemed gentle if I'd asked him to touch me. He's taking liberties, as he's known to do. Thus me busting his ass on *Gray Scales* two years ago.

Crime: Brock plays football. So did Nelson Barclay, who, until an unfortunate locker room incident, was a rising gridiron star and a closeted gay kid. That incident was engineered by Brock, and involved intricate paper arrows made out of the pages from gay porn magazines. The big block arrows were constructed with care I've only seen from my mother's arts-and-craftsy friends, and taped along the walls and lockers like directions through a maze. All pointing to Nelson's locker, where a huge sex toy had been rubber-cemented to the door in a way that would've forced him to hold it in one hand while he worked the combination lock with the other. Nelson never gave his cruel teammates the pleasure of seeing him fondle a plastic penis while suiting up. Instead, he left the locker room, never to return.

Punishment: I knew a secret—a couple actually—about Brock thanks to his brief relationship with Ocie back in the day (one of her lowlights if I'm being honest). As obnoxious and homophobic as he is, he's got a passion that he shares with his father. Comic books. Nothing wrong there, I've read a few myself, and can respect the art. It's more than a love for them, though. It's a lifestyle, at least part of the year. They do conventions. As cosplayers—people who wear intricate costumes in homage to a favorite fictional character.

We don't have any cons locally, which Brock's probably seen as a blessing. At the time of the Nelson Barclay incident, I had no way of tailing him to any out-of-state events. But this is one time where a little internet research did the job for me. There were plenty of photographers at GorgonCon, North Carolina. A whole lot of lists for best cosplayers. Guess who made the cut.

Brock and his dad. Or as their con buddies probably referred to them, Batman and Robin.

And, no, not cutie Robin from the late-nineties movies. I'm talking little green man-panties Robin. It took me all of fifteen minutes to find, crop, and post the photo on *Gray Scales*. Within a day, Nelson's sexuality fell off everyone's social radar as the school refocused on Portside's own Caped Crusader.

That was then. This . . . is something I'm not in the mood for.

I want to bite his hand and rip his shoulder from the socket. I also want to go back to being a Hall Ghost tomorrow. I can't let some hair frizz and the attention of an a-hole like Brock ruin my cover forever. I say, "Please take your hand off me."

He might've complied, and this might've ended quietly.

But Taylor smacks Brock's arm away. "Don't touch her, dick."

A whiff of masculine aggression raises hackles on the backs of onlookers. Now we're officially the morning entertainment.

Brock raises his hands, palms out, feigning peace. "My bad, Durham. Just wanted to know who the new girl is."

"Really?"

"I've seen a girl who kind of *looks* like you. Nerdy chick with glasses, antisocial, major stick up her ass. That can't be you, though. Unlike her, you're cute, in a future-hot-teacher kind of way."

"Oh, screw you, Brock." I realize the opening I give him a half second too late.

He says, "My bear costume is in the cleaners, but if you're still willing . . ."

A collective *ooohhhh* sounds along the hall, the hive-mind reaction to a well-timed burn.

Now the bad days are not just a memory.

I've time-traveled to when such jokes weren't just a Brock thing, but a Portside High thing. My bag's dropped from my shoulder, my fist clenching the strap while the satchel dangles an inch from the ground, heavy like the spiked ball of some medieval warrior's mace.

I say, "I prefer your superhero outfit," and I glance at his nether regions. "Those little tight shorts assured me there was nothing to fear."

The onlookers are laughing harder. Not at me.

Brock's not known for letting others have the last word. I'm not in a giving mood either. His chest expands, gathering air to say something nasty. Hall Ghost persona be damned—I'm not backing down.

Before it goes further, Taylor inserts himself between us, gets in Brock's face. "Back off."

Again, Brock plays like he's taking the high road. "I'm sorry, dude. This you?"

"This." As if I'm property to claim. I can't decide if I'm more offended by Taylor assuming I need him to fight for me, or the implication that I somehow belong to him. Wisely, Taylor shakes his head. "You know it ain't like that. Just back off."

Brock smirks, flicks a "You believe this guy?" signal to some nearby toady. "Sure will, Sheriff. I don't want no trouble with the law."

Brock forces his way between me and Taylor, bumping Taylor's shoulder hard enough to make him stumble.

I walk away, unwilling to lend credence to their childishness by being a witness to whatever happens next. If they fight, they fight. I won't let it be over me.

The resulting sounds aren't that of a scuffle, but of footsteps chasing me.

"Lauren, *bist du okay*?" He's asking if I'm okay, in German. Like he used to. Making me want to claw his eyes out.

"I'm perfect." I speed up, hoping to outrun this conversation. I can't beat his long legs, though.

"Brock's a messed-up dude." He says it like everyone who meets Brock doesn't get that instantly. Also, like *he's* not a messed-up dude. "I had to say something."

"Where's *your* shield?"

"My what?"

"All this time and I never knew your lying and backstabbing was an act. You're really Captain America, defending my honor."

"Lauren? Still?"

I'm visualizing the mace again. "No one calls me Lauren around here. Especially you."

Outside my homeroom, he stops, makes a quarter turn, like half of him wants to run while the other half needs to finish this exchange.

I say, "I'd prefer you don't talk to me. Ever. If you do feel the need, know that you've lost your 'Lauren' privileges." His back is to me now, and I expect him to walk away. "You call me Panda," I say, intending to add the stinger "It shouldn't be hard for you to remember, since it's the name you gave me."

Taylor's no longer paying attention to me. No one is and I'm feeling slightly shunned. I sidestep to see what's drawn everyone's attention.

Oh.

Keachin's back.

CHAPTER 13

MUTED COLORS, NO MAKEUP, HAIR UP and away. Keachin's taken a page from my Hall Ghost playbook.

Her friends form a protective bubble around her like a popularity Secret Service, escorting her through the stunned spectators. As she passes, a wave of gossiping murmurs follow. Keachin maintains a stiff spine, her chin high and eyes on the horizon. So dignified. She may be prom queen yet.

When she turns the corner, the volume cranks. Girls simultaneously pitying and cat-clawing, boys being crass or wanting to be the one Keachin allows to comfort her during this trying time.

"Wasn't expecting that," Taylor says.

"Me neither," I say with no snark. He seems shocked.

The warning bell rings and the crowds begin to disperse. Taylor gives me a long look that sets me on edge again. "I really need Mei's help, Lauren. I'd appreciate it if you considered giving me a pass on this one."

"I don't control what Ocie does."

"You've got more power than you think. I thought you would've figured that out by now."

"What's that mean?"

He shakes his head, and he's gone.

In homeroom I take my desk. The morning has already been a mix of rough and strange, and the school day has not started yet. I'm dreading what is sure to be a long, long Monday, and I reach into my bag to power down my phone. There's a text from a number I don't know, though the message reveals all.

> The bitch is back. Some ppl don't learn. A little *Neptune's Fury*
> would serve her well. BTW—like ur 'do. ;)

My hand rises, and I finger comb my spongy hair. He's here.

I glance at the surrounding desks, knowing my Admirer isn't that close. After all, me and Marcos don't have the same homeroom.

Dealing with Taylor and Brock distracted me, and I didn't notice if he was around. Observing. I should be creeped out. It's almost mandatory, right? But I'm getting used to his game.

He mentioned *Neptune's Fury* to bait me. After a weekend of silence. My strongest urge is to text back something mean. I fight it, cut my phone off instead, and leave it off for the entire day. I'm taking back some control.

Should've been playing hard to get the whole time.

Keachin Myer is not in my lunch period, but her presence is felt. Gossip is like wildfire; even when you think it's done, the ground is still hot. Ready to ignite again. It doesn't need a spark—it's already fire—it just needs air.

"She's the best-looking victim I've ever seen," Ocie says, not above the fray. "I hear she's a little testy, though. You know that theater girl? Melanie? Keachin bit her head off for staring."

"Doesn't that girl have an astigmatism?"

Some ppl don't learn.

Ocie shrugs, keeps chattering. If there's one positive to Keachin's return, it's eclipsed Ocie's irritation with me. The negatives, though . . .

"You think she thinks any of this is her fault?" I say, cutting Ocie off midrumor.

"Why would she? Coach Bottin's the grown-up."

I nearly say, "But what about Nina's crutches?"

That would be too much. A connection no one's made, and no one is going to make. What have I done here? Really? Is it possible that my pictures, and the subsequent scandal, have made Keachin *more* popular?

Ocie kicks my shin under the table.

"Ow! What the hell?"

She makes this really weird face, her lips pinched and twitchy, fighting a smile. She speaks through her teeth, "Don't look."

Of course I'm going to look, because she's cutting her eyes hard left. I should probably make sure I'm not about to be attacked or something.

Jalen Palmer and Mike Harris are checking us out like we haven't known each other forever. I glance to Ocie. "What's that about?"

"Your new look, dummy. You could've warned me you were glamming today. I would've switched it up, too."

"Wasn't on purpose," I mumble. Jeez, do I really look *that* different?

They stroll past flashing obvious eye contact, and Ocie's smile almost cuts her head in half. "I want Mike."

"You can have them both."

"Stop. They are cuties, and Jalen's in my next class. I can ask him about you. We could double."

"Do. Not."

Her grin retracts into something sinister. "You owe me."

"Just lattes, dear. Just lattes."

Dating is the last thing on my mind. Digital Photography is next period. Marcos will be there. He's where my head's at.

Except he never shows up. It's perplexing, and I want to ask his yearbook buddy Alyssa if he's gone home sick. But I've never asked after him before. It might tip him off. I remain silent, and can't concentrate for the rest of the day.

Can't help but wonder, is he thinking of me, too?

———

Ocie's pissed about me not signing off on the double-date thing. It's just . . .

I'm not a prude, 'kay. Not even a virgin. I had a boyfriend for most of sophomore year. He went to Stepton High, fifteen miles away. I knew him from my track days.

The beauty of the relationship was we got to miss each other because we were only together a couple of Saturdays every month. It worked for a while. I don't have anything against boys or dating in general. Jalen and Mike *are* cute.

I just haven't been open to dating someone from Portside in a long, long time. For me to get with a Portside boy, he'd have to be beyond special. Beyond lying, too.

In my room, I power up my phone and see the single missed text from my Admirer. *R U ignoring me?*

Drafting a text and flipping my MacBook open at the same time, I attempt to write back. Before I can send my message, I get *ping*ed through my chat program. There is a lesson here. Hard to get works.

> **SecretAdm1r3r:** We not friends anymore? I've been waiting to hear from you all day.
> **PandaD:** I'm surprised you're so impatient. You didn't have a problem keeping me waiting.
> **SecretAdm1r3r:** I don't know what you're talking about. :)
> **PandaD:** My photo was awesome. Admit that it stunned you silent all weekend, then maybe we can talk about the parameters of this "friendship."
> **SecretAdm1r3r:** *Neptune's Fury* was...okay.

Bullshit, okay. "Okay" doesn't take three days to comment on. "Okay" is what it is the first time you look at it. Not the second time. Not the seventeenth. I looked at *Dante* a thousand times. Every flickering flame, every charred piece of furniture. The framed print on the wall in *Dante*, it's not a painting. It's a movie poster, a one sheet from some old film called *American Graffiti*. That's how much time you spend on special.

> **PandaD:** Downplaying me is not cool.
> **SecretAdm1r3r:** The way you framed the sunlight was skillful, I'll admit.
> **PandaD:** You're a jerk!
> **SecretAdm1r3r:** I'm not saying the picture isn't good. I just think you can do better. I did.

What?

The email pops up in the corner of my screen. Title: *View from Heaven*. I click it open, then the attachment. My screen fills with a panoramic view of Portside, taken at night, from about thirty stories up. The hem of some baggy jeans and scuffed sneakers are visible in the bottom portion of the frame, dangling over the side of a mirrored glass skyscraper. The other buildings in the picture clue me in to exactly what I'm looking at. My Admirer managed to get on the roof of the Patriot Trust Building downtown and take this photo from the ledge.

SecretAdm1r3r: Are you stunned silent?

For a second, I am.

Something else in the photo catches my eye, and the panic attack I feel coming on subsides. I'm learning the rules of his game, and I already know my next move.

PandaD: Nice.
SecretAdm1r3r: Now who's downplaying who?
Panda D: You're a Rooftopper. Big deal.

It is a big deal.

There are whole sects of photography dedicated to taking dizzying, dangerous pictures from the tops of skyscrapers. I've seen a ton of photos like his on the web, in photography forums. Shots from Russia, China, India. Mostly because those countries have really awesome buildings. Also, it's easier to pull off infiltrating a rooftop in those places because there's generally less security to bypass. We're so paranoid about terrorists in America. Especially in *live* buildings—those that are occupied and in use. From what I've read, your social engineering and stealth abilities need to be government spy level to pull off that sort of thing.

PandaD: When did you take this?

SecretAdm1r3r: Last night. Why?

Because if you took it last night, you must have been up late. Were probably pretty tired by the end of today. Tired enough to skip DP class. Right?

PandaD: Just curious.

SecretAdm1r3r: Think you can do better?

PandaD: Am I still being blackmailed?

SecretAdm1r3r: No way. We're past that. I know you're in the game now. Good luck topping that though.

PandaD: I think I can manage.

SecretAdm1r3r: IDK, I checked the weather, no storms for a while. LOL!

PandaD: I'll have the picture by next week.

SecretAdm1r3r: Someone's feeling confident.

PandaD: I am. Hey, the text you sent me today, "some ppl don't learn," what did you mean?

SecretAdm1r3r: The return of Keachin Myer, of course.

PandaD: I know. But what was she supposed to learn?

SecretAdm1r3r: Karma's a bitch. ;)

My irritation from before is gone. My thoughts are on the city sky. I'm starting to like this game. The challenge of it. The possibilities.

We're all something we don't know we are.

I don't know what my Admirer—*Marcos*—is. Not exactly.

Whatever he is, I might be, too.

CHAPTER 14

IT'S A BUSY WEEK. A LOT of prep for the photo shoot that will top my Admirer's latest.

Marcos makes it to Digital Photography every day. I watch him closely from the corner of my eye, and I'm just as careful as he is not to give any indication that things are different between us. The one time I'm bold enough to speak to him, I ask for his thoughts on the Canon 20D—the camera SecretAdm1r3r mentioned in our first chat. His response: "Sweet rig."

That was all. But the way he said it . . .

Soon. Once I get this next photo, we can stop this part of the game and figure out a new way to play together.

Between getting ready to top *View from Heaven*, and school, and getting back into Hall Ghost shape, I feel like I'm working three jobs. The whole time, the scandal I sparked continues its rise toward critical mass.

Coach Bottin officially loses his job. But he also makes bail. Would he see that as a silver lining? Probably not.

Keachin cycles through a series of new looks each morning. From reserved on that first day, to loose locks and smoky eye makeup on day two, to bloodshot and teary on the day Coach is fired, to a barely-adhering-to-the-dress-code miniskirt on day four, to the Friday shocker . . . her formerly long and draping hair chopped short on one side, and shaved to the scalp on the other.

The worst part, it's fabulous.

She's run the board for the week. Five days of ensuring her name's never far from the lips of her peers. Flipping between snapping at peons who dare to breathe in her direction and milking sympathy from the sheep she herds.

It drives me a little crazy, if I'm being honest. She's the first to come back from a *Gray Scales* exposé stronger for the publicity. But I force myself to move on, focusing on the task at hand. Keachin Myer may still be due some comeuppance, but I won't be the delivery driver. Gray don't do repeats.

I make a couple of trips into the city after school for research that week. Dusting off some of my Gray-honed espionage skills to score some crucial information.

Really, it only takes one trip into the city to get what I need. The other trip—I wanted to get to the top of the Patriot Trust Building. If Marcos could do it . . .

Homework first, of course. That building belongs to the bank, but there are dozens of other businesses leasing space. Among them, AGG Technical Institute. A small for-profit computer-training school that offers tours and tech seminars to Portside kids in an effort to recruit them after graduation. A bunch of their pamphlets are in a rack in the guidance office.

Bright-yellow block letters on the front of the brochure scream: Make Your Appointment Today!

A quick call to their 800 number, and that's enough to get me past the lobby guard in the Patriot Trust Building. Hell, he might as well have walked me to the roof.

Exiting the elevator a few floors from the top, I find a stairwell, and make it to the roof access door. A red-on-gray sign reads: Alarm Sounds When Door Is Opened. Neither the sign nor the electric horn over it is much of a deterrent for me. Like I said, I did my homework.

These types of alarms have been handled by many Rooftoppers, and they're more than willing to share tips on disarming them. My newly purchased tool kit—screwdrivers, wire cutters, tiny pliers—is made for this kind of work. I pry the cover off the horn's circuit box, having memorized a half-dozen possible schematics to determine which wires to snip.

The job's already done. The wires I would have cut are unsheathed and frayed. Makes sense. He would've had to bypass the system, too.

My Admirer's done the work for me.

Rooftop gravel crunching under my feet is enough of a thrill for me. I don't bother to grab a ledge and dangle my feet. That's what he did. I must do better.

The Portside skyline twinkles like an alien solar system. I take it in before reentering the building and making my way back to the elevator. Excited about my next challenge, hopeful I've done enough prep to pull it off.

If I haven't, I may need to call up Coach Bottin and get his lawyer's number, so I can get out of jail as fast, if not faster, than he did.

Time to recruit the getaway driver.

I'm in Ocie's room, flipping casually through her calculus textbook as if it's interesting. "You know that photo contest I'm in?"

"Please tell me it's over and you won and you don't need my help again with something crazy. Though, I'm betting that's asking far too much."

Ocie's intuition. "Um . . . how?"

"You're dressed like a soldier."

Well, yeah, I'm in night-stalker attire. Black boots, dark jeans, dark hoodie. Not your typical grab-a-milk-shake-on-Saturday-night wear.

She breaks me down further. "And you've got the look."

"The look?"

"You look *interested* in something. Since you don't care about clothes, boys, and any of the other normal stuff *I'm* interested in, I know it's going to be something wild. What now?"

I may have lost her already, but if I have a chance in hell at getting her assistance, I can't hesitate or show any nerves. For once, I *am* nervous.

Getting through it the best I can, I tell her what I aim to do, try to make it sound less insane than it is. I don't do a good job.

She says, "No, no, no."

"Ocie, I'm not asking you to help me get the shot. I want you in the car, on the phone, letting me know if someone comes."

"Someone. You mean the police."

I shrug. The fire department and rescue squad are good candidates, too.

"It doesn't matter if you don't want me with you. *You* shouldn't do it. It's dangerous, and you're going to get in huge trouble."

"Not if you're there."

"I don't get it. What kind of contest would need you to do something like this? I'm not getting involved. I'm sorry."

I love Ocie like a sister, but here lies the problem in having a single, solitary best friend. If she's not down for the cause, there's no one else to draft. I have to convince her.

"I haven't told you everything," I say.

"Surprise, surprise."

"There's a boy . . ." I leave it vague because I know my friend.

Ocie fills in the rest. "I knew it! There had to be some testosterone in this bag of crazy. Who is it?"

"It's the guy from the contest, the one I told you about before."

"He's cute." Not a question. She's building my motive for me.

I nod.

"Let me see him."

I'm not prepared for that. I can tell she's not going to be down for this without a visual, something to satisfy the Cutie Quotient in her head.

I think fast, and go into the photo gallery on my phone. I have stock photos I've used for digital art projects. Plenty of male models to pick and choose from. I scroll to one that looks the least like Marcos. Tall, dark, clothes hugging his muscles like either they're shrinking or he's swelling.

When I show him to Ocie, her face lights up, "Oh, he's smokin', reminds me a little of—" Her mouth snaps shut.

I look at the picture, then back to her. "Who?"

"Never mind. This is really about impressing the hottie?"

I nod again.

She sighs, looks me in the eye, and I feel the "no" coming. "It's still crazy, Panda."

"But you said he's hot, right? We agree. He's our black."

A reluctant nod and sigh. "He is. Our tantalizing black."

"So . . ."

She raises her hand, shushing me. "Love is crazy. If this helps you embrace the insanity and get the guy, I'm in."

We drive downtown, the red, white, and blue signage of the Patriot Trust Building visible from the highway. We hit the surface streets and move beyond Winston Avenue and Noble, which house bars and clubs filling with the party crowd. Farther east and we're in the business district, which is as busy as a riot during the week, but feels like church on weekends. Only a few cars line the streets next to our destination, so parking's not an issue tonight.

Tonight's issue is something else entirely.

Idling in front of the Patriot Trust Building, I crane my neck, stare up its mirrored face. I imagine Marcos at the tip-top, legs dangling while his camera flash goes off like an exploding star, a winking jewel in the mane of the constellation Leo. That bit of imaginary astronomy gets me going, a boost to do the extremely scary thing I've come here to do.

I step from my car, turn away from the Patriot Trust Building, and face the unfinished structure across the street.

The Cablon Hotel. Due to open for business in the fall of 2016. When it's done, it will be Portside's tallest skyscraper, usurping the current champion . . . the Patriot Trust Building.

It's ten stories from being completed. The steel girders forming the frame of those final floors are in place, protruding from the fully built facade of its lower three-fourths like bare bones. From those high, unfinished floors it's a perfect downward view of the Patriot Trust roof.

That's where I'm going.

I pop my trunk, and remove a set of bolt cutters.

Yeah. Bolt cutters.

Ocie circles the block while I walk toward the Cablon site like I'm auditioning for Fashion Week. I'm in a red three-quarter-length trench, "borrowed" from Mom's closet. It's more suited for the clubbing crowd a couple of streets over than for tonight's exercise in Urban Exploration, but it proves its worth when a cop car passes and the officer inside doesn't look my way. Nothing looks more suspicious than someone in shady attire. You wear something bright, you *can't* be doing anything wrong.

Really, the key is confidence. Life Hackers and Social Engineers and Rooftoppers all agree there can be no hesitation—no doubt—when attempting a sketchy goal. The philosophy is summed up in three words.

Be bold. Belong.

I sneak to a dark corner of the hotel construction site, next to a "security" fence where I pull my gear from hooks I sewed into the coat's lining. Removing the coat altogether, I slip it into a heavy-duty garbage bag to keep it clean. Crouched, I make several quick snips with the bolt cutters, unmooring a section of fence that I can peel back, then slip through.

There's some sort of orange contact paper lining the inside of the fence, and my utility knife makes quick work of that. The chain links jingle like chimes on a cat's collar as I squeeze through, dragging all my stuff. Once inside, the paper conceals me; I leave the garbage bag by my entry point and move about the site freely, using the flashlight app on my phone.

"Please tell me you're not going to take the stairs, Bond," Ocie says. I'm wearing a Bluetooth earpiece, same as her, and she's keeping me connected to the outside world via cell.

"I'm not. Are things looking good out there?"

"All's clear, Bond," she says in a horrible British accent.

"Stop calling me that. You're so other, Ocie."

"No, you're so other, Double-O Nutcase. How are you going to get to the top?"

"I don't need to go to the top." Thank God. I only need to get higher than my Admirer got. I maneuver around bulky equipment that feels like sleeping monsters in the dark. A flock of birds takes flight, their wings batting the air, nearly taking my screams with them. I talk to Ocie more for comfort than any pressing need to explain my every move. "I'm taking the elevator."

"It works?"

"It did when I was here earlier this week."

"When you were— What?"

When it comes to Rooftopping you get bonus points for the height of the building, and the security you must bypass to reach the roof. News flash, getting to the very top of a building is not easy. The owners don't want daring (not to mention suicidal—or, I guess, homicidal) people on top of their buildings. In barring access to adrenaline freaks and psychos, artists like me and my Admirer have a lot of hurdles to jump. Locked steel doors, alarms, cameras—the kind I *don't* like.

Fortunately, they haven't installed all that stuff into this building yet.

Seems hotel investors are much less concerned about security before the fancy silverware and Egyptian cotton sheets get ordered.

Slowly, avoiding hidden holes, and scattered nails, and any number of other dangerous minutiae that litters construction sites, I make my way to the service elevator. The construction crew uses it to get supplies to high floors; later it will be the elevator that the hotel waitstaff uses to deliver room service to guests. I know this because of the notes I took for my school newspaper article. Never mind that I don't write, and my school doesn't have a newspaper.

Thumbing the up button parts the doors, exposing the dusty, paint-splattered car, with a flickering light bar casting the interior in a strobe effect that makes it seem like I'm moving in slow motion. I step in, select the forty-second floor, and explain my insider knowledge to Ocie because I can hear her nerves coming through the phone. I need her calm and focused.

Floors clank by while I talk. "I called the construction foreman from the school and pretended to be a guidance counselor. I proposed the foreman give a promising female student who's eyeing the architecture program at Commonwealth University a construction site tour since the building's nearly complete. A whole 'education is the way' kind of thing. I didn't think they'd go for it, but someone with clout is big on inspiring youth. Got a call back the next day. I came after school, and got shown around."

"That worked?"

She'd be surprised at some of the stuff I'd pulled off over the years. Confidence and willpower go a long way. "Sure."

"Why didn't you get your picture then?"

Because the foreman wouldn't take me to the unfinished floors. If he did, he probably wouldn't let me get near the edge. Even if those two unlikely events had come to pass, there was the other part. Being there, in the daytime, surrounded by burly men who would've been overly concerned about my well-being, would've made it . . . sanctioned.

None of the danger of Rooftopping. Nothing to top *View from Heaven*.

Nothing to admire.

All I say is "Didn't get the chance."

The elevator stops, doors open with a gust of wind that makes me feel like I'm back in that beach storm. Ahead of me, I see open air bordered by city lights and stars. This, from right here, is an awesome shot. The way the floor stretches toward the drop-off, a tunnel of exposed girders framing the sky, giving eerie depth. My camera's in my hand like I summoned it, and I twist on a fisheye lens for panoramic shooting.

Ocie says, "Panda, it's hard to hear you. You're breaking up."

The wind is loud, amplified by my Bluetooth. It's hard to hear her, too.

I shout, "I'm fine. Give me a few minutes."

The pictures I'm getting from the relative safety of the elevator would kill on many of the sites I frequent. Definitely could earn a few bucks selling these shots as stock online. But I need more.

The camera strap nestles into my shoulder with the feel of a safety belt. It's the only thing that feels safe in this moment. I remove a length of rope from my bag, and leave my backpack in the elevator so it wedges between the doors when they try to close. Venturing out, I break right, and cover half the distance—about twenty yards—to the view I want, Patriot Trust.

The wind's coming in at random directions, like a gang of ghost bullies taking turns shoving me then retreating to their spirit world. Within the last ten yards before the drop, I coil one end of my rope around the closest girder, securing it with a carabiner, like a rock climber. The other end locks onto the harness I'm wearing under my pants. Admiration is one thing, stupidity another.

The precaution is comforting, because the closer I get to the edge, the stronger the wind. Ten feet from the open air, I'm crouched, my center of gravity low. At the edge, the break between floor and sky, I forget to breathe. Still, I'm shooting.

The Patriot Trust sign. The gravel-topped roof. The shorter, less regal, surrounding buildings. What I have is nearly enough, but I need one more picture to make sure.

With my pulse pounding hard, louder than the wind now, I push onto my knees, rock back onto my butt. Extending my legs before me, I scooch until my feet slide beyond the solid plane, keep going until my legs can bend at the knee and my boots dangle hundreds of feet over the ground they walked not fifteen minutes before. Quickly, while I still have the nerve, I get a panoramic shot of Patriot Trust and the Portside skyline with my feet in the frame, toes pointed like a ballerina.

He's going to love this.

I'm done. Sliding backward, getting far away from the edge before the surrounding girders snap like a mousetrap, ensnaring me forever. Gasping, ecstatic, I undo my rope, moving back toward the elevator; I could cheer.

I *do* cheer, screaming into the wind while it screams back. Inside the car, going down, the ambient noise is gone, yet I still hear screams.

Ocie.

"Panda, Panda. Code red! The cops are here!"

I don't feel much like cheering anymore.

The elevator sails down. *Clank-clank-clank.* I watch the numbers on the floor indicator like a countdown. When it hits "1," I expect the doors to part, revealing cops, and SWAT, and Special Forces on the other side, peppering my dark clothing with red laser polka dots like in the movies.

The doors open, there is only darkness. Total, consuming. I don't dare turn on my flashlight app.

"Where, Ocie?" I hiss.

"They're, like, patrolling, shining their spotlight at the closed storefronts and alleys. They don't see me, but they're getting close to the fence you went in."

If they find that hole I cut . . .

I can't sit still, but I'm scared to move, to make a sound. An engine revs. My engine. I recognize the sound of my car coming through my earpiece, then my squealing brakes, followed by Ocie saying, "Officers, excuse me, I need help."

What is she doing?

Deep voices rumble in the background, too low for me to hear.

Ocie says, "I saw a couple of guys pushing each other around over by that club on Barnaby. It looked like it could get serious. I think one of them had a knife."

Oh my God, Ocie. You genius!

More deep, low voices. Quicker now. Slamming car doors and sirens sound simultaneously through my earpiece and in the air around as the cops peel out to stop the bloodbath Ocie fabricated.

"Panda," Ocie says, "if you're coming, it better be now."

I turn on my flashlight app and *move*, cautious of lethal construction site debris, but walking quicker than what's truly safe. The police might find something strange about the civic-minded Asian-ish girl when they find no weapons or hostility in the club district.

Once through the fence, I use plastic zip ties to resecure the cut links.

If I'm lucky, it will be days before anyone notices the damage, if they ever notice.

My car's waiting at the curb. I jog to it, carrying my gear like a bag lady. The passenger door pops open, and I see Ocie reposition herself with both hands on the wheel, a born wheelman. I dive in, and we're in motion.

I expect admonishments, a repeat of her storm rage. Instead, she's grinning, the excitement radiating off her. She busts a U-turn and peels out like the cops, but in the opposite direction, toward the highway.

"That. Was. Awesome!" she screams, and bangs one fist into the roof.

"I didn't expect that reaction."

She laughs, and hoots, and is in a better mood than I've seen all week. "That's our black, Panda!"

I agree quietly, "So not other."

We hit the on-ramp, and I feel closer to her than I have in a while. It's accompanied by a blast of guilt nausea—I've regained our bond with lies.

Shake it off, Panda Bear.

What's done is done. The question: Was the lie worth it? I won't know for sure until I get home and take a look at my photos on my MacBook. I'm feeling good, though. Confident. My shots are winners.

Ocie says, "Now that we just pulled off a caper, will I get to meet this guy?"

"Soon, I hope." This time, I'm not lying.

It's dark in my house when I arrive. The only light is blue and ghostly, flickering in the living room where my parents are watching a movie. From the sounds of punches and gunfire I know it's something Dad picked, yet Mom's hugging him like it's *The Notebook*.

I stop in the doorway to say hello. "Hey, guys."

Dad pauses the chaos. "You wanna watch the new Bruce Willis with us? You haven't missed much."

Mom offers their bowl of popcorn. "Extra butter."

Waving it off, I make my way upstairs. "Movie night is all you, guys." I like Bruce Willis, but since I just lived a PG version of *Die Hard*, I've reached my adrenaline quota.

In my room I import my pictures to my machine and I'm pleased with the results. I spend an hour on touch-ups before I click SEND and prepare myself for a long wait. I'm sure he'll want to battle again, but I'm not budging until Marcos admits who he is.

That's my plan, this bright and sunny fantasy about what me and my Admirer would be together.

How quickly it unravels.

The next night, Sunday, I'm fresh from the shower and pulling on my pajamas. My mail program sounds with an incoming message. The subject: *A New Game*.

Grinning—yes, my photos are game changers—I open the email. There's no message, only an attachment. I click it, expecting something amazing.

It's a plain, unflattering photo. Like a mug shot. Of Keachin Myer.

I don't get it. I respond and say so.

Less than a minute passes before I see the *SecretAdm1r3r wants to chat* request.

PandaD: What's the deal with that picture of Keachin? Did you get the photos I sent you?

SecretAdm1r3r: Got them. Keachin's our new subject.

PandaD: What's that mean?

SecretAdm1r3r: I told you already. Karma. I think I mentioned something about a bitch, too. It all lines up.

Um, no. It doesn't.

PandaD: You want me to get a picture of Keachin? Done that already. I like the other stuff we've been doing better.

SecretAdm1r3r: This had to happen. Tell me how you feel about it tomorrow.

PandaD: Feel about what? What had to happen?

SecretAdm1r3r has left the chat.

For an hour after I send multiple emails with no response. Irritating, but I don't think much about it—he's flaky, that much I know.

I doze off thinking about his "new game" and what it might entail. What's it got to do with Keachin? What else does karma have to teach her?

Whatever it is, I'm sure it's better than she deserves.

CHAPTER 15

THERE ARE NO NEWS CREWS TODAY when Ocie and I pull into the student parking lot. I guess bigger and better stories have drawn the flies to new honey.

Last night's weirdness from my Admirer—and the abrupt end to last night's weirdness—has me uneasy, and I mistake the palpable tension I feel when I step into the school as something internal, my personal anxiety. It's not. There's something in the air.

Voices are lower, and while the usual cliques are in their usual spots, there's hugging and hand-holding. A lot of PDA where there's usually none. Someone's sobbing, deep and throaty like a dog's bark. It's a football player.

Ocie's eyebrows bunch high, grazing her hairline. Her *What-huh?* look.

"What's happening here?" I say.

She spots some of her bandmates. "Hang on, Panda."

As she confers with them, I move to my locker, wishing, once again, I had someone to talk to other than Ocie.

Then he's there. Again. Taylor Durham. I so have to be careful what I wish for.

"Lauren, are you all right?" There's something weird about his voice. It's too soft.

And why wouldn't I be all right?

I say, "I was until you showed up. Are you, like, stalking me?"

He looks taken aback. When he speaks again, the sorrow has worn away. "Stalking *you*? You're . . . you're unbelievable."

Enough. "What's with you, lately? We haven't spoken this much in years. Am I radiating openness? Do you feel the warmth of springtime sun when I'm near? If so, please understand that sensation is actually my fiery disdain."

The muscles in his jaw clench, like he's biting back rogue words. A deep breath later, he says, "The way things have been going, I thought you could use a friend."

"Do you have a head injury that might explain the nonsense that's coming out of your mouth?"

His chest swells, like he's gearing up to blast me. But Ocie's suddenly between us, her hand pressed to her mouth. She looks to Taylor, and he says, "Mei, I tried. Okay. Can't do it anymore. You deal with her."

He goes and I'm so confused about his parting words—*you deal with her*—that I don't notice Ocie welling up. A tear falls from each eye and rolls down her cheeks.

"She's dead, Panda. She died last night."

I want to ask "Who?" But I can't quite manage. I remember the odd chat with my Admirer from the night before.

This had to happen.

Who else could it be?

"Panda? Where are you—?"

I'm down the hall and around the corner. Moving. Running. Bumping classmates aside.

Keachin's our new subject.

It's just a coincidence. It has to be a coincidence. Or I've made the wrong assumption. Ocie never said a name. The dead "she" could be someone else.

My mind's divided between flashes of last night's Admirer chat, backward twisted hope that I've guessed wrong on which of my classmates will never age beyond her yearbook photo, and the wholly pragmatic understanding that the nearest bathroom is not near enough.

Veering toward the closest set of doors, I barrel through into the auditorium, make it to a trash can just inside, and retch.

I'd skipped breakfast so nothing comes up, and I'm left dry-heaving into the can. A rending *whroa-oar* noise escapes my throat. Makes my ears hurt. So much so, it takes a second for the teeth sucking and disgusted groans to register.

Raising my head from the trash receptacle, I see a loose group of guys and girls—sophomores and freshmen; kids maybe too young, too out of the loop, or too disinterested to be affected by the morning's developments. They're twisted around in their auditorium seats, watching me. People have all sorts of hangout spots before class. The gym. The cafeteria. Here.

My stumbling nausea interrupts their Red Bull and earbud meditation. They are none too pleased.

A girl in a rainbow-colored knit hat with bulky designer headphones clamped around her neck like a collar says, "Damn, bee-yotch. Use birth control next time."

Her comrades cackle. I feel my complexion redden as I back out of the auditorium, considering if morning sickness and its causal condition might be better than everything swirling in me right now.

The warning bell sounds, and someone's moist wail ramps up in competition.

There is still a watery sensation in my empty stomach, and my knees feel only slightly less liquid. Somehow I make it to homeroom, my mouth sour. I don't remember walking, or sitting down, or the gradual filling of the seats around me. In the preclass murmurs I hear, for the first time, Keachin's name from somewhere other than my own head. She is the one.

Now her face, still and unremarkable on my computer screen, is all I can see.

I want to leave. And faint. And scream. At the same time.

No tears, though.

Can't bring myself to cry. I haven't done that in so long, not since the days when I was afraid to face the daily torment from my classmates. When I got strong, and became Gray, I promised I'd never shed another tear over anybody in Portside High. Promise kept. I hate myself for it.

I could've figured a way to go home, something that didn't have to do with the death of Keachin Myer, but I'm compelled to stay as the rumors grow in volume and scope. How she died. Where. Everyone's saying different things. With so many versions—which had to mostly be wrong—maybe the rumor itself is a lie.

I cling to that.

Maybe she's not really dead, just hurt in some mundane way that has nothing to do with any of the things I put in motion.

Those hopes are dashed when Principal Carlin appears on the closed-circuit TV with a suit and voice like a mortician, confirming that a student has passed away, but never mentioning Keachin's name. While more classmates break down, I feel a sudden rush of anger and the need to understand why he won't say her name. Is it a legal thing? A stupid law if it is.

Two of the girls in Keachin's clique are bawling in an unsettling register at the back of the room, creating a contagion. At least three people in adjacent desks start leaking tears. Mr. Graham ushers them all into the hall and down to guidance before the infection spreads. An unsuccessful quarantine.

It's a sullen seven hours from the announcement to last bell. I move among the afflicted, immune to the teary outward displays, though I suffer from different ailments. Shame and guilt.

The grief is heaviest in the cafeteria where chatter is hushed, like we're in church. Even Ocie dials down her usual gossip rant, mentioning only she heard it was some sort of car accident.

People die in car accidents all the time. If there's anything to hope for when it comes to an eighteen-year-old's death, I hope this bit of information is true. I hope for this, but I don't waste a wish on it. Wishes aren't real.

My Admirer is.

DP class offers only cold comfort. My routine is familiar, but looking at the class photos I've taken reminds me of *other* photos I've taken, and that line of thought makes the world tilt.

"Hey!" It's Alyssa Burrell, her tone high and chipper as always. It's unsettling today. A perky voice doesn't seem proper.

"Yeah?"

"You okay, Panda? You seem, I don't know, off."

I glance around, worried the whole class is as perceptive as Alyssa, who, on a day when "off" is the norm, sees me as more so. No one else is paying attention.

"I'm fine." Go away.

She doesn't.

"What, Alyssa?"

She reveals the camera she'd been holding behind her back, a loaner from the supply cage. "Do you mind if I take your picture? It's for my next class project. On grief."

Slap her.

The urge is so strong, my palm itches. Instead I nod, let her shoot—no flash—then she buzzes away, asking others for inappropriate poses.

Alone, I close my portfolio and lay my head on my desk. Ms. Marcella doesn't seem to mind. No one else—with the exception of Alyssa's ghoulish ass—is very productive today either. All here in body, but not spirit.

Except for Marcos Dahmer. Neither his body nor spirit showed.

I can't *assume* my Admirer did something to her. That's stupid, right? Doesn't that reek of self-importance on my part? Only *I* know the *real* killer, I'm *still* a step ahead of my classmates and the world?

That photo from last night wasn't coincidental, no. My Admirer somehow knew about Keachin before anyone else in school, and decided to be a creep about it. That's all. He's guilty of advanced knowledge.

When I get home, there's a chat request waiting for me. I see a version of myself slamming my MacBook shut and throwing it against the wall. Really dramatic, but not practical. The simplest thing I can do is tell him I'm done. No more Photographer Tag and late-night chats. I intend to break this off—whatever THIS is.

It's not fun anymore.

Was it ever?

> **PandaD:** Sending that picture last night was in real poor taste. I don't think we need to talk like this anymore.
>
> **SecretAdm1r3r:** You're afraid. Don't worry. No one's going to know what we did.

My chest tightens and my hands shake as an elephant dose of adrenaline saturates my blood. I type quickly, a flick of fingers.

> **PandaD:** *We* didn't do anything.
>
> **SecretAdm1r3r:** Why are you acting weird?
>
> **PandaD:** Someone died!

I'm giving him an out. His next words should explain it away. Last night's picture was mean, yes, but not . . . *evidence.*

> **SecretAdm1r3r:** When you say it that way, you make it sound so . . . accidental.
>
> **PandaD:** It's not funny pretending you had something to do with it.
>
> **SecretAdm1r3r:** Pretending? Let's be clear, this is very real. I finished what you started, Panda.

What I—? No. No, no, no.

> **SecretAdm1r3r:** Check your in-box. I think this photo is our best one yet.

An email comes through. No subject. Nothing clever or playful, and I don't want to open the attached photo because this feels like the first night he contacted me (*How do you get the color GRAY?*), the first time he showed me something I didn't want to see.

But how can I ignore this?

I open the image, and my legs kick involuntarily until my chair bumps my bed.

It's Keachin. Again. Not plain like last night's photo. It's brighter. More color. Particularly the snarling red gash along her hairline. The sheet of blood draped over the left side of her face. The bright-yellow candy wrapper tangled in her hair as the gutter water soaks the collar of her letter jacket.

The worst part, those *blue* blue eyes. Open and staring at things people in this world can't see.

Whatever tears I couldn't produce before come fast and hot now. I close my MacBook gently, unable to summon the strength to be forceful, or dramatic, or anything other than sorry.

Keachin was supposed to be a monster. One I hunt and slay. Not like this, never like this.

There *are* worse monsters out there. As Petra Dobrev says, "Once the beast's breath fogs your lens, it's too late to run!"

CHAPTER 16

MOM'S HOME FROM WORK, CHOPPING VEGETABLES for dinner when she notices me in the doorway, the MacBook under my arm.

"Are you hungry? It will be some time before I get this roast in the—" Whatever she sees on my face makes her drop her knife, its honed edge embeds itself in a halved onion like a trick she meant to do. "What's wrong, Lauren?"

I open my laptop and sit it next to the meal that will never get cooked or eaten. And I tell her everything.

Halfway through the story Dad comes home. Mom makes me start over and it's no easier to get through the second time. When I'm done there are questions. Mom mostly, flipping between English and German. Dad doesn't say anything. He keeps clicking and scrolling through *Gray Scales* with his mouth turned down. Every so often he shudders, like my site's a mirage he can shake off. Mom's questions get louder and *more* German, that is, when she manages to squeeze words between sobs.

Dad says, "The girl and that teacher, *you* exposed it?"

That question's coming from the sergeant, not my father. He's processing things quickly, strategically, the same way I do. He knows the threat assessment is bad without further enlightenment. I say, "Yes, sir."

"Now that girl is dead and you think this Admirer person is involved?"

"Yes, sir."

He stands and I'm eye level with the polo horse on his shirt, pink stitching on navy cotton. He stares at my forehead, I can feel the burn. Seeking cooler climates, my eyes drop farther, tracing the pleat in his pants before stopping at his square-toed shoes.

He turns toward the butcher's block on the counter. "Get your things. That computer, the camera, all of it."

My heart stops, pictures of him smashing my precious equipment with Mom's meat mallet go up on the IMAX in my brain. He reaches past the blunt kitchen utensil and grabs his car keys from the pegboard by the door.

"Where—?" I start.

"The police station," he says, cutting me off. "They need to hear your story."

The statement—the calmness of it—rocks me on my heels like he'd shoved me. I had to tell my parents what I'd been sent, what I'd seen. A piece of me knew the authorities would need to be involved, but I imagined two nice men coming by the house tomorrow or the day after to take a statement. The way Dad's acting is like my trip downtown is one way.

Mom's mouth opens, snaps shut. She has more to say, only not in front of me. They both eye me hard; the combined force of their stares pushes me from the room, but not too far. I crouch on the stairs to hear.

"We shouldn't tell anybody," Mom says. "Let her stay out of all this."

"Stay out of it," Dad says louder than I'm sure he intended, I would've heard him from my room. "If she's telling the truth, she caused it."

"Not someone's death. Just photographs."

"We hope. But I can't sit on this. We have to report it."

"Why?! She knows what she did was wrong and stupid. Keep the police out of it."

"I can't!" Glasses rattle and I know she's backed into the counter, knocking some bowl or cup askew. Daddy hasn't raised his voice like that in forever. When he speaks again, it's softer, the note of regret in his tone is almost lost.

"I work for a *government contractor*. Think about my security clearances."

His security clearances. The various statuses granted to government workers that allow them access to classified and top-secret information in order to do their jobs. Good-paying, difficult-to-acquire jobs. He talks about the clearances a lot with his friends and coworkers. How hard they are to get, and how easy they are to lose. He can't mean . . .

"Anything goes on in my home must be reported to the authorities and my company's security officer. *Immediately*," he says.

What I'm thinking—what I'm fearing—my mom says: "*You* can get in trouble for this?"

He doesn't answer, and that is answer enough.

I climb the stairs and prepare to be taken in.

At the police station we wait patiently on a bench like we've been told to do. There are magazines on the table next to me and a water cooler in the corner. An air bubble *GLUG*s inside the clear plastic water bottle, scaring a yelp from my mother. Neither me nor Daddy makes a sound.

It's not the chaos of police station lobbies in the movies, where hookers are handcuffed to chairs and some rowdy drunk is getting dragged in and processed. We're the only ones here; distant typing and air rattling through overhead ventilation is the soundtrack. This could be a doctor's office if not for the scratched and scarred bulletproof glass separating the desk officer from us.

A buzzer sounds and a door adjacent to the security window opens. The man who appears is my height, balding, with pink splotchy skin that could almost be polka dot. He's neat in slacks and a dress shirt. There's a badge and gun on his belt—both seem too large for him, like an eight-year-old's toys in the possession of a toddler—and a legal pad under his arm. He's disinterested. His eyes sail over us, trying to determine what it is he's drawn the short straw on. Checking the pad, he says, "Mr. and Mrs. Daniels?"

Dad slips his hand under my arm and tows me to my feet as he rises. He nudges me and I follow our escort into the depths of the station. Will I be spending the night—a lot of nights—here?

"I'm Detective Vincent," he says without looking back. "I'm told you have some information on a homicide."

"My daughter believes she does," Dad answers for me, "but we're not sure."

Detective Vincent pauses, looks us over again. He does not vocalize the "that sounds weird" expression that crosses his face. We come to a door labeled Interview Room #1 and he motions us in. There are chairs for us all, but it's cramped and hot. I expect one of those mirrors to be set in the wall, the kind where the glass on the other side is see-through, but the walls are solid. There is a camera set high in the corner, the tiny light next to the lens glowing red.

Detective Vincent sits across from us. "This is related to the Portside High girl we found last night, correct?"

"Yes," I say, "Keachin Myer. I—I might have some details."

"I'll be honest with you folks—it's unusual that people come to the station to talk about this sort of thing. Never seen it happen in my time. I'll be happy to take whatever info you have, but your statement will be recorded."

The camera draws my attention again. Would a jury see this sometime in the future?

"You okay, young lady?" the detective asks.

Choking back bile, I nod.

Detective Vincent leans toward me, puts both elbows on the table. "Look, folks, you came to us. At this point, I don't know anything beyond your names. If there's something you're worried about telling me, talk to a lawyer. Hell, the criminals get that option, the good law-abiding citizens should, too."

My heart jumps at the idea of having more time to be good old anonymous Gray. And, hey, getting some expert legal advice, I'm with that. I look to my parents and say with my eyes, *Yes, lawyer, please.*

Mom nods, agreeing.

Dad's a different story.

"We don't have anything to hide. Go on, Lauren. Tell the detective what you told us." A direct order.

Mom's jaw tightens, her eyes cut sharply toward my father. Yet she does not say a word.

Why would she? It's my turn to talk.

For the third time tonight, I tell the secret I've kept for as many years, stopping at the appropriate points to show off the accompanying photos. When I show Detective Vincent fiery *Dante*, he sucks in a whistling breath.

At the finale—my Admirer's final messages and the picture of a bloodied, dead Keachin—he stares at the photo a long moment before saying—to Daddy, not me—"Do I have permission to take this machine out of this room?"

I resent Detective Vincent not asking me since it is my machine and my photos. Beyond that, the stiff formality of the question makes me more uncomfortable, something I hadn't thought possible.

Daddy nods, and Detective Vincent is gone with my laptop under his arm. When the door seals, I face my parents. "Guys—"

"Shut it, Lauren," Mom says. Coming from her it stings like a slap.

I start to speak again, to—I don't know—defend myself, but Daddy grabs my hand and squeezes. Not hard, but enough to draw my eyes to his, which immediately cut to the camera I'd forgotten about. Someone is watching everything we say and do. Probably waiting for the moment when I show them something ugly and condemning.

The dark poetry of my circumstance is not lost on me.

CHAPTER 17

IT IS A HALF HOUR BEFORE Detective Vincent returns, and he isn't alone. A shorter, broader man accompanies him, and I wonder if the Portside PD is made up entirely of men who look like fire hydrants. The new cop has two shades of walrus whiskers—gray and grayer—sprouting wildly from his lips and ears. My open MacBook's in his hands now, and he plunks it on the table hard enough to make me wince.

He doesn't waste time introducing himself, only blurts, "How did you get this photo?"

"The guy I told Detective Vincent about, he emailed it to me after he confessed to—"

"You say email?" Walrus looks to Vincent. "You get that address?"

"I pulled it off her machine. Already sent it over to the tech guys."

Walrus redirects his attention to me. "Do you know the identity of the person who sent you this photo?"

He spins my laptop toward me so dead Keachin is staring me down. I flinch away like she's about to criticize my unkempt hair, bloodshot eyes, and rumpled outfit from beyond the grave. "I— Yes, I mean, maybe."

A notepad and pencil appear in Walrus's hand. It probably came from his pocket, but things are happening so fast it feels like magic. "Go on."

Glancing to my parents, I see they're leaning toward me, eyebrows arched and curious. Until now, I've not mentioned my suspicions about who my Admirer is. Despite all that's happened, I'm still hesitant to say his name.

But we've gone this far. "Marcos Dahmer. We go to school together. He's the yearbook editor."

Walrus scribbles the name, tears off the sheet, and hands it to Vincent. "Has he provided you with any more police property?"

"Any more—?" I'm stunned silent. *Police property?*

"You better speak up because I can't express how much trouble you will be in if we connect you with evidence tampering."

"Tampering? I'm trying to help."

"What is this about?" Mom asks.

Walrus points to the corner of Dead Keachin's photo. There's a number there. I noticed it before, but didn't examine it closely and mistook it for a time stamp.

"That's a case file number for this crime scene photo."

That sinks in. Feels like I'm turning that one over in my head for an hour.

I say, "*Your* photographer took these."

Detective Vincent explains to my parents, like I'm not in the room: "We've had leaks over the years. Photos and case details reaching news outlets before we're ready to provide them. I'm not sure why one of these dollar-chasing jerks has chosen to involve your daughter, but we will be looking into this."

The officers glare at each other, then to my parents, and I know we're done here. Relief is what I should feel, but this dismissal doesn't sit well with me.

Vincent says, "We appreciate you coming in. I've already made copies of the relevant files on your daughter's computer. I'm sure we'll need to follow up"—he checks his notes—"and I have your contact information here."

Dad says, "What kind of trouble is Lauren in?"

"We're not sure yet. You came to us and we will be submitting copies of her photos of the Myer girl to the district attorney to determine what value they have in upcoming proceedings. The DA will decide what's required of you folks going forward. In the meantime, I suggest you have Lauren take down that website she runs. What she's done is clearly an invasion of privacy—"

Internally, I buck at that. Vincent is not getting the big picture. Before everything with Keachin, my site *helped* kids. This situation is a mistake. The anomaly. *I'm not that different from you,* I think but don't say.

It goes on like that, them talking about how I need more discipline and supervision, staying on this tangent about leaked photos, ignoring what I'm really saying. The room is hot, I'm nauseous, and I can't understand why they're overlooking what I've told them.

So, I snap. "I'm not talking about some WikiLeaks asshole stealing crap from a Flickr page. I'm talking about a killer! He *murdered* this girl!"

There's a charge in the air and I resist eye contact with anyone who doesn't have a badge. My parents are shooting silent threats at me, like I'm five and throwing a toy-store tantrum. I won't be ordered to sit down and be quiet. I want to be able to sleep at night.

Something that may be more wish than reality going forward.

Vincent breaks the silence. "We have a suspect in the Myer girl's killing."

"You already caught him?" As soon as the words cross my lips I know we aren't talking about the same "him." Not Marcos.

Vincent nods. "Yes, caught him at his apartment. The car was parked out front." A thundercloud crosses his face, his next words angry, personal. When he speaks, I instinctively know this man has a daughter somewhere. "As if he hadn't violated that girl enough already."

He's talking about Coach Bottin. They think *he* killed Keachin. But . . . no. NO.

"What about everything I've shown you?" I'm looking to my parents now, begging them for backup. "My Admirer is a real person."

"I know," Vincent says, "but not a real killer. Trust me on this, darling. That yearbook kid is screwing with you."

"How can you know that?" I'm gripping the table so hard, I might leave behind a handprint.

"Because I just looked at photos of a bunch of people with reason to mess with your head." He motions to my MacBook. Really, he's motioning at the elephant in the room. The Gray one.

"Get rid of that site, kid," Vincent says. "If you're lucky, it won't come back to bite you."

With that he stands, meeting over. They have their man. Case closed. No need to make anyone work harder.

Me and my family are escorted from the station. Our demeanors no different from if we'd left a restaurant after a late dinner. The illusion disintegrates during the ride home.

"Lauren, tell me what the hell you were thinking putting that website together," Daddy says.

I mumble.

"Speak up."

"Justice," I say.

Uncomfortable seconds pass before Daddy says, "Are you insane?"

Remains to be seen.

Dad takes my phone, my camera, my lenses, and my Mac. Not before forcing me to delete the public folders, templates, and photos that make up *Gray Scales*. Because he knows computers from his job, he also makes me empty the little wire basket trash can in the corner of my display (where I'd planned to retrieve the files from later), permanently sending my beloved website into the Great Digital Beyond. Bashing my toes with a hammer would be less painful.

It's close to midnight before the warden finishes tossing my cell. No contraband makes it through inspection.

"School and home," he says. The sharp edge that's been present in his voice all night is worn, but not quite dull. "Nothing else. Not for a very long time."

When I don't respond immediately, he steps into my personal space and I have to fight the urge to back away. "Did you hear me?"

"Yes," I say, swallowing hard, "sir."

I almost expect an "at ease" before he leaves. It doesn't happen. Would've been insincere anyway. Nothing's going to be "at ease" from now on.

I can't sleep, and I hear noises through my wall, different from what I'm accustomed to from my parents' bedroom. No low and slow music, no squeaky mattress in a moment of lapsed restraint. Their voices are above normal speaking volume, argument voices. All because of me.

Murder. Cops. Mom and Dad sounding like an abusive couple in a Lifetime movie.

I manage to cry myself to sleep, clinging desperately to the thought that things can't get worse than this.

I'm wrong, of course.

CHAPTER 18

DAD DROPS ME OFF AT SCHOOL on his way to work. He says Mom will pick me up in the exact same spot after school. It's all he says.

The night before seems surreal. The memory of telling the cops my most guarded secrets are softening, drooping like the clocks in that famous painting, yet the stale cigarette smell from Interview Room #1 is still in my hair.

I'm caught up in my own head, fumbling my locker combination. When I get it open, I shuffle through the junk on my top shelf, remembering a forgotten treasure. A security blanket in these uncertain times.

Wedged in the far corner is a palm-sized plastic rectangle. A tiny point-and-shoot camera, won in some long-ago raffle, good for quick-and-dirty shots when all the DP cameras are checked out. I pull it to me, intending to check the batteries, and notice the tightly folded paper square—something foreign slipped through the locker vent. It tips off the edge of the shelf and drops between my feet like a dead bird. When I crouch to pluck it up, my fingers freeze an inch from touching it.

It's him. My Admirer, choosing more traditional/intimate ways to communicate now that we've bonded over blood. What will this twisted love note contain? A lock of Keachin's hair? A tooth?

Forcing my hand to move, I grab and unfold it, bracing for horror and anticipating the vindication I'll feel when I show this to all the adults who doubt me and say, "See, this Crazybags is still out there!"

The note is not made of skin, or written in body fluid. It is a love letter. Or a sex letter, with vivid descriptions of things both contorted and damp. Not for me, though. It's addressed to Corra Oliver, my locker neighbor.

My heart slows and my breathing deepens while an angry red beam shoots through my head.

Can a person be relieved and furious simultaneously?

Corra approaches with her bestie, Marnie Davenport, and pops her locker.

"Corra"—I push the note toward her—"this was in my locker, but it's for you. I read some of it. Sorry."

There is a knowing look on her face when she takes the note, but Marnie's the one who explains, "Moody can't seem to get her locker right. Last week's note ended up on the other side of the school."

Moody—not a description of temperament, but a name, as in Derrick Moody. Most likely he couldn't remember Corra's locker number because of all the ditch weed he smokes, when he's not selling it. I thought he might've been a prime target for Gray at one point when I heard rumors of him strong-arming younger/smaller druggies. It never panned out.

Corra rolls her eyes, used to her boyfriend's ditziness. "Thanks, Panda. Me and Moody aren't a secret or anything, but this is a bad time for any personal deets to be floating around. Gray's on a rampage."

My mouth does not tic. "How so?"

Now she's bug-eyed, excited to be someone's first source for gossip. "You didn't get the email?"

I shake my head, urging her to get on with it.

"He's putting someone else on blast today! You know how Gray do."

While Corra is beaming, Marnie looks as uncomfortable as the positions described in Moody's note. She says, "It's kind of a douche move to do it so soon after Keachin."

Corra, with effort, reins in her desire to see another student humiliated. "Totally. Respect the dead, yo."

The warning bell rings, and Corra finishes at her locker. She and Marnie move along while I stay rooted, my camera/security blanket offering little comfort over what I just heard.

My stomach's sinking and I want to find Ocie for the full scoop, but her locker's a hike, and she's probably already in homeroom since she had to get up at the butt-crack of dawn to catch the bus. Crap.

Gray's exposing someone today.

I make it to my own seat just as final bell rings, and the anticipation makes homeroom queasy. Infinite minutes pass, torturously.

That misery ends, replaced by new pain that comes during Spanish class.

It's not sudden or subtle. I hear the telltale buzz of someone's silenced phone rattling in their bag. The rule is you power down during school hours, so the sound alone is enough to get your phone taken. This is Mrs. Vergara's class, though, and she's hard of hearing, so you're being considerate if you bother to turn down your ringer at all.

Twisting, I see Holden Goldweather fishing the cell from his satchel and checking the display the way a vain person checks their hair in a hand mirror. Mrs. Vergara's a little blind, too.

Facing forward, I try concentrating on verb conjugations—*yo veo, tú ves, nosotros vemos*—when Holden says, "No effing way! Pan—"

The second syllable of my name is drowned by a sudden explosion of hornet-nest vibrations and forgot-to-silence ringtones. At least a dozen phones go off at the same time. The exposé we've all been waiting for.

There's only one person who could/would impersonate me now. Only one story worth exposing.

There's a vibration at *my* desk as well. Not a phone, but my hands. Shaking. With such force that I have to lay my pencil on my paper because my last conjugation had become a scraggly line of dips and peaks, like an erratic heartbeat on some hospital monitor. The combined whispers around me are too loud, not really whispers at all.

Another phone sounds. Late, but the loudest of all with its upbeat mariachi music. Mrs. Vergara, alarmed by the surge of classroom interest, shuns the very rule she's supposed to enforce, retrieves her phone from her desk, checks the display.

She plucks her cat's eyes glasses from her nose and stares me down. "*Señorita* Lauren! You are Gray?"

Sí, señora. I am.

At the class break, I step into the hall, head down, still trying—and failing—to be a ghost. I am officially and permanently undead. All eyes aren't on me, but I can't imagine the sensation being much different if they were. There's a sense of pressure, like walking under deep water. Getting deeper.

"Yo, Gray, that thing you caught Tam McNamara doing was sick!"

I speed up, until a pair of girls I don't know start clapping. The unexpected applause slows me down, and someone in the crowd says, "I want an autograph."

Now I'm at full stop, taking in words and expressions. Everything I see is a mix of awe, and good humor, and appreciation.

Until I spot Nina Appleton at her locker. She's looking my way and I smile slightly, a silent but humble admission. *Yes, I'm Gray. I stood up for you.*

Nina's mouth turns down. She gives a slight head shake and fades into the crowd. What's that about?

I want to chase her, and would have. A powerful hand clamps on my arm, hard enough to bruise. I'm dragged into the bathroom, wedged between the sink and the perpetually empty paper towel dispenser before I'm released.

"Is it true?" Ocie says. Her outfit is red-on-red today. She's dressed for anger.

"Ocie," I say, and try to step toward her.

She shoves me in the chest and I stay cornered. She's a dwarf enforcer.

The hurt in her eyes makes me want to lie. Not because it will help anything, I know it won't, but like a snake hiss-coiling, or an opossum playing dead, the instincts want what the instincts want. I know everything about her, and she thought she knew everything about me. We've both been betrayed today.

"Are you Gray?" she asks.

I inhale, ready to admit what she already knows.

A bathroom stall door swings inward, and Godzilla's niece steps out, her cell phone in hand.

"Yeah," the giant, stone-faced girl says, "are you?"

Her name is Danielle Ranson. Younger sister to Darius, the former baseball star/doper whose academic and athletic career Gray—I—ended.

I take it she's not a fan.

CHAPTER 19

LIE. LIE. LIE.

Danielle skulks toward me. Her big, clopping Sasquatch feet smacking the always-moist tiles. She's six feet tall, with hips as narrow and shoulders as wide as anybody her brother might've competed against on the field. Her freakish size makes me wonder if Darius had been buying the 'roids for her.

The bell rings, and, as that old saying suggests, I think I'm saved. "We're late."

The giant blocks my way to the door. "Then we don't gotta rush."

"Danielle, I don't know what you think—"

"My brother was gonna play ball for UVA, or the farm league." She plants her palm on the empty towel dispenser by my head, a slow, deliberate THUNK! The cheap aluminum box bows inward. "He was going to buy us a house. You know where he is now?"

She lets it hang, wanting me to give some inadequate answer that somehow adheres to the script in her head. This is a play, and the finale is her pummeling me, no doubt.

"He's a sales associate," Danielle says, bringing me back to her. "In the mall. At *Footlocker*."

Words bubble up my throat, not the whimpering plea or shamed apology she's expecting. *I don't care where he is as long as he's not on a baseball field because he shouldn't have been a bully and a cheat.*

"Back off," Ocie says before I blurt, saving me from myself. She wedges herself between me and Danielle, like a little dog facing off against a pit bull because she doesn't realize they are different sizes. Ocie shoves the hefty girl back a few feet. "You got a problem with her, get in line."

Whoa! Ocie's aggression warps my mind. We're both learning something new about each other today.

Danielle seems less impressed. "Shouldn't *you* be the Panda, Horton? Aren't those bears from your freakin' continent?"

"China's a country, not a continent. And I'm from America, thank you."

"Whatever. Get back before I dip you in some duck sauce and take a bite."

Ocie's head tilts. "Now that's just racist!"

Danielle sweeps Ocie aside, all talk done.

She draws back her meaty fist, ready to whale on me, when our vice principal, Ms. Del Toro, enters, her trademark walkie-talkie stitched to her hand. "What's the commotion in here?"

Danielle reaches past me as if checking the dispenser for towels: "Darn, empty."

Darn?

"You're supposed to be in class."

"Sorry," I say, slipping past Danielle and hooking Ocie's elbow so we're leaving together. "We're going now."

We're halfway down the hall before Danielle leaves the restroom. I glance back at her, knowing what I'll see. A promise. She and I aren't done.

Around the corner, Ocie shakes loose.

"You were awesome in there," I say, knowing this isn't *that* kind of moment, but desperately wanting to avoid a fight with her. "That was our black."

"Don't even," she says, and her fierceness is dampened by tears. She goes to her next class, which is in the opposite direction of mine. Mrs. Del Toro rounds the corner, watching, so I can't chase my friend. Maybe that's a good thing.

Enough truth has caught up for now.

There's rumbling around me for the rest of the day. Nothing as in-your-face as the bathroom showdown, but the news spreads. *I'm* the center of attention, the exact reverse opposite of what I've strived for my whole high school career. Some of it is . . . gratifying. Some of it gives me eerie flash-backs of Keachin's final days. I cut those thoughts off. They spiral into dark places.

I skip lunch once I peek through the cafeteria window and see Ocie sitting with some bandmates instead of at our usual table. I know she's mad, and may be that way for a while. I get it. I just hope she doesn't take too long to get over it. I . . . I need her right now.

As much as people seem to be taking my secret identity in stride, it's foolish to think there's more goodwill than bad out there for me. I mean, okay, I think a lot of people—most, probably—appreciate what I do. Or did. They might outnumber the douche bags I caught unawares over the years. But I can't count on any of them to have my back like Ocie does. Or did?

Unlike Darius Ranson, most of my targets still roam these halls. They were always bigger predators than me. I think I can deal, though. I know who they are, and what to expect.

It's the unpredictable predator that worries me. Especially since I've got a class with him next period.

Only, DP class doesn't put me face-to-face with my Admirer. Marcos doesn't show. Again!

What if he's absent because the police picked him up? What if they kicked his door in a second after he sent the email blast that exposed me and is now in Interview Room #1 trying to explain his whereabouts when Keachin died.

What if this is over?

I want to believe me and my Admirer are through.

But he's surprised me before.

Fifteen minutes after the last bell, Mom's a no-show. With no cell phone to summon her, I turn back toward the building to call her from the main office. Through the foyer windows I spot a familiar face.

Nina Appleton waits for the automated door to finish its slow opening. When the gap is wide enough she hobbles through. She hasn't spotted me yet. I approach with a wide, unnatural grin. Emphasizing my friendliness. "Hey, Nina."

The sun's behind me, and I can tell she doesn't know who's calling her. She returns my grin until I step beneath the awning and become fully visible. She doesn't scowl or flash the sign of the cross, but she shuffles on her crutches, glancing over her shoulder like she wants to duck back inside.

You know you can't outrun me, I think. It's mean, and I'm sorry as soon as the words skim the surface of my brain. But, really, what's up with her?

I close the distance between us. My jaws aching from smiling. "Nina, you got a second to talk?"

"I guess, Panda. What do you want?"

Okay, straight to it then. "So you heard about my secret? That I'm Gray?"

"I heard." She's gazing down the fire lane in front of the school with a cold sort of panic, like a bank robber whose getaway driver is late.

I say, "Are we cool?"

Her eyes are all over. Everywhere but on me. "We don't really know each other like that, Panda."

"Yeah, I know." My smile's gone, and my patience is right on its heels. "What I'm saying is, do we have a problem?"

She's taken aback, shuffling away from me an inch or two. We're alone, and I'm being aggressive. Not Danielle Ranson's level of aggro, but if there were bystanders present, this might come off as me threatening a beloved disabled girl. I soften my voice, clarify. "You've been giving me weird looks and I'm trying to understand what you would be mad about since I only wanted to help you."

"Help me?" She shuffles forward and her voice has the edge now. Totally aggro. "How does your creepy perv act have anything to do with me?"

Creepy perv act? Is that one of her jokes? The Old-Time Appleton Humor. If so, that one falls flat. "I went after Keachin because of what she did to you. The way she shamed you. I got you some payback."

"She didn't get paid back, Panda. She got killed. You know that, right?"

I blink rapidly, like she'd triggered a flash an inch from my eyes.

For a second, I'd forgotten that Keachin was dead.

I'd pushed it down and behind today's events. Lumped her with all the other Gray targets, exposed and well.

"I don't know what sort of weakling invalid you think I am," Nina says, "but I don't need your kind of help. Not ever. When all this stupid Gray stuff blows up, make sure you don't mention my name. I didn't make you do it. The devil didn't either. It's all you, Panda."

The same way she lands a punch line—with expert timing and the perfect inflection—is the way she closes an argument. Crisp, clear. As strong as a Danielle Ranson jab, I imagine.

There are no benches outside of the school entrance, but I need one. Nina's backlash is dizzying. I nearly ask if I can borrow one of her crutches.

"Are you okay?" Nina says. She hobbles closer like she somehow plans to catch me if I collapse.

"Fine," I say, and wave her off. "Skipped lunch."

A motor approaches, Nina's father's minivan.

"Eat. Soon," Nina says. She goes to her ride, done with me.

I'm not done with her, though. I need to know something. "Nina."

She whips around in a way that makes me think she might overbalance and fall. There I go, underestimating her again. Of course she stays upright, her gaze communicating a clear *make it fast*.

"The day after I posted the pictures of Keachin and Coach, I saw you. You were cheesing ear to ear. What was that about?"

She lowers her head, thinking. She's struggling to recall the moment. When our eyes meet again, I have a spark of intuition. I know what she's going to say—some version of it anyway—before she says it, and I cringe before she speaks.

Nina says, "I don't know for sure. I'm happy about a lot of things, and I don't keep score like you do."

If she'd breathed fire on me like a dragon, it would've burned less.

Her dad parks the van, gets out, circles the vehicle to open her door for her. When she climbs into her seat, he asks, "Friend of yours?"

"No way." Nina doesn't spare me another glance.

My mom arrives as Nina's dad seals her into their vehicle. Mr. Appleton climbs behind the wheel and pulls away. I only stop watching when my mom honks. *Come, Panda, come.*

I strap myself into the passenger seat. Mom examines me, the frown lines around her mouth strained. "What is the matter?"

"Nothing. Can we just go?"

She's not satisfied, but she honors my request and shifts to drive. I zone out, resting my head against the window, staring into the side mirror. I'm thinking of what Nina said, and trying not to think of it.

I notice a car—an old, dark-green Jetta—parked behind my mom's. A young guy's driving it. Somebody's brother or cousin, I figure. When Mom pulls off, so does he.

Oddly, he doesn't pick anyone up.

CHAPTER 20

MOM'S ERRANDS. I GO ALONG—GET DRAGGED along. It's something I haven't endured since I was too young to be trusted home alone. That I'm, again, not trusted to be home alone is an insult on par with Nina's painful statements.

How had it come to this?

At the post office and Home Depot, I'm allowed to wait in the Honda, fiddling with radio stations, desperately missing my iPod and all the other modern tech I've been stripped of. It's hard to get lost in music when you don't pick the songs and mattress ads keep breaking in. I can't get my confrontation with Nina off my mind.

I don't keep score like you do.

I'm feeling a familiar regret, that sensation of coming up with perfect comebacks an hour after you need them.

"It's not about *me*," I should've said. "The assholes I exposed, that's not *revenge*. I could've easily done nothing, let them all keep tormenting their respective whipping boys and girls. I could've been a coward like everyone else. I could've—"

She got killed. You know that, right?

That is the ultimate comeback, isn't it? The rebuttal nuke, destroying all others. Or am I just keeping score again?

Mom exits the hardware store with . . . whatever. I don't really care. I'm anxious to get home and sulk in the privacy of my room.

"I must make one more stop," Mom says. "Groceries."

I shrug, and Mom drives us a couple of blocks to the supermarket, which is located next door to my favorite bookstore/café. When she parks, I get out, too.

"Where are you going?" Mom asks, though I get the sense she already knows the answer.

"For coffee." Not that I really have a taste for the caffeine; I just want a familiar distraction. "I can meet you back here when you're done."

"Nein!"

"Ich habe Geld!" I've got money!

She stares at me over the roof of the car. *"Es spielt keine Rolle, dass du dein eigenes Geld hast. Du kannst nicht einfach tun was willst. Zumindest nicht mehr."* So what if you have your own money. You do not get to do as you wish. At least, not anymore.

This is my world now. Simply desiring a beverage incurs the wrath of others. I'm Panda the pariah.

I switch back to English—quiet English—because she's loud and people are watching. "Fine. I'll wait in the car."

Mom checks her volume and language. "Did you not just hear me? Come on, the shopping will go faster."

I look anywhere but my mother's face because it's so crazy-making.

To the sky for some divine intervention. Around the parking lot for some kind stranger with out-of-state plates who might take me away from here.

It's then that I notice the dark Jetta and its driver—the same from the school—on the row across from ours, parked a few spaces closer to the store. He does that thing guys do when they get caught staring at your butt or boobs, jerking his head in the opposite direction, as if that busted LeBaron he's parked next to had his attention the whole time.

"Lauren! I do not have all day."

Following Mom into the supermarket, my eyes stay on that car. The driver resorts to gazing at his lap. He reminds me of someone.

Me.

I've been in similar situations when tracking Gray targets. Suddenly, the offender is looking in my direction, and I'm willing him or her not to notice me. I was certainly smoother than this guy, never getting caught until recently. But that's the rub.

Who is he? And why is he following me?

The last person to tail me was my Admirer.

Marcos.

I'm 99 percent sure they are one and the same. But 99 percent sure isn't sure at all, is it?

Suddenly, the grocery store—with its bright lights and crowds of afternoon shoppers—doesn't seem so bad.

Tearing her shopping list in half, Mom gives me my own cart and tells me to find her when I've gotten everything. I seek the sundry items, but I'm also noting every single face I come in contact with, glancing over my shoulder every few seconds. Is he in here? Watching me now?

I get my answer in the detergent aisle, when I'm alone, grabbing a gallon of Tide, and he comes straight at me, the man from the Jetta. No stealth, no hesitation. Just a tall, brown-haired guy in wrinkled khakis.

Hit him with the jug of soap. Run him over with my cart. Scream. All options scroll through my mind, and I don't know which I'll settle on. A few feet from me he extends his hand like I'm the store manager and he's here to interview for a bag boy position.

"Hi, I'm Quinn Beck. Lauren Daniels, right?" He checks something on the phone in his other hand. "You go by 'Panda,' though."

Um, what?

My silence seems to fluster him. He retracts the hand he offered and pulls some sort of laminated card from his breast pocket, holds it out for me to see. "Sorry. I'm from channel nine news."

I look at the card—an ID badge actually—and see the station's logo. Next to it is the name he gave me and a pasty, overbright picture of his face. He's pastier in person, like he hasn't seen the sun in about a year, but it's definitely him. "You're a reporter?"

"An intern, actually. I'm a sophomore at Commonwealth University, the Broadcast Journalism program."

That information answers none of the billion questions I have. "How do you know my name? And my nickname? Why have you been following me? Why are you talking to me now?"

"*Gray Scales*, the website where the Keachin Myer sex scandal originated, right? I was hoping to reach you first. I want to discuss the genesis of the site. What prompted you to become this sort of school yard whistle-blower, revealing the secrets of your classmates to the world?"

His phone is now held between us, at chin level. Recording our conversation. The wrongness of this all sets off alarms in my brain, yet I can't bring myself to walk away.

I don't say a word while his phone's in my face. Terms like "self-incrimination"—something I heard on some cop or lawyer show—float to the surface of my mind, and it's terrifying that my thoughts are going there.

Now I'm certain this guy is not my Admirer. He might be worse.

He sees me eyeing his phone, lowers it. "Okay, off the record, then."

"How do you know *anything* about me?"

He blushes, two red blossoms on his sun-deprived cheeks. "I'm a fan. A bunch of people in my program are. The way you get scoops, we all thought you had to be some PI's kid, like Veronica Mars, or something. I thought for sure you'd be a guy"—he shrugs off his own sexist assumption—"when you revealed your identity today. It sort of blew my mind."

I shake my head. "No, not me."

"You didn't—?"

More vigorous head-shaking on my part. "You said you want to talk to me because you were hoping to be the *first*. The first what?"

"The first reporter to get an interview."

"I thought you were an intern." I'm missing the point here. My mind is protecting me from what he's actually saying.

"Well, yeah. But if I land some time with you, it could mean big things."

I'm looking around, willing my mother to become impatient and find me. "I'm not eighteen, can you even be talking to me?"

"Sure, there's no rule against interviewing minors, unless this thing becomes a criminal or civil matter."

"What thing?"

"Your involvement in the Myer girl's murder."

I spin my cart away, nearly taking a couple of his toes with me. He leaps back. "Hey!"

"I don't want to talk to you. I have to go." I'm rolling away, but he jogs ahead and cuts me off. As I reconsider running him over, he shoves a card at me. It's so sudden, I raise my hands defensively, and end up with it in my palm though I never intended to take it.

It's somebody else's business card, but with the name and number scribbled over and replaced with Quinn's contact info. They really don't pay interns anything.

"Look," he says, "I *get* what you were doing with your site. When you want to get in front of this, you'll want a friendly telling your story. Trust me."

Get in front of this.

There it is again, the implication that there's something more going on than this weird meeting in the soap aisle. I stuff his card into my pants pocket and swerve my cart around him. I zoom past aisles, catching glimpses of lightbulbs and dog food and breakfast cereal, until I spot my mom. She's on the coffee aisle, grabbing a bag of Dad's favorite blend.

"Mom, can we go? Please?"

She's not looking at me, she's looking in my cart, taking inventory. "Where is the rest of my list?"

"Mom, I'm sorry, it's just—"

She gives me *the look*, the one children have feared since the dawn of time. Despite being on the verge of a total anxiety attack, I turn my cart around and return to the other side of the store to finish Mom's shopping.

When I pass the soap aisle, Quinn Beck is gone.

We ride home listening to Mom's classic rock and I don't mind because the guitar riffs and synth-keyboard solos of her eighties metal bands provide sufficient distraction from the weirdness of having my biggest secret in life exposed for all to see. I want to tell her about the reporter—the intern— from the store, but I'm drained from, well, all of it. I stay quiet, and it's a bad call, because talking about it might've meant a tiny bit of mental prep for what awaited when she made the turn onto our street.

The curbs by our house are crowded with at least three numbered vans. A dozen people mill about our lawn like we're hosting a yard sale. Reporters and their respective crews, cameras ready. Seeking today's juicy news story.

Me.

CHAPTER 21

WE DON'T TALK TO THE REPORTERS. To their credit, they aren't rude and don't block our way as we run for our front door, abandoning the groceries in the trunk. They shout their questions, though, and those questions prick.

Why were you stalking Keachin?

Do you think she'd still be alive if you hadn't posted those photos?

Do you regret what you've done?

Mom slams the door, then presses her back against it like the reporters are a zombie horde attempting to break it down and she must protect me with her body. We stare at each other, and there's no anger in her gaze. I almost wish there was.

She peels herself from the door and goes to the nearest cordless phone. Calls Dad.

She says, "We have a big problem."

The reporters wait for my dad to arrive, and hit him with a similar batch of questions. He doesn't answer them, but politely requests that they stay off the lawn. They continue their barrage until he's inside, then they shuffle to the concrete driveway.

All of it is visible from my window. The neighbors are on their porches and lawns. More than a few provide additional coverage by recording the chaos with their cell phones. In that moment, I hate them. The reporters are doing their jobs, the people I've grown up around are just being nosy jerks.

"Lauren!" Dad shouts. "Get down here."

I go. Mom's beside him, hugging herself. I shouldn't be getting used to seeing this kind of tension in them, but I am.

"What the hell is going on?" he asks.

I tell him what the Admirer did, about how everyone knows I'm Gray. He starts pacing about halfway through my explanation, running his hands through his thinning hair.

The next hour consists of a repetitive Q&A session with my dad asking me over and over what "I did" and how "I let this happen."

My interrogation only ends when Mom puts dinner on the table. Big hunks of sourdough, deli meat, and leftover potato salad. Our newly purchased food is still in the car. When she spreads mustard on Dad's bread, her hands shake.

After dinner I'm banished to my room, and with no connection to the outside world—not even a TV—I sit at my windowsill and watch the reporters like they're my ant farm.

My story isn't big enough for them to camp out, not yet anyway. They pack their vans as the sun sets. By the time the moon rises, my street's empty. You can almost believe what just happened, didn't. Almost.

Sleep doesn't come easy. My parents' tense conversation quiets long before the noise in my head does, but sometime after midnight, my brain shuts down, too. It's a restless slumber. No dreams I can remember. When I open my eyes again, the sun is back, and it feels like I blinked instead of slept. I lie in bed staring at the pandas on my wall; they seem sadder today.

I shower, dress, and get downstairs before Dad, wanting the morning to go as smoothly as possible for my parents' sake as much as my own. When I pass the kitchen, I'm grabbed and nearly scream.

Mom tugs me close, and speaks in a whisper. "I do not want you to go to school today, but your father insists."

She presses a familiar rectangle into my palm, and I have to suppress a smile at the return of my cell phone.

"Do not let him see," she says. "With those reporters and your angry friend who told your secret around, I want you able to contact me if you need to."

I nod, and drop the phone into my bag. Dad's heavy steps thud down the stairs a moment later.

He gives me a strange look before his gaze floats to Mom. "I'm going."

She says, "You are."

My breath should be visible in this climate.

The ride to school isn't much warmer, but we don't run into reporters. Since the whole school already knows the secret, maybe things can get back to normal.

Or maybe I'm an absolute dumbass.

Yeah, definitely the latter.

CHAPTER 22

OUT OF MY FATHER'S LINE OF sight, I power up my phone. Texting Ocie is my first intent, let her know I'm back on the grid and we need to talk. Before I do, I'm overwhelmed by the number of missed texts that are waiting for me. More than thirty taunts, all from the Admirer.

How's it feel to be tattled on?

This is a hard lesson, but you will thank me for it someday.

Are you ignoring me?

Answer me!!!

That one stops me dead in the middle of the crowded hall, and I get bumped by passersby. Hard.

It happens a couple of times, like it's a game I don't know about. Jostle the Panda. The last collision is hard enough to knock my phone from my hand and send it sliding like a hockey puck. Taylor plays goalie and stops it with his foot.

He says something that I miss because, um, what the hell? How many times is he going to beam in like that?

When he scoops up my phone, I snatch it back. "What are you doing?"

"Me?" he says. "What about you? Why did you come today?"

"Why wouldn't I?"

He leans in close. "Because people are saying you got Keachin killed."

"I . . . got . . . ?"

"Come on." He grabs me by the hand and I have a flash of awkward memory. A lingering fleck of fondness staining my disgust for this boy.

Taylor leads me through the halls, beyond the dirty looks that have multiplied exponentially since yesterday's Gray reveal. We leave Junior Lane, navigate Sophomore Row and the Freshmen Slums until we reach the library. Only a pair of early-morning study hogs are present. He sits me down at a corner table as the warning bell rings.

He takes the seat across from me, then scans the room like he's my bodyguard assessing threats. I nearly laugh because he's so tall and skinny, a stickman in baggy clothes. He couldn't protect me from a breeze.

However, that I've treated him like crap and he still feels this need to do whatever it is he's doing saps some of the humor. What's going on here?

When he's satisfied with our seclusion, he stares me down. "It would've been best if you stayed home."

"You know what's best for me now?"

"I'm trying to help you. Chill, for once."

"Don't tell me to—"

"Haven't you seen what they're saying about you on the news?"

That shuts me up. Because I haven't seen. Other than the reporters mobbing us on my front lawn yesterday, I don't know what they're doing, or saying, or showing.

You'll want a friendly telling your story. Trust me.

Taylor's examining me, his mouth pinched. "So, you don't know."

"How about you tell me, Taylor."

"The local stations started talking about your website in their broadcasts last night. They didn't say *Gray Scales*, but everyone knows. Then someone posted a link to one of the segments on the memorial page—"

"The what?"

He rolls his eyes. "For someone who stalked her you sure are uninformed."

"I'm not a stalker."

"Whatever. It's a Facebook page for Keachin. It had five thousand likes."

"Keachin's RIP page has *five thousand* likes?!" Yes. That sounds shitty. Still. Really?

Taylor shakes his head, and I mistake it for him judging my pettiness.

He clarifies: "Had. It *had* five thousand. After those news stories aired, and the link started making the rounds, it's up to"—he checks his phone—"thirty-five K."

Thirty. Five. Thousand. Likes.

It's sinking in. She's dead. Thirty-five thousand people have expressed some level of mourning with a mouse click.

So what do I—the one who "got her killed"—get? What's the opposite of a Facebook like?

The bell rings. We're both late. I couldn't care less.

I should, though. I really, really should.

Squeezing my eyes shut, I mull over what he's said. "I get she was popular, but she wasn't nice, Taylor. Has everyone forgotten that? What? Don't look at me like that."

"You're not lying, but"—he squirms in his chair—"she got run over by a car."

"I don't mean it disrespectfully. It's just blowing my mind. She's every-one's best friend now?"

"My mom once told me people have a way of turning shiny when they die."

"What's that even mean?"

"It means people exaggerate the good stuff about dead people."

"So she's going to be prettier even though she was already gorgeous? The time she *didn't* ream some poorly dressed kid becomes her feeding the homeless?"

"Do you hear yourself?" He looks away, motions toward the library's double doors, and beyond them. "You've got bigger problems. Yesterday, when they found out you're Gray, that was like shell shock. Now they've had time to go home and yak it up with their friends, let some talking head tell them what to feel. They've been supplied with an opinion. That opinion says you got the school's most beautiful, sweetest, smartest girl murdered. Now you're as big of a monster as Coach Bottin."

"I don't get it, Taylor. Why are you trying to help me? Why aren't you mad at me, too?"

Surely, by now, he's realized he was my first target. The one who started it all.

His eyes remain on the door when he speaks again, nonchalant. "I've always known you were Gray."

CHAPTER 23

"YOU . . . WHAT?" I STAND, BACK AWAY like he'd just flashed hidden claws and vampire fangs.

"That first picture, me with the jockstraps. Hell, yeah, it was you. What other *photographer* was that pissed at me?"

That is the reason I don't do personal.

"If you knew, how come you never . . ."

"Confronted you? Blew up your secret identity? Because you were right to do it to me. I had it coming."

This sounds something like an apology. Not quite, but it's so much closer than anything he's ever attempted before.

"I don't know how to take that," I say, honest.

"However you take it, I suggest you do it later. When we've dealt with the fallout of you going crazy and telling everyone your secret. What was that about? Did you feel guilty?"

"It's not what you think. I was—"

"Let me guess," Vice Principal Del Toro says, having entered the library unnoticed, standing now with hand on hip and an annoyed stare. "'Just on your way to class'?"

Taylor rises. He knows what's coming, as do I. He tries to save me. "It's my fault. Lauren shouldn't be punished."

"I don't doubt you're at fault for something, Mr. Durham. You and I have been here before. Ms. Daniels is still responsible for her own class schedule. Besides, she can probably use a break today."

She knows about my recent unmasking. Everyone does.

Ms. Del Toro thumbs her walkie-talkie. "Mr. Mitchell, I'm bringing two students to the ISS room for skipping class."

ISS. In-School Suspension, aka Siberia.

Ms. Del Toro holds the door open and hurries us along. On my way out, I glance into the stacks and see a kid ducking behind the podium where the huge dust-covered dictionary sits. He's actually skipping class, but *I* have to go to ISS?

He sees me seeing him, perhaps wondering if I'm going to tell Ms. Del Toro.

No worries, kid, I'm not ratting you out.

Too bad I couldn't count on him to return the favor.

The ISS room is located on a desolate back hallway, right across from the old special-needs classroom. There's one window, and an air-conditioning unit partially blocks the sun attempting to stream in. What light remains shines through milky, yellow glass that's stained from the days when kids used to smoke their cigarettes behind the school. Inside the room, eight or nine desks are arranged in an unrecognizable pattern. Not rows, or a circle. More like chaos-lite.

When we arrive, there are already two kids in lockup. A couple of burnouts who look old enough to be seniors but still have lockers in the Freshmen Slums because, well, burnouts.

Behind the big desk, Mr. Mitchell, the Automotive Arts teacher I thought was pervy until I uncovered the king faculty perv. I can't believe they leave him alone in a secluded room with children, though. Have they learned nothing from Bottin? I feel his eyes on my boobs already.

"Hand over your student IDs," Ms. Del Toro says.

Taylor—obviously familiar with this routine—has his in hand. He passes it over to Mr. Mitchell and takes a seat toward the front of the room. I have to root in my bag for mine, Ms. Del Toro sighing impatiently while I do. Before I find my ID, my fingers graze the camera I took from my locker yesterday, forgotten in the nightmare that's been my life ever since. It cheers me up a little.

"Today, Ms. Daniels," Ms. Del Toro says.

"Yeah, sorry." I hand over my ID. When I take my seat, it's in the corner farthest from Taylor. I'm still processing his claim to have known about my exploits all along. I need some distance.

"I'll be notifying your parents about your misconduct. Provided you hold it together and don't give Mr. Mitchell any trouble, I may consider letting you go back to your regular classes tomorrow. In the meantime, you will work in silence for the rest of the day."

I didn't bring any work with me, leaving the option of napping like the burnouts. But within twenty minutes, an office runner arrives. I barely notice until he begins handing out class assignments passed along from the teachers we won't be seeing today.

Taylor takes his, leafs through the pages, gets to work.

Both burnouts tuck their assignments in the baskets under their desks as if the papers are for someone who will be along later.

When the kid gets to me, he drops my handout on my desk and leaves the room in a hurry.

My assignment is four pages stapled together. I peel back the first page and understand his rush. Sticky blue bubble gum, thick and moist, is pressed between my papers. A not-so-subtle message.

Now I know what the opposite of a Facebook like is.

A different runner brings my second-period assignment. No gum this time. Just spit.

The third-period runner just scrawls the word "KILLER" in red crayon on the back page of my history worksheets. I spend most of the period wondering where he got crayon from.

Fourth period is lunch for the ISS kids. We go before the first regular lunch period so our isolation is not interrupted. The silence rule is supposed to be maintained while we eat, but Mr. Mitchell has had enough of it by then—he's got no one to talk to either—and leaves us alone in the cafeteria while he does whatever suits his mood when he's not eye-humping young girls.

As soon as he's gone, Taylor's next to me, whispering, "I'm sorry I got you in trouble."

"This isn't your fault." Me, saying *that* to him. So many surprises this week. "Besides, I'm getting the impression ISS might be the safest place for me right now."

"What?"

I tell him about the various assaults on my schoolwork. It's no surprise to him. "A lot of people are mad. Why'd you blow your own cover?"

"It wasn't me," I said. "I was outed."

"By who?"

"That . . . is complicated."

"We've got time. Like nine minutes, but time."

The burnouts have stopped murmuring to themselves, keying on our conversation. I can play Secret Squirrel and try to conceal the truth, but it hasn't been my week for subterfuge, now has it? I tell as much as I can in eight minutes. Not the whole story, not the parts about *Dante* or scheming my way into the Cablon construction site or Keachin's crime scene photo because I'm still not sure what to make of all that, but Taylor gets the gist.

With a minute to go, he says, "Someone you don't know followed you, photographed you in stalker mode, then used your own mail list to show the world what you do when no one's looking." He cocks his head, squints. "And you think this person *admires* you?"

I shoot him a look.

"Just wondering."

A sharp whistle interrupts the conversation: Mr. Mitchell signaling the end of the lunch period, ushering us from the cafeteria like lepers unfit to be seen by the good and free students of Portside High.

I leave my seat, contemplating what Taylor said. I'd been so caught up in *what* happened, I'd never considered *how* it happened. I never saw the message the Admirer sent when he did what he did, but the buzz leading up to it had everyone thinking *Gray* was making the reveal. Taylor asked why *I* exposed myself. So did Quinn Beck. People think *I'm* doing this because the Admirer's using my own system against me.

Stupid, stupid, stupid, Panda.

Mr. Mitchell stops us outside the cafeteria doors. "Hang tight, prisoners. We've got some new inmates joining us."

More burnouts, I presume. Ms. Del Toro rounds the corner. I'm very wrong.

She's walking Danielle Ranson down the hall, and the girl's staring me down. Her hair's pulled back, slick and greasy with Vaseline. Her ears are bare, the chunky, gaudy earrings she usually wears absent. Her forearm muscles dance as she flexes her fists.

Our bathroom encounter from the day before is so fresh, I focus on Danielle first, neglecting the other two girls accompanying her. There's Simone Presley, who missed part of last year because my pictures got her sent to rehab. And there's Lanie Jackman, Keachin's freshman cousin. I have photos of them hanging together in the days before the coach scandal broke. Lanie idolized her older cousin.

Del Toro says, "They all seemed quite determined to get tossed in ISS today, Mr. Mitchell. I'm more than happy to oblige."

Mr. Mitchell shrugs it off, either ignorant of the conspiracy unfolding before his eyes, or indifferent. "The more the merrier."

C H A P T E R   2 4

I'M FIRST THROUGH THE ISS ROOM doors, but Taylor's on my heels, risking a few words, in German no less, before Mitchell brings in the rest of the herd: "*Setz dich zu mir.*" Sit by me.

The solitude may have made me chatty in the cafeteria, but I'm not about to let him be my personal security in a room where evil looks are the worst thing that can happen. I won't look weak.

I sit where I sat before; he does the same, shaking his head.

The burnouts enter, taking their old seats, though they twist them slightly to allow a peripheral view of me and whatever entertainment they think this new ISS dynamic will generate. Danielle and company enter, each taking desks that are much closer than I like.

I expect the glares and threatening gestures to begin right away, but they adhere to the ISS rules. Silence. Eyes ahead. Simone's particularly studious, pulling a science book from her bag and burying her nose in it.

Mr. Mitchell takes his place behind the big desk, pulling an MP3 player and earbuds from his shirt pocket. Seems the man enjoys his tunes after lunch.

Things are uneventful. For about twenty minutes.

Simone raises her hand, speaks before the gesture is acknowledged. "Mr. Mitchell, I need to use the ladies' room."

There's a dreamy lilt to her voice, sort of gaspy. It's weird, and Lanie's glancing back at me like I smell.

Mr. Mitchell—loud, because his earbuds are still in—tells her to come up for a pass. When she rises, she wobbles. It's exaggerated, though, like someone playing drunk. She makes it to Mr. Mitchell's desk, then lurches, catching the edge for support. "Oh, I don't feel so good. Can you walk me to the nurse's office?"

Mr. Mitchell looks wary; a creeping dread fills me. I know what this is. Why doesn't he?

He yanks his earbuds. "You better not be messing with me, girl."

"I'm not," Simone whines. "I feel really hot and dizzy."

Mr. Mitchell grabs his walkie-talkie and thumbs TALK: "I'm walking Simone Presley to the nurse's office. Gonna be out of ISS for approximately five minutes."

I don't know who he's talking to, but the kids in the room are paying attention. Every. Last. One. Of. Us.

He says to us, "No monkey business while I'm gone."

He doesn't have to worry about monkeys in here. When he leaves, this is going to be something more vicious. Sharp teeth and claws. I pull my bag into my lap, reach into it.

Mr. Mitchell "helps" Simone along. When they turn the corner, she flashes a smile to Danielle, confirming what I already know.

She's the distraction.

Seconds . . . heartbeats . . . lifetimes . . . pass in the space between the alternating clacks of Simone's heels on the hall tiles, quieting with distance, a countdown. She and Mr. Mitchell are away, too far to hear anything that happens next.

And then the jackals pounce.

CHAPTER 25

DESKS SHIFT SUDDENLY. CHAIR LEGS SCRAPE the floor, a sound like screeching howls.

"Yeah, Peeping Tom." Danielle rises to her full height and advances. "No one's gonna save your ass now."

I'm up, too, and regretting my seat choice. Not because of Taylor's implied protection, but sitting in the back corner leaves very few escape options. Backpedaling, I hit a wall, keep digging in my bag. *Come on.*

Danielle's charging me, a half second from ripping my head off. My hand closes on the point-and-shoot in my bag. I yank it free of my junky satchel, and trigger the shutter release without aiming, hoping to blind her with the flash.

Would've been a great plan if I'd been pointing the camera in the right direction.

As it is, the flash blinds me. My field of vision goes stark white, then explodes with red and yellow dots. I'm so stunned, it takes a few seconds to feel Danielle's man-hands wrapped around my throat.

Confession: for all the badass secret agent/private eye stuff I've done over the years, for someone who's a *soldier's daughter*, I've never really picked up any fighting skills. I'm going to get right on that, though. Should I survive.

The lack of oxygen does wonders for my spotty vision. Danielle snaps into sharp focus, as do the burnouts clapping and cheering behind her.

Taylor crosses the room, puts Danielle in a half nelson, prying her off me while she curses and spits. The burnouts boo him for it.

"Lauren," he says, riding Danielle like a rodeo cowboy. "Are you okay?"

Air burns my throat, but I cough out the word, "Okay!"

Lanie, whom I'd forgotten about, forms an immediate rebuttal when she punches me in the eye.

"The hell?" I say, on a slight delay from the extraordinary pain that comes with the expertly delivered blow.

She answers with a second haymaker to my other eye. Somehow, I'm staring at the ceiling.

Lanie drifts into my field of vision. "This"—a kick to my side, forcing me into a ball—"is for my cousin, you night-skulking"—another kick—"freak!"

She winds up for another kick, but doesn't deliver. She's crying too much.

This is how Mr. Mitchell finds us when he returns. Me on the floor, Lanie sobbing, Danielle and Taylor conceding a grudging respect for each other's wrestling skills. We all get a trip to the main office. I'm happy to go.

I'm sure the people are much nicer there.

Waiting. A large sandwich bag filled with ice pressed to my swelling eyes. Taylor's called into Ms. Del Toro's office first, and is quickly dismissed back to ISS for the rest of the day. The look he gives me on his way, it feels like good-bye.

Danielle was also taken in right away, since whatever parental wrangler was called in to deal with her special kind of crazy got here fast and was already waiting in Principal Carlin's office. The rest take their turns one by one.

I'm left in awkward silence with Lanie. She'd doesn't grill me with evil looks, just pretends I'm not there. Her fists have already delivered whatever message she had to send.

Pressing ice to my eyes, I pretend not to notice how the person who beat me down is now treating me like I don't exist.

"Thank goodness!" Miss Carney, the old-lady secretary, screeches. I lower my ice to see if this "goodness" was going to make my day any better.

It was only Rozlynn, Taylor's student tech support protégée, rocking a style best categorized as Gypsy Frump. Her tie-dyed skirt brushes the ground despite her height. Her blouse's collar hugs her neck, and she's got a denim jacket that distorts any possible curves.

She enters the office and goes straight for the secretary's PC.

"I don't know what's wrong with it," Miss Carney says. "I was trying to open my attendance reports and it froze."

Hunched and as awkward as ever, Rozlynn motions for the old lady to give up her chair, takes a seat. Gently, showing none of the frustration I'm feeling from the secretary's high-pitched voice, she says, "Do you remember the trick I showed you? Control-Alt-Delete?"

Rozlynn spaces her hands and keys the command to demonstrate.

Miss Carney smiles sheepishly. "I tried that Contour-App-Delete nonsense, but it didn't seem to do a thing."

"You're right. It isn't working. I'm going to try a hard reboot."

"Will it take long?"

Rozlynn says, "A few minutes."

"Do I have time to grab a cup of tea from the lounge?"

"Go crazy."

Miss Carney gives an excited little clap, then motions toward me and Lanie. "Keep an eye on these two while I'm gone. They've been little troublemakers today."

"I will keep the lighthouse in your absence."

The old lady leaves, and Vice Principal Del Toro calls Lanie into her office. I'm left alone with the freshman computer geek. She flits glances my way.

"How'd you score such a cushy gig?" I say, needing the weird silence to end. Before she answers I lean my head back, and press the ice bags to my eyes, creating a cold blindness. I don't want to see Rozlynn's dismissal if she has soured on me.

She says, "You're talking to me?"

Wow, how shy must you be to think I'm talking to someone else when we're the only two in the room. Poor kid. "Yes. You."

If I wasn't freezing my eyeballs solid, I imagine I'd see her blush from the attention.

She says, "I'll tell you if you tell me how you got those shiners."

"A master negotiator," I say, hoping she takes it as praise. A confidence boost. Be nice if I did something good today. "Deal. But you first."

She takes a deep breath, like a runner before the starter pistol fires, and says, "There weren't many—or *any*—girls in student tech support. When I asked my guidance counselor if I could join, I think he got nervous and pushed my request through. Like, affirmative action or something. You know?"

I do know. Something similar got me a guided tour of the Cablon construction site. Sometimes the gender card works.

She says, "I get training on some cool computer stuff. Stuff I can use when I get ready for college. I might be able to get some scholarships."

"You and my friend Ocie would get along well," I say. "Fixing all the raggedy computers must make you the It Girl with the faculty."

"Don't know about that. I'm nowhere near as famous as y—" She tries to catch herself, not wanting to offend me. The effort alone makes her friendlier than most these days.

"I believe the word you're looking for is 'infamous.' You're Rozlynn, right?"

"Yeah. But people call me Roz."

"I'm Panda." Of course, she already knows that.

"So, what happened to your face?"

Shrugging. "Karma, maybe."

"I can see how your, um, exploits might piss off people."

My phone vibrates in my purse. I lower the ice, retrieve my cell, and read the message. It's from him.

SecretAdm1r3r: Look Up.

Dozens of my schoolmates pass by the big office windows. Only one is still, staring at me through the glass.

Marcos.

CHAPTER 26

MY ICE BAG SLIPS OFF MY lap, crunch-splashing on the floor when I rise. Despite its absence, I'm chilled.

Marcos smacks the glass then motions with two fingers: *Come here.*

If this was night, and he was at the mouth of a dark alley, I might've made a different decision. But midday, in a crowded hallway . . .

I snatch my purse strap and make for the door.

"Hey!" Roz says. "I'm supposed to watch you."

I point to the window. "Well, watch."

Outside, hall stragglers give me the evil eye. I ignore them and move toward Marcos, slowing as I draw near, leaving a few feet between us. Escape room.

"So, Gray," he says.

"And what should I call you? Does 'Admirer' work, or does 'Sack of Crazy' feel more fitting?"

His eyes narrow, and his forehead creases. "What?"

"We're done with the games, right? No more mysterious chat sessions"—
I hold up my phone—"or creepy texts?"

"What are you talking about? I don't have your number. I don't *want*
your damned number. Not in a million years."

"But, this text, you just—"

He sidesteps slightly, closes the gap between us. He's quick, the exact
opposite of what I am since I'm puffy eyed and half blind. I rotate a
moment too slow, and let his forward motion intimidate me. He backs me
into the window/wall. I can only get away by doing a clumsy side shuffle.
If he touches me, I'll scream.

"For what you did," he says, "that beating you got today is too good
for you."

"Are you threatening me?" I search the hall for someone to help, but
we're alone. The period bell rings, and for the first time in Portside history,
it seems no one's tardy. Except Marcos. But he doesn't seem concerned.

"Not threatening. Explaining. In case you don't know what a bitch
you are."

Anger sears the center of my skull, and the throbbing in my eyes
doubles, pounding like bongos. I shove Marcos in the chest. He stumbles
backward.

"Is that the lesson you taught Keachin? What a bitch she was?"

His crinkled face goes slack. "Don't you ever talk about her."

"Where have you been, Marcos?" Did the police have him? Did he con
his way out of his cell? "You're the one who sent me her picture. You told
me it 'had to happen.'"

"I have no idea what you're talking about, Daniels. All I know is, you
got my friend killed."

"Your—?" *What?*

"You want to know where I've been? At Keachin's house, with her parents, crying my damn eyes out." To demonstrate, twin tears crawl down his cheeks.

"Since when were you and Keachin *friends*?" I try to imagine the scent of deep-fried hush puppies exuding from his pores and mingling with her three-hundred-dollar Brazilian perfume. His worn army surplus jacket next to her silk blouse as they enjoy a Saturday afternoon matinee.

"That's none of your business," he says, "but minding your business is a concept you obviously don't get. She was trying to get away from Bottin's crazy shit, to end it on her own terms. You dragged all that into the light, and look what happened."

Keachin was trying to end her affair with Coach? And Marcos knew about this *before* I exposed it?

But he can't have been Keachin's friend. He's *my* Admirer. He *has* to be.

"Two days ago I thought a twenty-five-year-old *Star Wars* geek who preys on teen girls was the worst person in this school. That bastard killed my friend. Yet, I'm thinking he runs a close second to you." He says it between sobs.

Marcos leaves me. When he's down the hall and around the corner, I start breathing again. Roz stares curiously through the glass.

She couldn't have heard what he said. Or felt it. That's the only relief I can find in the moment. The only way I'm able to face her.

When I'm back in the office, she says, "Is everything okay?"

"Peachy. He's a fan."

"Somehow I doubt that. He looked kind of intense."

He did. But intense enough to be my Admirer? I don't know anymore. I don't know anything.

"Roz," I say, "you're good with computer stuff. If I asked you for a favor, do you think you could help me?"

She tenses. "Depends on the favor."

I get it. I'm a walking bull's-eye right now. No one—even people who don't despise me—wants to stand too close. This won't require standing. "I've got a phone number and I need to know who it belongs to. Can you do that?"

"Is this a *Gray Scales* thing, because if it is—"

"No. It's not like that. Someone's been messing with me. For a while now. I need to know who he is."

She nods slowly. "I can try a couple of reverse-lookup sites. If it's a cell, maybe I can figure a way to ping the GPS. It'll be a challenge, though. We haven't really covered that stuff in my tech support training. A lot of times we just play *Zork*."

"Play what?"

"Just know it won't help you. I'll try, though."

"Good enough." I grab a Post-it off Miss Carney's desk and scribble down the number my Admirer's been texting me from, along with my own contact information. Handing over the note, I add, "One more thing?"

She waits.

"Can you figure out who in the school has the skills to hack my email?"

"I think so. Should be a short list."

"That guy I was talking to is Marcos Dahmer. I want to know if he's on it. I want to know if he's—"

Principal Carlin's door opens and Danielle exits, followed by an adult in a black-and-white-striped referee shirt. The Footlocker name tag pinned to the chest identifies him to shoe shoppers, but I don't need to read it.

Darius Ranson sees me and places a gentle hand on his sister's shoulder. The picture of restraint.

"Darius," Principal Carlin says, "please express to Danielle how easy it is to derail herself at this age. She'll have some time to think about it."

"Yes, sir," Darius says, a display of respect I didn't know he was capable of. "I know. It's just me and her, and I won't let her mess her life up over stupid stuff."

Danielle stares absolute death toward me. Darius catches her doing it and his grip tightens. "Come on. She's not worth it."

A former beefed-up sports tyrant just told his sister that I wasn't worth the trouble she's brought on to herself. I never thought there would be a day when I'd consider if Darius Ranson was right about anything.

He escorts Danielle away to begin her suspension, and Principal Carlin says, "Come on, Lauren. Your turn."

The principal is looking past me, at my mom, who just arrived, not a trace of pleasant on her face.

She examines my swollen eyes. "Are you all right?"

"I'm fine," I say quietly.

I read the response in her stone expression. It says, *Not for long.*

Carlin's office beckons. I step forward to face my school punishment, knowing it will be mild compared to whatever awaits me at home.

CHAPTER 27

THE START OF MY SUSPENSION IS quiet and terrible.

Mom stays home from work that first day, occupying my time with whatever task is farthest from her. Anything so she doesn't have to be close to me, or talk to me, or look at me.

That hurts, though I kind of get the not-wanting-to-look-at-me part. I'm not too fond of mirrors right now. Not with two bad-getting-worse black eyes.

The throbbing, puffy pain stopped, but the purple bruises circling each eye have turned into ebony rings. My nickname has never felt more fitting.

I keep my mind off my mangled face by focusing on Mom's long list of chores. Or non-chores. It's stuff no one really does, like, ever. Things like polishing all the lamps in the house, and ironing the sheets in our linen closet. The mundane nature of each assignment is almost admirable, showcasing Mom's creativity in the art of domestic torture.

When Dad comes home that evening, he just glares with unhidden disgust and makes a show of leaving whatever room I enter. He's been that way ever since he learned I'd be missing at least ten days of school over this "picture nonsense."

I nearly tell him, "No, it's actually over some '*punching* nonsense.'" Didn't think he'd appreciate the quip, though.

My parents aren't too warm toward each other either. That's the new normal during this ordeal. If there's a bright side to being in our house of disdain, it's that Mom's too busy being irritated with Dad to remember that I still have my phone.

When I'm not being a domestic slave, I wait for word from Roz while trying to ignore my Admirer's texts. All apologies.

I didn't know you'd get in so much trouble. I'm sorry.

We were both mad and took things 2 far. I forgive u. Do u forgive me?

I consider showing my parents and telling them, "See. It's him. He's real."

But I know the way things are, at this moment, it doesn't matter if he's real.

There's stuff Dad wants to say, angry things. He saves them for when he and Mom are in their room. Like now. There's an empty drinking glass on my desk. I upend it, fling off residual drops of water, press it to the wall. With my ear to the glass, I try to decipher the warbling mess. I get, like, every fifth word.

"She . . . think . . . Vicky."

Aunt Victoria?

I struggle to hear more, but they're moving around and I stop hearing anything useful at all. Lowering the glass, I consider the possibility that I'm being a total narcissist and every beef my parents have with each other doesn't necessarily revolve around me. They're talking about my evil troll of an aunt.

Totally unrelated.

I was allowed to sleep in yesterday. I suspect it was so Dad could leave the house without having to acknowledge my existence. But today, he rocks my bed frame, a gentle motion.

"Lauren, wake up. We need to talk."

When I roll over, my parents are positioned exactly as they were the night we first talked about Coach Bottin. Dad on my bed, Mom in the doorway. Something uncomfortable is about to happen.

"What is it?"

"Look," Dad says, glancing away from me, "we've been talking about everything that's going on, and after some consideration, we've decided it may do you some good to spend time with your aunt Vicky down in Georgia."

"What kind of time?" I'm standing. This isn't "sit down" news.

"She'll be up for Thanksgiving," Dad says, meeting my eyes, getting stern. "She's got plenty of room at her place, so you can fly back with her after the holiday."

"Thanksgiving is three weeks from now."

"We'll come down to see you at Christmas. You'll be settled by then."

The man is crazy. Mom. She's not insane, I can talk to her. "Mom, I don't want to go. We can't stand Victoria. Tell him."

She swipes at her eyes. "*Liebste, ich weiß, dass du es nicht hören willst—*"

"Speak English!"

She is stung, like I intended. For a moment. She hardens, and her voice takes on the same sternness of Dad's. "Your father and I have discussed this at length. You are not doing well here, Lauren. A change may suit you."

"I don't want a change. Not like this. I was set up. You get that, don't you? There's some crazy guy that's turned everyone in school against me.

Now you're turning against me, too?"

"We're not against you, Lauren," Mom says.

"It sure seems that way."

"Stop being dramatic." Dad rises like we're done.

"I'm not," I say. "I just don't want to live with your evil sister, Dad. She hates me."

"If she hated you, she wouldn't be *willing* to let you live with her."

"Listen to me, okay. This isn't my fault. The Admirer—"

"They're talking about expelling you, Lauren! And locking you up. Do you get that?" Dad's in my face, and I'm not strong enough not to flinch. A string of spittle stretches from his lip to the bottom of his chin. I smell what he had for breakfast.

Expulsion. Lock me up.

It's like I've got an ice pack on my face again. My skin feels so cold. I say, "*Who's* talking about that stuff?"

"The school board, and the lawyer they're recommending."

"But we were with the cops the other night. They didn't even care."

"Then, Lauren. Things change. It's time you learned that."

"But, I—"

"Shut. Your. Mouth!"

My father has never, ever spoken to me like this before. The closest I can recall was when I was five and he barked at me to get my hand away from our stove's blue flame. Then I'd run, ashamed for disappointing him. Sticking my hand in fire would've been better than this.

Mom's left her perch in the doorway and is pulling him back, trying to. "Come. Everyone needs a break. You should rest and she should rest."

He allows her to lead him from my room, but not before he speaks again. "You're going to Georgia. That's the end of it."

When they're gone, I slam my door, lock it. Drawing the curtains and cocooning myself in my comforter, I wait for my parents to return so we can argue, or they can apologize, or they can tell me they aren't banishing me to the Peach State.

No one comes.

I'm dozing on a moist pillow when I hear shaking. I mistake it for Dad jiggling my doorknob, his apology singing in my imagination. Rising from my cocoon, the sound becomes clearer and I know *exactly* what it is.

My vibrating phone shimmies beneath the sweatshirt I stashed it under, dragging the garment toward the edge of my desk. I save my cell from a falling death, and read the incoming text.

> **[unidentified number]:** Ur list of possible hackers is on the way
> **Me:** Is this Roz?
> **[unidentified number]:** Close.

At first, I think this is some Admirer trick. Then, no. His tricks are angrier. And, maybe, bloodier.

> **Me:** Who is this?
> **[unidentified number]:** Roz's boss. You'll b getting a bill for our services by the end of the week
> **Me:** Taylor?
> **[unidentified number]:** UR as sharp as ever, I see.

Smart-ass.

> **Me:** What do you know about the list I'm looking for?
> **Taylor:** U recruited my mini-me. She's good, but has a lot to learn

> **Me:** So ur Portside High education makes u a tech expert?
>
> **Taylor:** Just check your email

I switch apps to view my in-box and there's a new email titled *Portside Hackers* but from an almost nonsensical email address: THX778083@Searchmail.net.

The message says:

> *Panda, sorry for the delay, but I needed a hand with compiling the list you requested. You know Taylor Durham, right? He's my coach, and I don't know EVERYBODY in school, and, anyway, he walked me through. Here you go . . . Dudes with mad computer skills at PHS:*
>
> *Durham, Taylor*
>
> *Flynn, Eduardo*
>
> *Goldweather, Holden*
>
> *Joshi, Raj*
>
> *McCoy, DeQuan*
>
> *Parham, Brock*
>
> *Hope this helps. Let me know if you need anything else.*
>
> *Roz.*
>
> *P.S. You'd asked about Marcos Dahmer. Best we can tell, he's got NO tech skills. If he's your guy, he had help.*

Switching apps, I text Taylor back.

> **Me:** You're at the top of this list. Should I be looking @ you?
>
> **Taylor:** Isn't it alphabetical order?
>
> **Me:** Fine. Got me there. What about Marcos Dahmer?
>
> **Taylor:** He's not on the list for a reason. He edits the yearbook

and can barely use Word.

Me: Are you sure?

Taylor: Why are you?

My concerns about Marcos are too long to text. Plus, I'm not ready to tell him everything about *Dante, Neptune's Fury,* and the rest.

Me: If I'm ruling U out, which one of these a-holes is the likely suspect?

Taylor: I'm thinking the biggest a-hole. Do I need 2 clarify?

Me: You do not.

Brock Parham, then. I never knew he was good at anything besides being a D-bag, but if Taylor's saying he's got the computer skills . . .

That's only half of the equation, though. My Admirer is a photographer and a techie. Best I can tell, neither Brock nor Marcos fits both criteria.

Or one of them is hiding a talent. Not unheard of. I should know.

Taylor: FYI—Roz was a good draft pick

Me: I thought she needed ur help

Taylor: She's green, but she's also a fan of Urs

Me: ????

Taylor: You see her email address?

Me: Yeah. What's it mean?

Taylor: Ask her. Or look up the hex code 778083. U know what a hex code is?

Me: Ur question w/ a question thing is getting annoying. Yes, I know what a hex code is.

Taylor: Text back once you see it.

Hex codes are six-character designations for colors across a visual spectrum. Mostly used by designers, illustrators, and, on occasion, photographers. A code of all zeroes—000000—is solid black. FFFFFF is white. When I search for 778083 on my web app, I get a pleasant surprise.

The color gray.

> **Me:** THX778083 means "Thanks Gray"? What's she thanking me for?
>
> **Taylor:** Not my place. I'll let her tell it. Just thought U should know EVERYONE hasn't turned on U
>
> **Me:** It's a small comfort
>
> **Taylor:** What now?
>
> **Me:** Now, I figure a way 2 get my sentence shorted. Parental lockdown over here.
>
> **Taylor:** That sux
>
> **Me:** Yep. Then I have a little chat with Brock.
>
> **Taylor:** Don't you mean we?
>
> **Me:** I don't.

There's a long break with no text. Maybe I pissed him off. If so, it's not intentional. This time. Him admitting the total dickishness of what he'd done to me, and helping me gather some intel on potential Admirer candidates, is appreciated. I don't want him thinking that we're Team Hug now. That we're rekindling something.

Perhaps it's time to lift his Ocie ban. Her tutoring will give him something else to do.

My phone vibrates again.

But it's not Taylor.

SecretAdm1r3r: School's not the same without you here.

Ignore. Ignore. Ignore. It's the smart thing to do. I do the other thing.
Five letters, keyed in a blur.

Me: Fuck U

Acknowledging him is a mistake; I'm too angry to care. Getting beat up,
grounded, and being told you're getting shipped off to Warden Vicky's . . .
it can have that effect. I send my message again.

Me: Fuck U
SecretAdm1r3r: I guess I had that coming. Sorry. Okay.

Okay? *Really?* No! It's not okay. It's pretty freakin' far from okay. I let
him know with yet another colorfully worded text.

SecretAdm1r3r: I said I'm sorry. How long r u going 2 throw it
in my face?
Me: You ruined my f'n life, asshole.
SecretAdm1r3r: By telling the world about GRAY? I didn't ruin
you. I freed you.
Me: U R Crazy! Making me like u with those photos and your
little mind games. I'm done.
SecretAdm1r3r: No. Ur not. You don't get 2 b done with me.

Whatever I felt I had to say to him, I'm not feeling it anymore.

SecretAdm1r3r: So lets continue

Continue what?

There's a crawling sensation at the base of my skull, like my spine is the water spout from the itsy-bitsy spider nursery rhyme, and the little arachnid is doing a short-lived victory dance at the top.

Staring at my phone, I anticipate his next taunt. The inactivity stretches ten, twenty minutes. I glance at the clock: eight thirty. School's started. Unless he's sneak texting between classes, I won't hear anything for the rest of the day.

Seven hours of waiting for him to say something. Or send something. Or—this is the scariest one—*do* something.

Swinging my feet from under my comforter I stand, then crouch, retrieving Victoria's collapsed makeup mirror from beneath the bed. On my dresser I unfold it, and flip on the battery-powered light, illuminating my battered face in three separate panes. I wince at the initial sight, like my reflection's going to punch me, too.

It's not so much the bruises that stun me. It's the thought of my aunt Victoria having the perfect makeup to cover them while giving me the smoky-eyed look of a runway model. All because everyone thinks *I'm* the lunatic, and everything that's happened is my fault.

Maybe the Admirer's right. I don't get to be done. He's going to regret letting me in on that little secret.

CHAPTER 28

MOM AND DAD LEAVE ME WITH a list of weird tasks, as usual. I buckle down and fly through everything in under three hours, giving myself six hours before either of them will be home. Time to do some real work.

Getting my equipment back is easy. It's all locked in a backyard shed, same place Dad used to hide my Christmas presents. Dad keeps the shed key on him. No issue. When I taught myself to pick locks, I practiced on the very padlock I'm breaking into now.

Inside, the smell of lawn mower gas is cloying, swirling around me on a cool breeze. There's a dust-free plastic tub in the back corner by the garden shears. Inside I find my camera, laptop, and a few other useful items Dad confiscated in his sweep. Decorative bricks, left over from the flower bed Mom created in the spring, are arranged on a shelf. I drop a couple in the tub to throw Dad off should he make it out here in the next few days and move stuff around, then I transfer most of my gear to my car trunk. I won't need my camera or the other stuff inside the house, and my MacBook will be easy enough to conceal when my parents are around.

Back in my room I make the most of my alone time, arranging every-thing I've ever gotten from my Admirer in a single file. I sit back, viewing it all as one big picture, each item layered in cascading windows, looking for clues with the scrutiny I reserve for Gray targets.

Everyone I ever exposed, I had to get to know from afar. Their friends and their patterns. Of course, I always had a name and a face to start.

He's awesome with a camera. Able to get into places other people can't get in, either through his charm or stealth. He can get his hands on crime scene photos from secure police servers. He's a meticulous planner. If he wasn't we would have never crossed paths because he'd have cooked him-self alive trying to get the *Dante* shot.

What *don't* I know?

I spend the afternoon combing through Marcos's and Brock's Facebook pages, Twitter, Tumblr, whatever I can find. They're my only suspects. Yet, I can't find anything to suggest either one of them could pull off what my Admirer has.

All I get for my effort is a dose of torment. My social media accounts are filled with hate messages from everyone who's turned on Gray. Me.

The most brutal posts have as many as three hundred likes. I con-sider deleting my page altogether, but there's a single friend request. Roz Petrie.

I accept and spend some time clicking through her photos because old habits don't die. Mostly selfies of her hiking, or canoeing, or lying in bed making goofy faces. Nothing spectacular, though she is pretty when she's not hunched and shuffling.

Aunt Victoria pops into my head: *She could look like a young blah, blah, blah, with some effort.*

My hands retract from the keyboard and rest on my thighs. Those were Victoria's words, but not her voice in my head. It was mine. Making the same judgments as my annoying aunt and soon-to-be roommate.

One hand darts to my Magic Mouse like a squirrel snaring an acorn, moving the cursor and clicking things until I reach the MESSAGE icon on Roz's cover page. I start a private conversation with her that she'll answer at her leisure though it eases my conscience right away.

> Roz,
>
> Thanks for helping me. For being a friend. You're awesome. Taylor explained your email address to me. THX778083 = "Thanks Gray." Tell me what I did for you.

For a while I surf aimlessly before returning to Facebook and seeing the little speech bubble icon lit up with a red "1" in the top corner of the page. I open my new message, Roz's response, and I'm excited. Who doesn't like reading praise?

> Hey Panda (Gray . . . hehe). So you know I'm a fan now. ::blushes:: Okay, I thought I was being clever with my email but Taylor got it right away. No surprise there, he's like a genius. What can I say? Us nerds love our Easter eggs and double meanings, and love decoding them even more. Speaking of, have you ever read Ready Player One by Ernest Cline? It's awesome and Taylor could totally be a gunter. Go Parzival! ☺
>
> Anyway, I digress. I'm thanking you for Randy Sigell. A lot of Gray Beards owe you for that one.

Ah, Gray's third exposé. A classic bully known for robbing neighborhood kids, boys *and* girls, of whatever cash their parents had entrusted them with, then bragging about it.

I caught him vandalizing a teacher's house by sprinkling chlorine pellets on the lawn during a late-night rain shower. I don't think he got in much trouble, but he calmed down significantly before his family moved to Maryland last year. A minor victory.

Her gratitudinal email address is now clear. But her note generates other questions and not about "Gunters" and "Parzival," whatever those are.

Two words are what I send.

Gray Beards?

I don't wait long.

You don't know? Gray Beards are like Browncoats, or Rihanna's Navy. Here, see what I mean:

A link follows. It takes me to another Facebook page. A private group that I can now join thanks to Roz's hypertext invite. The Gray Beards.

My official fan club.

Okay, okay. I sought out Roz because I needed a pick-me-up, but this? This is going to Starbucks for caffeine and getting heroin.

There are 204 members, a bunch of kids I know from school—including a few from my DP class. Several of my revealing photos are visible in the news feed and thumbnails. No one here is trashing me. I scroll through and learn that "Gray rocks" and "bullies suck" and, and, and . . .

Perked up and curious, I click the link that always interests me most on FB pages, photos. There are two albums. One is named "Gray Scales" and is a compilation of everything from my site. The other, it makes the bottom of my stomach fall out.

It's called "The Game."

Click.

There are dozens of photos, with hundreds of comments spread among them. I look through many of them. Selfies, photobombs, landscapes. Amateur shots from fuzzy to awesome. On the better photos there's a trend of some commenter giving begrudging praise ("Sweet, but peep this . . .") then linking to another photo meant to outdo the last. Exchanges I've become very familiar with in recent weeks.

There's no *Dante*, or *Neptune's Fury*, or any of the other visual capital my Admirer and me have traded. Certainly no plain, bleached picture of Keachin, or the richly colored snapshot of her cracked skull, with a convenient link back to the profile of whoever posted the pics.

The game I thought so unique to me and my Admirer appears to be a common thing here. That's the bad news.

The worse news: I just gained 204 new suspects.

CHAPTER 29

WHEN MY PARENTS GET HOME, I have to tuck my Mac between my mattress and box spring, then get back to it after they're in bed. I don't mind the break, because the challenges I'm dealing with are frying my brain.

Next steps? Well, in the immediate, the plan doesn't change. I talk to Brock first. From the technical angle of my undoing, Taylor likes him as the prime suspect. Also, it's less sanity-destroying than printing off a list of Gray Beards and throwing darts at it.

While I comb through Brock's online profiles, I get pinged by the actual culprit—whoever he is—several times.

SecretAdm1r3r wants to chat.

I don't care what he wants.

Near midnight my eyes are burning, and my temples pulse. I shut the machine down and lie on my bed, my phone on my chest. It's Friday. Me and Ocie's night when I'm not in solitary confinement.

It's still our night.

Me: U up?

Ocie: what?

Me: I'm sorry about what happened.

Ocie: Took u long enuf.

Me: Been grounded. No phone.

It's a lie. I could've been texting and emailing all day the same way I've been communicating with Taylor and Roz. Just forgot. Focused on the mission. Probably best not to mention that.

Ocie: What u did was cray, for reals. A lot of people r mad @ u

Me: I'm sure. Just like I'm sure most of them have Gray Scales in their favorites. Whatever.

Ocie: What do u want? It must b something.

Me: All I want is 2 make sure we r cool & 2 pass the time while I serve my sentence.

Ocie: My mom doesn't think it's a good idea 4 us 2 hang anymore.

That knocks my thought train right off the track. I didn't see that coming. Not in a million years.

Me: Do u agree with her?

Ocie: Idk. Would've been clearer if it didn't take U 2 days 2 hit me up.

Me: I told u I was grounded and couldn't text

Ocie: Funny. Taylor told me something different. Guess it's not so stupid 2 deal w/ him these days.

She's still been talking to him. She knows I've been talking to him. Crap.

> **Me:** It's not what u think.
> **Ocie:** Right. Because UR the same old mind-reading Panda. U know what I think b4 I do.

This is going bad. Fast. Face-to-face will be better. Then she'll understand.

> **Me:** Sorry. Okay? When I'm out of solitary, lattes for a month. Deal?
> **Ocie:** G'nite Panda.

Mrs. Horton doesn't want me and Ocie together anymore? Of all the ways my life's gone to pot since my secret came out, this feels most surreal. The most excruciating.

No. I'm losing everything else. Not my best friend. I'll speak to Mrs. Horton myself and explain that I'm not some low-life bad influence. Make her see it's all a misunderstanding. That I made a mistake and I'm sorry. All that good stuff parents like to hear.

Once I get out of this house.

———

The next morning, Dad's up early and off to the gym. It's his weekend ritual. Which is why I was up even earlier, waiting.

The hiss-spray of the shower in my parents' room comes on. It's time.

Sticking my head in their bathroom, I say, "Mom, I've got your grocery list and the credit card. Be back in an hour."

"What?" She pokes her lathered head from behind the shower curtain, her eyes sealed against the sluicing soap.

"Early start to the chores. Up and at 'em. See ya." I run for the stairs.

She yells, "But that's not *your* chore!"

I don't slow, and don't look back. I figure I'm halfway down the block before she can get to her bathrobe. There's a stop sign at the end of my street, then a left to get to Ocie's.

I go right.

I'll fix things with Ocie and her mom, for sure. After I pay Brock a visit.

A small delay in my repentance isn't going to kill anyone.

CHAPTER 30

BROCK'S NEIGHBORHOOD ISN'T KEACHIN-LEVEL SWANK, BUT his family is a couple of rungs above mine on the affluence ladder. I pull to the curb by his brick-and-siding McMansion and stare across a lawn so perfect it looks like a green swimming pool. The street is silent except for the *swish-swish-swish* of a nearby sprinkler. Brock's probably sleeping soundly.

Enough of that.

I dial the cell number I pulled off his Facebook profile. Convenient for me, but tarnishes my theory that he's my guy. My Admirer's tech savvy, and most tech-savvy people know to adjust their Facebook settings to hide such info. Still, a conversation is in order, if only for the sake of elimination.

The phone rings and rings, then goes to voice mail. I hang up and dial again. This cycle repeats three more times before a groggy troll picks up.

"Who is this, you freakin' dickbag?"

"Come outside, Boy Wonder." I kill the call and wait.

Within a minute he's stepping onto his porch wearing basketball shorts and pulling a Portside Football T-shirt over his admittedly ripped torso. He crosses the lawn in bare feet, squinting in the daylight. He's close enough to touch my car when recognition hits.

"Morning, Brock."

He leans forward with his elbows on my window frame. "I thought you, like, skulked in the shadows and shit. Doesn't sunlight hurt you?"

"No, but your morning breath does. Please direct it elsewhere."

He inhales deeply then blows a slow blast of foulness into my vehicle. It smells like warm Dumpster juice.

No one ever said interrogations were fun.

"So what do I owe this visit from Portside's Most Hated? You wanna take me up on my previous offer of free lovin'? I still don't have a bear costume, but my mom's got this fox fur stole. I can tie it around my head like a bandana if that works for you."

The same old Brock, with the same old tired jokes. It's hard to fathom him being as scary original as my Admirer. Still: "I came to talk about Keachin."

His joker grin recedes. "You should've come to her funeral yesterday. You could've given the eulogy."

"Screw you."

"I thought we covered that already." He backs away from my window and makes a show of slow-scratching his crotch.

"Did you know she was involved with Coach Bottin? Before?"

"If I did, why would I tell you?"

"Because I've still got pictures of you that I've never shown anyone. These photos make your Robin costume look like a Tom Ford suit."

His Adam's apple bobs like he wants to say something, but if he has a comeback, it never makes it into the world.

A subhuman like Brock probably does so much dirt that the prospect of any one of his nefarious deeds being dragged into the open is terrifying. I hope that's what's on his mind. Because there are no pictures. His super-hero affinity is the best I've got. He doesn't need to know that.

He's leaning back into my car again. "Unh-uh. Didn't know about her and Bottin. That scoop was all you, Gray."

"I thought you used to hang. You weren't close?"

"Not as close as I wanted to be. None of us ever had a chance. Everyone knew she dated older dudes, but I always thought she was into Common-wealth U guys. Not grown-ass men."

"That piss you off?"

"Not me. I smash hot chicks all the time. One tease don't affect the Brock."

If he was my Admirer, and was really behind Keachin dying, he wouldn't flat-out admit to anything I'm trying to get at. I know that. But, God help me, though Brock's mean and disgusting, I don't think he's a liar. You have to care what other people think to make lying worth it.

My phone vibrates in my lap. I ignore it to finish here.

"Two more questions. Did you hack my email and tell everyone I was Gray?"

"If I'd done it, you wouldn't have to ask. I would've had a T-shirt made."

"Last question. You secretly into photography?"

"Only selfies." He uses one hand to lift his shirt and give me a profile shot of his perfect abs. I shift my car into gear and pull off with him still leaning on it. He stumbles backward onto his dew-damp lawn.

Swinging a U-turn, I drive back the way I came, back to having a couple of hundred theories but no solid leads on my Admirer's identity. Even if Brock lied about everything, what do I have for proof?

My phone buzzes with an incoming text. There's a strip mall at the mouth of Brock's neighborhood. I pull into the lot so I can read the messages my Admirer's been sending.

> **SecretAdm1r3r:** UR ignoring me, or ur distracted. Either way, the game goes on.
>
> **Me:** ur crazy!
>
> **SecretAdm1r3r:** Even crazy requires a certain level of commitment. Which u currently lack. Don't worry, we'll fix that.

A final message comes through. It's a photo. As plain and badly composed as the one I got the night Keachin died. It's his next target.

Ocie.

Reckless. In so many ways.

Ocie won't answer my calls. I'm passing cars on streets not meant for passing. Laying on the horn when someone waits a half second too long before turning on red. At the intersection, a block from Ocie's, I get caught at the light myself. I would run it if there was a break in the traffic. A congested boulevard keeps me from saving my friend.

Tires screech around the corner, out of my line of sight. The green light comes. I stomp the gas hard, revving my engine to a strained roar that I've never heard before.

"Come on!" I scream, pounding the wheel with my fists.

My car's on two wheels—or it feels that way when I make the turn onto Ocie's street. I come up on a stopped Hyundai too fast. I slam the brakes as hard as I stomped the accelerator moments before. My car's mechanical whine is like a cry for mercy. I skid to a stop inches short of the abandoned vehicle. Its yellow hazard lights are flashing, and the driver's door hangs open like the wing on a lame bird.

"Help!" some person screams.

I shift into park and leave my car, rounding the vehicle blocking my way. A stranger is crouched, phone to his ear, rambling about ambulances and blood to a 911 operator.

Ocie is motionless in the street, with her legs at wrong angles and fluid leaking from her skull. Ocie's parents are summoned by the commotion. Watching their faces go from curious to concerned to horrified as they push through the crowd is almost as bad as seeing Ocie's broken body.

Sirens are fast approaching. My best friend in the world is posed grotesquely on the pavement.

I'm not distracted anymore.

CHAPTER 31

MY BEST FRIEND MIGHT DIE.

My parents should be punishing me for, well, everything. They're letting me off the hook so I can sit in an uncomfortable chair in the ER waiting area. No one says why because it doesn't need to be said.

The worst might occur, and whatever I've done, I don't deserve to be locked in my room while she's fighting for her life. She needs my moral support, and I need to be in a position to provide it, Mom's words and Dad's blessing.

Me, I see it slightly different.

I'm *still* being punished, forced to endure the torture of knowing one of the people I love most may lose her life because of what I've done. Or didn't do. Or . . . God.

I'm hunched, face in hands. I press against my healing eyes, making them ache again. I can't apply enough pressure to stave off my tears. Visions of strobing emergency lights, and Ocie's crumpled little body. The paramedics stabilizing her with a backboard, a medieval-looking device that straightens the spine and immobilizes the head with a bunch of Velcro straps. I recognize it from the gruesome teen car accident footage we watched in Driver's Ed, a class Coach Bottin taught.

The memory makes me shiver even though I'm sitting under a ceiling vent blasting warm air. I don't want to think about Coach, or Keachin, or the Admirer. Especially the Admirer.

I have as much success stopping those thoughts as I did stopping the car that ran Ocie down.

He did this. It's not a prank played in poor taste, and it's not a game. I've been terribly mistaken to ever think of anything that's happened in terms of fun and play.

Mom sits with me for hours. When Mr. Horton comes down and gives us an update, I focus on his mouth. Not his eyes. They are dark and glassy, sunken like the eyes of a fresh zombie head on *The Walking Dead*. Usually he's vibrant, as bubbly as Ocie, with his eyebrows sitting high on his forehead while telling me and her some joke we don't get. Now, he's sluggish and robotic in tone, the personification of a PSA.

"Mei woke up, but she's incoherent. They gave her something for the pain. Her legs are broken, so's her left arm. There doesn't appear to be any internal bleeding, but there's some concern about her head. She"—his voice cracks, he quickly pulls it together—"she's not out of the woods yet."

Mom asks if there's anything we can do. Mr. Horton says pray.

By 10:00 p.m. Mom's antsy, wringing her hands, pacing, looking like she could claw her own skin off.

"Mom, you know that bacon and potato casserole we make"—by "we" I mean "her"—"I was thinking the Hortons might like some."

She bites, anxious to get away from this place. "Yes, yes. That is a wonderful idea. I can cook it tonight. But what about you?"

"I'm going to stay until I hear something else. If that's okay." We drove in separate cars, and no one seems pissed that I took mine without permission, considering all that's happened. She agrees, kisses my forehead, and tells me she loves me. Once she's gone, I resume the hand-wringing, and pacing, and desiring to claw off skin.

Four more hours, fatigue starts to set in so I take a short walk to stretch my legs. Standing in an ER isn't a smart move. Seats fill fast.

With my chair gone and the day wearing me down, I eye a clean corner occupied by a potted plant. I'm not above crawling behind that plant and taking a nap. As I'm about to settle in, Mr. Horton appears again. His eyes more sunken than before, the corneas pink and moist, his shoulders slumping.

He gives me the last update.

Mr. Horton sits next to me, holding my hand, comforting me through my sobs. I feel horrible for taking his attention from Ocie, but I'm afraid to let him go, or even speak. Like he might take back what he said.

"Mei's talking. Not a lot of words, but enough."

"When can I see her?"

"It could be a while. She's not up for visitors yet."

"Tell me again, so I know it's real. She's going to be fine, right?"

Now he's tearing up. "Yes, the doctors believe so. There are still tests to run, and she's got some painful rehab ahead. We'll help her through that."

Yes. We will.

"I need to ask you something, Lauren."

"Okay."

"I told the police you might've seen something. Did you?"

A couple of officers questioned me earlier. I wondered what keyed them to me. Now I know. I told Mr. Horton what I told them.

"I got caught at the light on Highmore. I heard tires screeching. By the time I got there it was over. Oc—I mean, Mei—was in the street. But I thought I saw a car speeding down the block."

He nods. "A Mustang?"

"I'm not sure. Maybe."

"I suppose it doesn't matter. I was speaking to the police a few moments ago, before we got the good news about Mei. They found the drunk son of a bitch who did it, and there's"—he stammers here—"*evidence* on his car so it should be a slam dunk when they prosecute him. I was sure you'd seen something, though. If that was the case, it would only help our side."

A lot of things compete for space in my head, fatigue being the heavyweight contender, but I have questions. "It was a drunk driver in a Mustang?"

Mr. Horton shifts from relief to mild rage. "Repeat offender. Guy's got more DUIs than teeth. Maybe this is enough to put him in jail once and for all."

"Why were you so sure I'd seen something?"

He shrugged. "I thought I heard that funny horn tap you do."

Honnk-Onk-Onk-Honnk. Come, Ocie, come.

Mr. Horton heard my honk? Did Ocie? Is that why she stepped into the street?

I can't believe the person who tried to kill my best friend is a drunk driver. The same way I can't believe a humiliated former coach killed Keachin Myer.

My Admirer is playing us all.

Voicing my suspicions is not an option. The last time brought on this snowball of misery; to do it again might bring on the avalanche.

No more talk, then.

Mr. Horton relays more of the info he gathered from the police. How they found the fall guy passed out drunk on his couch, his blood-spattered car parked in his driveway like he'd just come back from a beer run.

How does someone pull *that* off?

"I know you've had some troubles over the last few days," says Ocie's dad, drawing me back to our conversation, "and I want to be clear that I don't approve of what you've been doing in your spare time, but I do approve of your friendship with my daughter. I'm glad you're here, and she's going to be happy to see you when she's able to handle visitors. Until then, I think you should go home. If you give me a moment to go up and see Mei, I'll come back and drive you."

"No. She needs you more than I do. I'm okay to get home."

I've been given a directive. No more distractions. Ocie's going to be okay. That's all I need from Mr. Horton until I can see Ocie myself. The rest of my energy goes into exposing the bastard that put her here.

Mr. Horton hugs me, promises to call when Ocie can have visitors, disappears into the depths of the hospital.

I don't leave right away. Something—possibly a very stupid something—bubbles up in me. I'm tempted to draft an angry, curse-filled text to my Admirer, but don't. His flawless plans, everything he's done to me, is not because he's some all-knowing god.

It's because I'm predictable.

Right down to how I honk my car horn.

Everyone I ever caught, I caught in some routine. Some habit, shady or otherwise. People get into a comfort zone and if you wait long enough, you can get right into that comfort zone, with them.

I start a new text, send it, but not to the Admirer.

Me: You still want 2 b friends? We should talk.

Despite it being 2:00 a.m., Quinn Beck, the college intern/wannabe reporter who tried to warn me that my life was about to go to hell, responds promptly.

Quinn: When and where?

CHAPTER 32

IT'S NO SMALL FEAT LEAVING MY house the next day, even with Dad away at the gym again (fittest man in the world lately). This is where, I'm ashamed to say, Ocie's injuries come in handy. My parents spoke to the Hortons, and they know she's not allowed to have visitors yet. I have another angle, though.

"I want to buy her a pair of shoes. For when she's able to walk again." Low, I know.

Mom doesn't buy it as is. "It has to happen today?"

"No. But, if I sit here and do nothing, I'm going to have a breakdown, Mom." This is not a lie. I'm on edge. For reals. "My best friend almost died yesterday."

"Fine. Go. If you are not back in two hours, be prepared to live in your room until your aunt comes for you."

"Deal." I kiss her on the cheek and note her scent, soap and vanilla. How long it will take me to forget it once I'm gone to the Peach State? Shaking off the thought, I drive to the library, where Quinn and I agreed to meet.

The Portside public library is small, brightly lit, a hard place to sneak. Still, my paranoia is on another level. My Admirer could be Satan himself, hopping from body to body like a winter cold.

Every single person who crosses the library's threshold is a suspect. An elderly man paying his fines is my number one suspect, until he's replaced by a mother pushing her child's stroller. How do I know that's a real baby and not some plaster-and-paste facade meant to conceal cameras and torture devices? Skateboard-toting middle-schoolers en route to the computer lounge, a notary public meeting some suspicious cardigan-wearing grandma-type to stamp her documents, the maintenance guy fiddling around in an exposed electrical socket. All enemies until proven otherwise.

"You're early."

I suppress the urge to jump. I'm tired from waiting at the hospital and didn't notice Quinn Beck's arrival because I was too busy profiling all the others in my vicinity. Stupid. My Admirer could've slipped in, too.

My phone's clock reads 1:45. "So are you," I say.

He sits, dropping a heavy satchel between us. He removes a slim, silver digital recorder from a side pouch and puts it on the table, the mic pointing toward me.

"Put that away," I say.

He frowns. "I thought you wanted to talk."

"Not to your little machine. Not yet."

His smile returns. He puts the recorder away. "What's this about, Lauren?"

"Stopping a very bad person."

A slight head shake. "I'm not following. I thought you called to talk about cyberbullying. An insider's perspective."

The "cyberbully" thing is a pinprick to my eardrum. Me? The bully?

This is where we are. Moving on: "This is about catching Keachin Myer's killer."

Something between the smile and frown now. Quinn says, "Her killer is already in jail."

"Coach Bottin didn't do it. I don't think."

"Who, then? Because best I can tell, the only other person who showed potential for extreme hostility toward her is you."

"What if I told you a fan of my site has gone too far?"

"I'd say it sounds like hyperbole."

"I can show you proof. Messages. Photos."

"Of this fan?"

"No. I'm hoping you can help me there."

"Lauren, I'm trying to get my news career started. For that, I need news."

"Aren't there such things as investigative reporters? I'm asking you to investigate something that you can later report. How's that not helping your cause?"

He sighs, looks around like he's hoping someone will drag him away from me. "Show me."

"Off the record," I say, because I've seen people on TV say it.

Another sigh. "Off the record."

I boot up my laptop, which I snuck from my house, sliding my chair around so I can properly walk him through things from the beginning.

Twenty minutes in, he's hooked.

Beck's laptop is next to mine, he's keying in notes and questions. The skeptic vibe is still strong, but he's taking me seriously for the moment. Maybe he has nothing better to do on a Sunday afternoon. I'll take what I can get.

"One thing I'm wondering," I say, clicking to the photo of Keachin's split skull, shrinking the image so no nosy passersby or librarian thinks we're looking at torture porn. "The police told me this was a crime scene photo. They also said they've had problems with people selling them to journalists. You know anything about that?"

"I know there are better ways for people to make money than"—he makes finger quotes—"stealing photos from the police."

"Not getting the sarcasm, Beck."

"I've heard of photos making their way into the hands of journalists when they aren't supposed to, but it's usually some cop doing the selling. You know, they picked the wrong horse out at Colonial Downs and don't want to get evicted. That sort of thing."

"You think the cops lied to me."

He shakes his head. "I doubt it. Don't see a reason in it. I'm just saying, since your connection to all this became apparent, I've paid close attention to our coverage as well as to the other news outlets. This is my first time seeing this photo. Your guy didn't sell it to anyone around here."

"Just for me then."

"I guess. He must be a real romantic." Beck pauses, says, "Did you get the sarcasm that time?"

"I did."

We're sitting side by side. Beck grabs his chair, does this weird lift-turn thing so he's facing me. I think he expects me to do the same. I don't comply, because I recognize this as the heart-to-heart position. He's about to talk some sense into me.

"Lauren, look, this stuff is compelling—"

"Don't do it, Beck. I'm not crazy."

"That's not for me to determine. Whoever this Admirer is, he's screwing with you. There's a reason the police look at husbands, wives, and lovers when someone gets killed. Those people *tend to be the killers.* Bottin's had a bad go the last few months. His career was done. He was facing possible prosecution as a sex offender. Wasn't like his life was great before that. He'd lost almost everything in a house fire and was living in an apartment he could barely afford. I'm surprised he didn't snap sooner."

"What did you say?"

"I'm surprised he didn't snap sooner."

"No"—I switch to a different photo on my Mac—"Coach Bottin's house burned down?"

"Yeah. I read about it in the story notes at work."

I maximize the photo of a burning room. *Dante.* "Is this his house?"

Beck shifts uncomfortably. "I don't know. I only saw notes. No pictures." Then, like he's breaking bad news, "This doesn't mean there's a connection."

"There's a chance, though." More than a chance. "When I asked my Admirer how he got this photo, he said he 'lit a match.'"

"Your criminal mastermind murderer-hacker is also an arsonist?"

"Maybe."

"Maybe not." He navigates to a secure site for channel 9, logs in, and brings up some bookmarked files. "The notes also said Bottin admitted to leaving candles burning near some drapes. The fire was his fault."

That stumps me. My hot connection fizzles. "Is there any way I can get a copy of those notes?"

"Absolutely not. I could get fired for passing you internal documents. Since I'm an intern, you can appreciate the psychological damage I'd suffer if I lost a job that doesn't actually pay me." He's giving me the judgment stare.

"I'm not crazy."

"You keep saying. Really, I don't think you are."

"What do you think?"

"I think you're looking for some way to not have to shoulder the load of all this."

"A way for it to not all be my fault?" I say.

"That's not what I mean."

It's what *I* mean.

He's gathering his things, like he's the one with the midafternoon curfew.

"Beck, wait. I need to ask another question."

"Here I thought *I'd* be doing the interview today. Go on."

"Do your notes say where Coach Bottin's new apartment is?"

He drums his fingers on the tabletop. Then, he opens his laptop again, bringing up another internal document. He makes a show of looking in another direction. "You didn't get this from me."

Bottin's address is on the screen. I note it in my phone. "Thank you."

"You're welcome. The next favor comes from you, though. Don't text me again unless you're willing to go on the record. The cyberbully angle is timely and with you as a source, I can pitch it to my boss."

"In other words, you want to build your career on my personal misery."

"You wanted to be my friend. There's a reason I don't have many. Good day, Lauren."

In the hour before I'm due home, I forgo the mall and Google Map Bottin's apartment. His complex is in a cropping of recently built "luxury apartment communities," each having a unique visual flair. Cobblestone facades, or shale, or wrought-iron railings on the stairs and balconies.

The complex I'm interested in is called *Preserve*, and has a tagline on a plaque below its cedar plank signage that reads: "Nature's Home." As if the geometric sections of warm autumn colors—orange, and brown, and burgundy—like a Lego tree house set, didn't sell the theme already.

I bet Keachin loved coming here. The newness of the complex makes it look more ritzy than it probably is, enough to impress a shallow girl.

It's not real luxury, though. Actual rich people would've put a wall around this place to protect it from prying eyes and potential intruders.

Like me.

Twisting in my seat, I lean back so my gearshift pokes my kidney. It's enough to keep my camera lens from protruding beyond my open car window as I shoot.

There are about a dozen blocky buildings, some containing maybe six apartments, with a few taller buildings housing eight. Each building has its own number for postal purposes. Bottin's is the third I zoom in on. I note the security door, and the digital keypad/intercom next to it.

My phone rattles in my cup holder. I glance around the street for any occupied cars, anyone who might be watching me.

Taylor: I heard about Mei. Do u know anything? Is she all right?

I've got enough shots for my next steps. Holstering my camera in its case, I send a quick text back to him before driving home.

Me: She'll b fine.

More texts follow, but I don't answer. I have research to do. Plans to make. I have a game to win.

Taylor's concern can wait.

CHAPTER 33

THE NEXT MORNING CHIMES PIERCE THE darkness. An unfamiliar sound that calls me from a thick, lead-limbed slumber. I manage a one-eyed glimpse at the phone glowing, shaking, and tolling on my pillow, inches from my face and a drool puddle. It's sloppy, leaving it out like that. If Dad saw or heard it, I'd lose it. He hasn't been in my room since the Aunt Victoria fight, so thankfully the risk is low.

My mouth is dank with the aftertaste of coffee and cola, the fuel from last night's marathon dissection of the Gray Beard's FB page. Based on what I know about the Admirer, I was able to cross off eighty-four of the Gray Beards as potential suspects. I'm almost certain I can knock off another fifty today. If I don't eat, or bathe, or blink.

First, I swipe through notifications on my phone, trying to figure what that sound is about. A red "1" is plopped on top of the voice mail icon.

Nobody I know bothers with voice mails when a text will do. Is my Admirer frustrated with me ignoring him? Maybe he's left some salacious message, which excites me. His voice is another clue for my growing file. I hit PLAY.

"Lauren, this is Mr. Horton. Wanted to let you know that Mei said it was okay for you to come by this afternoon, if you like. Take care."

Hmph.

I replay the message.

Mei said it was okay for you to come by this afternoon, if you like.

Of course I'd like to come by. Why wouldn't I?

Something in his tone, the words, feels off. Or I'm just tired, reading into things that aren't there. That's all.

Right?

<hr>

The middle of the day is spent eliminating more Gray Beards, while simultaneously bumping a few higher on my list. Like Lance Winslow, whose brother, Logan, I once exposed. Strange that he'd be part of my fan club. He also has a photo in "The Game" album. It's a photo of his butt. Still.

Then there's Durrell Pierce. I never dealt with him in my Gray persona, but he's shown a certain amount of bitterness because I turned down his invitation to prom last year when I was a sophomore and he was a junior. He noticed me despite my best Hall Ghost efforts, and acted like his attentiveness somehow indebted me to him.

"You should be happy someone sees you for how beautiful you really are," he said when I declined his invite. Because that's not creepy. I don't know if he has talents that fit my criteria. He's worth looking into.

In the afternoon I give Mom a call and make a case for another exemption on my grounding to go to the hospital. She agrees, making it clear it's for Ocie's sake, not mine. Okay. Fair enough.

I pull away from my monitor and get dressed to visit my friend. Unexpected butterflies flutter among the sloshing caffeine and junk food in my belly.

I'm at the hospital in time to see some band kids exiting the main entrance, their arms linked, their vibe a mix of joy and solemn concern. I watch them from my parked car, where I'm ducked down, huge sunglasses concealing my bruised eyes while I peer over the dashboard.

They're Ocie's tribe, and they're leaving. Visit over.

They pile into a vehicle and drive away. Coast clear. I enter the hospital wondering how I—Ocie's *best* friend—am so late to the party.

On Ocie's floor, I'm moving on the balls of my feet, quick and silent. My intent is to stroll right past her room, sparing a sideways glance to see who's present. If anyone else from school is there, I'll come back later. There's a lot of traffic in a hospital corridor to conceal me. It's a technique I've used many times when chasing Gray targets.

I speed up to do the pass. Doorways sail by, I'm reading the placards by each door with sidelong glances until I spot *M. Horton.*

Glimpsing a boy from school at the foot of Ocie's bed, I keep moving, ready to leave and come back. I'm a few yards beyond her room when his face registers.

Spinning on my heels I fast step into the room, hoping I'm doing a good job of concealing the edge in my voice. "Taylor?"

He turns to me, casual. "Hey, Lauren."

Hey, Lauren?! "Why are you here?"

"To see me, probably. That's just a guess." Ocie's voice is gruff, drawing my attention to her bed. I suck in a sharp breath. I should thank Taylor for the initial distraction.

Both of her legs are in casts, and one has the addition of a metal halo, secured with long silver screws drilled into the plaster. Her arm isn't much better in its shell and sling. Bandages circle her scalp, but her face is, remarkably, unaffected. Aside from heavy bags under her eyes, she looks just like she did the last time I saw her.

A gasp slips past my lips.

Taylor rises from the chair, offers it to me. Out of habit I wave off the gesture even though there's nowhere else to sit. He says, "Mei, I'm going to go."

"No. Stay."

I shoot her a look, but she's focused on him, communicating silent eye messages the way my parents do. Like she's telling him not to leave her alone with me. I don't react, not visibly.

Taylor glances at me, says, "We can talk later."

At her bedside he touches her bare arm, a reassurance. For an insanely possessive moment I want to smack his hand away.

He gives me a respectful nod that I don't return, and he's gone. I feel comfortable taking his seat now. "So . . . ," I say. I've got nothing else.

She says, "I totally understand why people get addicted to drugs. These painkillers they've got me on are awesome. I'm going to be a junkie when I grow up."

I laugh. It's forced.

My eyes bounce around the room, land on the massive bouquets of balloons and flowers that crowd the narrow space between her bed and the window. I didn't bring anything. We both notice my lack of decorum.

"It's okay," she says. "I think there's, like, a limit. Too much stuff gets in the way of the nurses doing their jobs. Or something."

It's nice of her to give me a pass, because I'm sensing she's having

difficulty with graciousness at the moment. Difficulty that wasn't a problem when it was just her and Taylor, I'm sure.

"How's your head?" I ask.

"It's getting there. Still hurts. I don't remember much after Friday
night."

"Nothing about the accident?" Does she remember hearing my trademark honk? I hope not. I don't want her connecting the accident to me.

She shakes her head, stares toward the window.

Screw this. "Are you mad at me?"

She doesn't say anything for a long time. When she speaks, all pleas-
antries are gone. "You mean *still*."

"What?"

"Am I *still* mad at you for having a whole secret life for, like, years? Yes.
I am."

Okay. I asked. We can deal with this. "I'm glad you told me. When
you're feeling better, we can talk about it. You probably shouldn't get
worked up—"

"You are being so other right now."

*Me? I'm so other? How is it your band friends, and Taylor, and whoever
else has been here knew you could have visitors before I did? Because there
are a bunch of squiggly, colorful signatures on your cast, and so many bouquets. Too many to have all come today. That is other. So, so other.*

I don't believe that Mr. Horton was fudging the truth when he said
he appreciated me being Ocie's friend, or that he would call me as soon
as she was up for visitors. I do believe he would delay notification at his
daughter's request.

Mei said it was okay for you to come by this afternoon.

Those things, I think. All I say is "I know a lot of stuff has come to light recently. Stuff I should've told you myself. I can't change that, but I think we'll be better friends for this going forward. I do."

"You think we'll be better friends?" Her face scrunches. "God, you just don't get it. I shouldn't have told Daddy to let you come here."

"You shouldn't have—" It's coming, a tidal wave of all the blame and accusations and attacks I've endured from everyone. The cops, my parents, the school, the media. Now Ocie? My friend? Who's supposed to have my back? Some dam in me breaks, the verbal flood comes to crush a person I care so much for, who I thought cared for me.

I say, "You're going to act like this over my stupid website? You've been my freaking number one fan since I started. You couldn't get enough of the gossip, and the guessing who Gray might be, and saying how cool it is that we've got some secret agent spy-type at the school. You're mad? You should be happy. You're friends with a local celebrity. It's your dream come true, so stop being a hypocrite."

I'm panting, the exertion of going too far.

"Wow," she says, blinking tears, "say what you really mean."

"I'm sorry, Ocie," I say, but in the way that's about hard truths instead of apologies, "I—"

"No, you're not. And stop calling me that. I hate that shit."

At first I'm confused. Stop calling her what?

She rolls her eyes, face pinched like the painkillers wore off. "That's not my name. Yours isn't Panda. Since we're going for absolute honesty today—that's what you want, right?—let's talk about these stupid nicknames that you won't let go. I'm not an obsessive compulsive. I'm just neat and care about my clothes. There's nothing wrong with that, and I'm sick of you making a big deal of it because you've embraced constant frumpiness. Though, the more I think about it, I see what you were doing. It was like camouflage so no one would think you could be Gray."

I don't tell her she's right because she might confuse it for being right about all the other things she's saying. She's clearly not.

She goes on: "Here's the thing—you trashing me didn't have to be part of your cover. You just like doing it."

"I don't *trash* you."

"*Avatar* when I do blue. *Leprechaun* when it's green. *Little Shoulder Devil* when I do red. You've always got a joke. You're always a little mean."

"Ocie—*Mei*, that's just our thing. Our black."

"No, it's not!"

How loud is she? I can't tell, but I'm afraid that a nurse, or a security guard, will be here any second. I keep my eyes on the door because it's easier than looking at her.

I can fix this. Of all the things that have gone wrong, this—her—I can handle. I say, "Do you hate me?"

"No. I don't hate you. I don't really know you either."

Smile. Keep voice light. Don't show the pain.

It's so hard to do. "I think we have a misunderstanding to work through."

"We broke into a skyscraper!" she says. "I still don't know what that's really about because your cute-photographer-boy story seems like more of your Gray BS. You want to fill me in on what we were really doing there, and at the beach during that storm?"

Instead of answering her question, I pick up a red Sharpie resting by her toes. "Can I sign your cast?"

She shakes her head. Hesitates. Are things that bad between us that she doesn't want evidence of our friendship mixed in with all the signatures of people she likes better than me right now?

I put the Sharpie down, still capped. "You're in pain. You should rest. We'll talk when you get out of here."

I'm not sure we will.

As I exit, I nearly collide with Ocie's mom and dad. Mrs. Horton swishes hot tea from her paper cup, burning her hand.

I'm sorry. It's what I intend to say. I'm crying too hard. Wedging myself between the Hortons, I move as quickly as I can without running because there are nurses and other visitors in the corridor. More damned band kids—how many are there?

When I turn the corner toward the elevator lobby tears are drizzling off my chin. It's only fitting that Taylor is there, leaning on the wall by the up and down buttons, playing some game on his phone.

"You play *Candy Crush*?" He doesn't look up. "Level eighty-eight is hard as hell."

"What are you doing here?"

"Slow elevators."

Not that slow. He left Ocie's room ten minutes ago.

"Did that list Roz sent you help?" he says. "Do you know who your Admirer is now?"

With the back of my hand, I attempt to mop up the crying mess that is my face. "That's really what you want to ask me about right now?"

"No. It's the least awkward thing I can think of at the moment."

The floor indicator chimes and the silver doors part. A stubble-chinned male nurse and an elderly man in a wheelchair are parked in the center of the car. Taylor steps into the gap beside the chair, and I go to the opposite side before we're sealed in.

I say, "She asked you to come see her."

"You're wrong, Lauren. I caught a ride up here to drop off a get-well card. I saw some kids from school and they told me she could have visitors now, and I hung around. That's all."

"So you say."

The old man in the chair giggles. "Lovers' spat."

"No," I say. "It's not."

The nurse joins in. "It's got that kind of vibe, sugar."

"Really."

There's a *ding* and the elevator opens. The nurse spins the old man's chair and backs him onto the second floor. The doors close and we're on the way down. Alone. In a confined space.

"Since when have you and her been so close?" I say, breaking the silence between us.

"You gotta stop this, Lauren. We go to the same school, me and her have classes together."

He thinks I'm being bitchy. I've conditioned him to think that, I suppose. "I didn't mean it that way. I want to know the deal with you two. What I missed."

We thump to a stop, and the parting doors reveal a number of people waiting for a ride. We sidle off the car as they stream in. When there are no more people between us, Taylor motions to some empty chairs in the lobby. "You want to sit down?"

I do not. I want to leave, keep hunting.

"Sure," I say, because I also want to be on someone's good side today.

There's a row of five vinyl chairs with lacquered armrests dividing them. Taylor sits, and I follow, keeping an empty seat between us.

"Mei and I had Earth Science together freshman year. Remember? She sat next to me and—you'll be happy to know—shunned me, at first."

"So what changed?"

"I got humiliated. This whole jockstrap-sniffing incident. You might know something about that."

I nod.

He says, "Even then, Mei tried to hate me. She loves you that much, I guess. It was a long year. I wore her down with charm and an uncanny grasp of tectonic plates. We've been cool ever since. I made a point to never let it be known when you were around. We knew you wouldn't react well."

"Am I that transparent?"

He shrugs.

"Why help me, Taylor? Why the concern over everything that's happened. I've been terrible to you."

He looks at me now, straight and plain. "You lost your way."

"Excuse me?"

"The people you put on blast were all assholes. Me included. I didn't get in your way because, I don't know, I was the one who . . ."

I don't like the sound of that. "The one who what?"

"Created you."

Oh. Hell. No.

"You didn't *create* me. You don't get to take credit for what I've done. Sure, I started with you, but *Gray Scales* is more than Taylor Durham payback. God, your ego! I helped a lot of people. Me. Not you."

"You think Keachin would find you helpful?"

His low blow takes my breath.

"Maybe I didn't create you, but I feel some responsibility. You don't see how far off the rails you've gone. Did you even understand what you were doing when you posted those photos of Keachin and Coach Bottin?"

"I was—I mean . . ." The old arguments come to mind. What Keachin did to Nina, her general shrewlike behavior, and so on. Yet as much as I've said these things in my head, I'm struggling to vocalize them.

Instead, there's Ocie's voice—*You're always a little mean.*

"When that stuff went down back then . . ." Taylor stops, starts over. "When I wrecked your rep after that night at your house, I was shredded on the inside. I saw what it did to you and the guilt felt like . . ." He motioned with his hands, trying for the proper words.

"A corkscrew in your stomach?" I offered.

"Yeah. Right. When you showed those jockstrap photos it was almost a relief. With all that's happened between Keachin and Coach, I can only imagine what you're going through."

"You mean since I'm the reason she's dead and he's in jail."

"I don't believe that."

"You might be the only one." I feel tears prick at my eyes again.

Taylor rises, moves into the empty seat I'd placed between us. "I'm going to hug you now. Don't claw my eyes out."

When his arm slips around me I don't fight his touch, or the memories of how I used to love his touch.

My phone vibrates, the buzzing is almost expected. I'm scared to look. But I'm going to. My Admirer knows I will.

There's a photo and message on my touch screen.

The photo is of me and Taylor waiting for the elevator on Ocie's floor.

The message: *Panda? Another distraction? Some ppl never learn.*

CHAPTER 34

"WHAT'S WRONG?" TAYLOR SAYS.

He's still sitting, I'm not. Every passing face, every hand on a phone that could be taking my picture right now has my attention.

"Lauren?"

Ocie's floor.

I run to the elevator and stab the up button repeatedly.

Taylor's next to me. "What's wrong with you?"

The elevator's five stories up. "Come on."

Taking the door beside the elevator, I climb the stairs two at a time, not pacing myself, barely breathing. When we reach the fourth floor I'm winded and gasping, a far cry from my track days. Taylor arrives a few seconds later, his breaths fast but regular. We turn the corner onto Ocie's hall and I expect blood-soaked walls, dead bodies littering the walkways. The Admirer is a horror-movie slasher, a supernatural monster, an unstoppable force.

The floor is brightly lit and gore-free. The sounds of laughs and chatter flit toward us from Ocie's room.

I say, "I need you to do something for me."

Taylor cocks an eyebrow, not agreeing or disagreeing.

"Can you go back to her room and make sure she's okay?"

"What?"

I think I feel an organ fail when I say the next word to him. "Please."

"Okay, okay." He starts down the corridor.

"Taylor, one more thing."

Slight annoyance passes over his face like a storm cloud. "What?"

"Can you take note of who's in the room?"

He rolls his eyes and keeps moving.

Retreating into the elevator lobby, I examine the photo on my phone. It's taken from behind me at a high angle, the back of my head taking most of the frame while Taylor's face is fully visible over my shoulder. It's low-res, lacking the quality of the Admirer's more polished pieces, but better than the dull photos he's sent me of Keachin and Ocie.

How does he keep getting *this* close to me?

My paranoia ramps up when I notice a ceiling-mounted security camera, hidden inside a black glass bubble over my head. Can he access the hospital security? Is he watching me right now?

I smile for the camera and slowly uncurl my middle finger.

"Guess you really don't like hospitals," Taylor says. Startling me.

Jesus, Panda. Now *he's* sneaking up on you?

"Is she okay?" I ask.

"She's got a bunch of broken bones."

"No! She's the same as when we left her, right?"

"She's fine. A bunch of people are in there. She's happy."

I'm glad and hurt. Happy wasn't how *I* left her. "What excuse did you use for coming back?"

"Said I lost my cell and thought it was in the room."

Smart. Plausible. "And?"

He turns his palms to the sky, a half shrug. "And what?"

"Who was in the room?"

"Her parents. A few other kids. From the band, I think."

"Like who?"

"Declan Brand, Michaela Holland, Carlos Goya, two other kids I don't know."

My phone's vibrating again.

Taylor says, "You feel like telling me why I'm gathering intel on Mei's bandmates? Are we bringing down a secret criminal organization? The High Step Mafia?"

Telling him what's happening is not what I want to do. I opt for my phone, regretting it instantly. Three messages.

> **SecretAdm1r3r:** U keep picking the wrong friends, Panda
> **SecretAdm1r3r:** No one knows us like us
> **SecretAdm1r3r:** Do I have to be ur last option b4 u get it?
> We'll see.

"Who's texting you?" Taylor asks. He sounds concerned. The fourth message arrives; he should be.

It's Taylor's picture, as bland as the shot of Keachin I received before she died. As badly lit and unflattering as Ocie's picture prior to the hit-and-run.

No.

Turning away from Taylor, putting yards between us so he can't glimpse my phone, I respond.

Me: I will not let u hurt anybody else. Never. I'll destroy u.

"Lauren?"

I take a few more steps so that I'm almost in another corridor. As if that makes him less involved now.

The response comes. I read it. Then again. Time rewinds a few weeks, to me and my Admirer's first contact. The conversations were long and exciting. The best I've had since . . . before. Flirty, but always with the air of competition. The pursuit of a win.

This message is six words. A challenge, perhaps the final one.

SecretAdm1r3r: You have to catch me first.

CHAPTER 35

THERE IS LAUGHTER WHEN I ENTER Ocie's room. Whatever's so funny has everyone distracted, unsuspecting. They don't notice me. My gaze drifts over the faces of kids I've seen every day but whose names I barely know. Ocie's my only friend here. Maybe. For her, I'm one of many. It tugs something in me to see her be as natural and fun around them as she is—was—with me.

Taylor fills the door behind me, stops short of running me over.

"Which one of you did it?" I say, bringing all but one boy's awkward giggle to a halt. I key on him. "Was it you?"

Mr. Horton stands, a cautious look on his face. The same look I've seen on people approaching a strange, unfriendly dog. "Lauren, are you okay?"

I sidestep him. Focus on the boys I don't know. "Which one of you has been fucking with me?"

"Hey!" Mr. Horton says. Mrs. Horton slips to her daughter's bedside, putting herself between me and Ocie. Between her daughter and the threat.

"Look, one of these creeps is the one who hit Oc—I mean, Mei. He killed Keachin Myer, too. I've got all his messages on my phone. He followed me here, even took a picture of me and Taylor."

Taylor shakes his head. Mouths, "What?"

"I can prove it." Everyone with the exception of Taylor, Ocie, and her parents have cell phones in hand. "Whoever you are, you messed up. You just texted me. Your number's in my phone."

Dialing. No one breathes while we wait for the telltale ring that will reveal the killer.

It doesn't come.

A generic voice mail message sounds through my speaker; it's not loud, but everyone hears it in the crushing silence.

"No," I say, all set to redial, "his phone's on silent. Or it's off."

One of the boys holds up his lit and powered phone like a shield. "Not mine."

The others follow suit. Even the girls. All phones are on. Even if the ringers were silenced, the vibration would've given him away.

"Lauren." It's Ocie. Such disgust in her voice. "Are you done?"

I struggle for something to say. A hand lights on my shoulder. "Come on."

Taylor's touching me, motions to the hall with a slight head tilt. If I didn't get the hint, Mr. Horton clarifies, "It's probably time to go, Lauren."

No offer to drive me, not this time.

I turn and fast step away. In the hall, I'm jogging.

"Hold up," Taylor says.

Not like I have a choice. I'm back at our favorite hangout, the elevator lobby. Waiting.

"What was that?" he asks, the same wary, in-the-presence-of-a-rabid-beast look on his face as everyone back in the room.

"He's trying to ruin me. Or kill you. Or both."

"I'm sorry. All I heard was 'kill me.'"

"The Admirer."

"The guy you told me about in the cafeteria."

An empty elevator opens, and it's time for Taylor to know the whole truth. Not here. *He* might still be watching. "Let's go. You're in danger."

"That's sounds really dramatic, Lauren."

If only . . .

CHAPTER 36

AS FAR AS MY PARENTS KNOW, I'm still at the hospital with Ocie. Visiting hours end at eight. I can reasonably pull off an eight thirty return without raising eyebrows. I do the calculations while I drive Taylor back to his place.

We cruise past my neighborhood, and Ocie's, and we are never even close to Brock's. This is the part of town where there's litter in the streets, and it's gloomy even on a blue spring day. At a red light, there's a guy leaning on a shuttered window, blocking spray-painted profanity with his body and eating something fried from a greasy paper bag. When I look his way, he flicks his tongue at me.

We pass a dilapidated playground where all that remains of the swings are broken chains dangling from rusted A-frames, and a sloping metal chute resembles a sharp-toothed cheese grater more than a slide. Kids are about, girls and boys, propped on benches and picnic tables, but show no interest in the playthings meant for them. With puffed bulky garments and unsmiling faces, they seem ready for older things.

Finally, we reach the lot at Taylor's apartment building, having to wait to park while the neighborhood boys play a down in their street football game. Once the play ends, they allow us to pass, and I park between a Cadillac SUV with mirror rims and a stripped-down Toyota sitting on cinder blocks.

Taylor exits, begins moving toward the building entrance, while I pop my trunk and grab my camera bag.

"Afraid someone's going to take it?" He laughs after he says it, overselling the nonchalance about his unpleasant, slightly scary neighborhood.

"My Nikon goes where I go."

He joins me and peeks at the photographer's arsenal in my trunk. "And the rest of it?"

"What about it?"

He sifts through my stuff—tripod, some bulbs, a flash kit, along with other things thieves might usually expect to find in a car trunk. I fight the childish urge to yell, "Mine!"

Instead I say, "The camera's the most important thing."

"At least you've got your priorities straight."

He walks away before I can determine if that was a dig. I close the trunk and follow him into a faded brick building that is identical to six others on the street. No illusions of luxury living here. Definitely not "Nature's Home."

We climb three flights of metal stairs and arrive at an apartment where the door isn't thick enough to muffle the childish screams inside. Taylor lets us in and I'm greeted by two munchkins treating the couch like the world's best trampoline.

"Hey," he says, "you're just going to keep jumping right in front of me."

The girl, talking like a Brit, says, "Ye have no authority here, peasant."

I look to Taylor.

"She's obsessed with the BBC. Don't ask me why."

The boy pauses, gathers, and does a backflip off the chair. My heart stops while he's in the air. I envision an incomplete rotation and shattered vertebrae. He lands on his stockinged feet, stumbles slightly, then regains his stance like an Olympian.

"You're going to break you neck one day," Taylor says, echoing my concern, though laughing as he does. The boy bows at the waist. *Ta-da!*

"What happened to your eyes?" the boy asks me. I keep forgetting my bruises.

Taylor says, "That's rude!"

"It's fine." To the boy I say, "I flipped off too many couches."

His mouth puckers. "Oh."

Sighing, Taylor introduces me. I never got a chance to meet his siblings before. "Lauren, this is Aaliyah and Jaiden. Midgets from hell, this is Lauren."

"Ohhhh." Aaliyah abandons her across-the-pond accent. "You said the H-word."

"Like you don't say the S-, F-, D-, B-words when you don't think I can hear you." To me, he says, "You should hear the crap that comes out of her mouth sometimes. Samuel L. Jackson might be her real dad."

Smiling at the joke, I can't help but wonder about Taylor's dad. Sure, I've avoided being within thirty feet of Taylor in the last couple of years, but that doesn't mean I haven't heard things. About his parents' divorce, and his family's move here, where jumping on the couch was probably a better, safer option than the postapocalyptic playground we passed.

"Let's talk in my room," Taylor says. Leading me, though I could easily find it on my own. I can see every door in the apartment from where I'm standing, and there's not many to choose from.

Jaiden jumps in my path, landing in a crouch. "I'm Spider-Man and you have to take my picture for the *Daily Bugle*."

I say, "I thought only Peter Parker takes pictures of Spider-Man."

He gives me a knowing smile. We're in the Cool Club together.

Raising the Nikon, I say, "Parker's going to be mad at me for doing this, but how can I refuse you, Spidey?"

I snap three quick shots, the first pictures I've taken for fun since . . . God, when?

I'm into it, getting Jaiden to do some poses, and another couch flip that I catch midair. Aaliyah joins the act as Storm of the X-Men, and I'm ready to bring in some props and extra lights when Taylor gets my attention. "I thought I was in danger."

"We've got a pair of superheroes here, so you're good."

The children giggle, but Taylor's right. We've got things to discuss. I tell the kids, "We'll do this again. I promise."

You promise? Really, Panda? Where's that coming from?

If anyone else finds my sudden commitment to the Durham siblings strange, they don't let on. Taylor nudges me into his room, where two twin beds are pushed against opposite walls. There are no chairs, so I sit on the bed with the Spider-Man comforter.

He sits opposite me. "Now, who's trying to kill me?"

Perhaps I'm getting good at telling the story, like a veteran teacher delivering a patented lecture. By the numbers. I'm not stammering through the sordid history of me and my Admirer, like I did with my parents. Not feeling the need to justify, like for the cops. Not desperately trying to sell an idea, like I was with Quinn Beck. I'm telling Taylor a cautionary tale, a warning of what's happened and what could happen. It is what it is.

He nods a lot, doesn't interrupt. He was always a good listener. It's one of the things I liked most about him back then.

When I finish, he says, "I thought Coach Bottin killed Keachin. And the guy who hit Mei is locked up, too. That means your guy set them up. How's he pull something like that off?"

I consider his question. Not the logistics of how the Admirer could engineer a murder, a hit-and-run, frame two people, and only arouse *my* suspicions—that's been troubling me long before he asked. I'm taken by his lack of condescension. Mostly everyone I've told has treated me like I escaped from the mental ward when I float my theory. Taylor's assuming I have an explanation.

He's wrong. The vote of confidence is nice, though.

"I'm not sure. If I find his real identity, everything falls into place, I think. That's the problem."

"I get it. You're not calling him the Admirer for fun. You got any thoughts on who it could be?"

"He goes to Portside. I'm almost certain of that."

"Okay, a boy at Portside. That's only half the school. What else you got?"

"He's incredible with a camera." I hand over my phone so he can see *Dante* and *View from Heaven*. "My first thought was Marcos Dahmer . . ."

"But he doesn't have the tech skills you've been looking into." Taylor swipes several times, looking at all the photos I've received from the Admirer. When he winces, I know he's seen Keachin's crime scene photo.

"Right," I say, "you told me Brock's a techie, which was news to me."

"He wants Zuckerberg's money. That's all."

"I went to see him."

Taylor meets my eyes. "And?"

"Even if he's got the skills, nothing about him screams photographer."

Taylor refocuses on the photos in his hand. "Yeah. All this is a little too detail oriented for him. He's more of a sexting-pictures-of-his-junk kind of guy."

He keeps going through my phone, pauses on a photo and stays there awhile.

I say, "Do you see something?"

"Not really, it's just . . ." He trails off.

"What?"

"How'd your Admirer get my driver's license photo?"

"Your—? Let me see."

He gives the phone back, displaying the photo of his face taken under harsh lights, a DMV trademark. How did I miss this?

I've seen Ocie's driver's license. She's often flashed it as a badge of dishonor since she doesn't have a car. That's why the picture I got on my phone before her accident was familiar. I was too amped up to see it then.

The plain shot of Keachin before she turned up dead . . . a driver's license photo, too?

How *would* the Admirer get those? None of this makes sense.

Except the one thing.

I swipe back to *Dante*. "This picture was among the first he sent me. He was proud of it. Showing off. I think it means something."

"The photography stuff is your world. I'll take your word for it."

"He's all about the double meaning and slick talk." His "Panda in a blender" riddle and the pretentious names for his photos gnaw at me. "Dante's *Inferno*. You remember reading it in freshman English?"

"I recall the *Wikipedia* page. Sorta."

"Okay, slacker. Dante pretty much walked through the circles of hell and watched people get punished for their sins. There was all kinds of torment, but the fire was reserved for really bad people in the lowest circles."

"What's your point?"

"Coach Bottin's house burned down." I tap my screen. "Maybe the Admirer was punishing him."

"For what?"

"Getting with Keachin. A lot of people had a thing for her, right? What if my Admirer had it worse than most? What if he found out about her and Coach way before me, and did this?"

He frowns. "Do you know for sure that's Bottin's house in the picture?"

"No. But I'm going to find out."

A small, boxy TV sits on the dresser. I motion to it. "That thing get cable?"

"Yeah, why?"

"Do you mind turning it to CNN or some other news channel? Make sure the volume's real loud."

He looks skeptical, but complies, turns the volume up.

Dialing the number I recently added to my contacts, I wait for someone in the Preserve rental office to pick up.

"Thank you for calling Preserve, Nature's Home. This is Renn, how can I help you?"

"Yes, this is Patricia Parker from channel nine news," I say, only extra fast and twangy with an exaggerated Southern accent—*Yaaayesss, thisis-PatriciaParkerofchannelninenews*. "I'm doing a quick follow-up fact check on a quote we got from one of the property managers in your complex. Is it true that Mr. Bottin's apartment has yet to be vacated?"

"Lord, am I ever going to hear the end of that pervert?"

"That's a yes then, sir?"

"He's paid up through the end of the month. Even then I gotta wait ten days before I can put his filthy things on the street. It's like the state wants his pervert germs making my other tenants uncomfortable. And who's going to have to clean it all up? Me. I've got half a mind to—"

"Thank you, sir!" I end the call.

Taylor's ogling me like a tentacle's curling out of my ear. "That was impressive."

"Thanks. Don't go trying to take credit for it." I honed those skills long after me and him. "I'm going to check out his place tomorrow. Try to find anything that ties him to *Dante*. At least that gives me a direct link to him and the Admirer."

"Us."

"'Cuse me?"

"It gives *us* a link. Don't look at me like that. It's my neck on the chopping block, right?"

He's got a point. "Fine. I'll text you as soon as I'm done to let you know what I find, then—"

"I'm going with you."

"Oh no, you're not."

"You said your Admirer goes to Portside."

"Probably."

"So if he's really trying to kill me, skipping school is like self-defense."

"It's more like bullshit. You think I'm still off the rails. I don't need you to protect me."

"News flash, Daniels, it's not all about you. Wanna know something? Keachin was never mean to me. I know she could be an asshole, but sometimes she was cool. She shouldn't be dead right now. If the person who hurt her is really what you say, if he hurt Mei, too, and you—*Gray!*—are taking him down, I want in. If I have to sit in front of your house tomorrow, I will. It's going to be hard for you to sneak out if your parents see me."

"Who says I have to sneak?"

"You, with the way you keep checking the time on your phone. I got them Sherlock skills, too."

Hardly. He's right, though. It is getting late.

Standing, contemplating, I say, "Text me tomorrow and we'll go from there."

"You all right getting home?"

"I'm not the one with the target on my back." I'm only half joking. Then I say, "Be careful."

"You should tell him that. I'm not some girl."

"He's not some boy. With what he does, he's something else altogether."

Taylor walks me past the couch where Jaiden is already asleep and Aaliyah isn't far behind.

We tiptoe to the door and into the hall. There's nothing else to say, but it feels weird leaving him. The weirdness makes me angry. At Taylor. At Ocie. Of course, at the Admirer.

"Stay alive, please. Everybody's seen me with you, I don't need any more heat for something that's not my fault."

He huffs, "No wonder you attract such charming dudes."

This snark feels right. Normal.

"Thank you." I touch his arm and take the stairs. That's enough for one night.

CHAPTER 37

THE NEXT MORNING I'M THROUGH THE door like thirty seconds after my parents leave for work. I pick Taylor up at his place, and we make the drive to Coach Bottin's. We park on the street, a block away from Preserve.

"Let's go. Try to look like we belong here."

He falls in line, moving quickly, casually. We walk the lot for several hundred feet.

Taylor notices the security panels at each door. "You don't have a pass code, do you?"

"I don't."

At Bottin's building, I approach the door and press the plastic buttons mounted beside each unit number. I detect faint buzzing from inside the building with each push and fight the increasing anxiety when I don't get an answer. The longer we're standing still, the more memorable and suspicious we become. I get lucky on the fifth try.

"Yeah," some guy I plan to never see says through the intercom.

"This is FedEx." I check the number of the last unresponsive condo I buzzed. "I've got a delivery for unit 204; the order says I can leave it at their door, but I don't think they meant *this* door. I don't want to have to take it back if I can help it, because it's marked urgent, and—"

There's an angry buzz from the other side of the security door and a loud *ca-clunk* of a lock releasing. Taylor grabs the handle and we let the oblivious neighbor in 205 get back to his day.

"I can't believe the crap you do works," he says.

"Sometimes it's hard for me to believe, too. Good thing we weren't coming to kill whoever's in 204."

"At least the guy in 205 could buzz the cops in afterward."

Coach Bottin's apartment is on the third floor. Aside from the sound of hushed TV voices flitting from other apartments, the floor feels abandoned. Great. If taking too long to get buzzed in was suspicious, what comes next will definitely get cops called should we get caught.

"Watch my back." I crouch in front of Bottin's door, pull my lock pick set from my jacket pocket.

Taylor's face droops. He turns away, watching the stairs and other doors on the hall, tapping his thigh in a nervous rhythm. He whispers, "How'd you learn to use lock picks?"

"YouTube is a second-story man's best friend."

"A what?"

"If we're going to do this more often, you gotta learn the lingo."

A deadbolt is the only lock on the door. Tougher than padlocks, but not as tough as the average homeowner likes to think they are. My tension rod goes in first, then I work the pins with my C-Rake. A quick flick of the rake—like swiping a debit card through the reader on a gas pump—will sometimes be enough.

This isn't one of those times.

I give up on the rake and opt for my short hook, which requires a more delicate (time-consuming) touch than my previous tool. Deep breaths are necessary to keep a stressed hand tremor at bay.

Taylor says, "Are you trying to get someone to call SWAT on us? Hurry up!"

"Don't rush me. You asked to come."

"I didn't think we'd be doing this. If I acted like you, I would've been locked up a long time ago. Must be nice on the other side."

That makes me pause, only for a moment. He's right on one thing. I need to hurry.

The next three minutes feel like three years. Aborting the mission is starting to look like an option when—

CLICK.

There's give, the tension rod turns. I never get tired of that feeling.

We step inside, and I close the door gently, reapplying the locks. I ask, "The other side of what?"

He plays dumb amnesiac. I remind him, "You said 'must be nice on the other side.' The other side of what?"

His annoyance is unhidden. "The other side of getting away with stuff. You're a girl, and you look"—he shrugs—"you don't look like me."

"You mean I don't look black enough." Ghostly echoes of elementary school teasing haunt me.

He rolls his eyes. "I mean no one assumes you're a criminal, even though you really are. For me, it's the opposite."

"Oh, boo-hoo! Guess what, you just broke in with me. You're a criminal now. Leave if you want, but don't go full a-hole over something I have no control over because you're scared. I'm scared, too. We're in, so look around."

He does. "Someone's been here."

Drawers and kitchen cabinets are open, revealing mismatched drinking glasses and dinner plates. Furniture's shifted wrong, the couch is at an odd angle from the wall. Blotchy residue powders the TV screen, and the counter, and the glass door leading to a balcony. Fingerprint dust.

I say, "The cops are building their case. Let's not leave any extra prints, in case they come back. That's how smart criminals do it." My lock picks go in my right pocket; I pull a balled-up pair of latex gloves from my left.

Taylor gives me the stink eye.

"What? You didn't bring any?" I let him stew before I pass him the extra pair I always keep on me.

"What are we looking for?" he asks.

"Maybe a photo album. He might have pictures of himself in his old place. I can see if it looks like *Dante*. Speaking of pictures . . ." I brought along my trusty point-and-shoot, give it to him. "Photograph the whole room. The memory card's big, so take a thousand shots if you have to. I want to examine everything when I get home."

"Question."

"The shutter release is on the top right."

"That's not my question. Why are you just now trying to track this guy down?"

"He hurt Ocie and ruined my life."

"Before that. You did some poking, but you didn't think to use all your secret agent skills to find this guy's identity sooner?"

"I got sidetracked. I haven't been myself."

"Which self? You're like three people."

What's he want to hear? That I liked the game at first? I thought the Admirer was someone like me, someone I'd been looking for without knowing it. I'm feeling a certain nostalgia for working alone.

"Let's get this done. I'll be in the back."

Taylor gravitates toward glass and metal shelves in the corner of the living room, home to a few books, but mostly an extensive DVD and CD collection. I move into the back rooms. A bathroom, home office, and the bedroom. I shudder, thinking of Keachin making this same walk with different intentions.

The *man* smell in the bedroom lingers though the place feels long vacated. A mix of overly sweet deodorant and a laundry hamper that's decaying in his absence. The silk bed linen is a coiled mess, the fitted sheet snatched from the mattress, exposing a full third of yellowed pillow top padding. The dresser is like the kitchen, drawers extended and picked through. The closet door is open. I shift a few dangling golf shirts aside, but find nothing of interest hidden behind them. No safe. No secret perv dungeon.

The shelf above the closet rods are full of neatly folded towels, and jeans, and novelty tees featuring familiar characters on the creased shirt faces. Darth Vader. Wolverine. Superman's *S* in primary colors.

The comic tees would've seemed cute and quirky if not for Bottin having youthful tastes in more than his clothes.

On the closet floor, a few more shirts lie scattered. More cartoony kids' stuff, except for a faded Portside Pirates shirt and an AGG Tech shirt that's stained with what might be grape juice.

I take several shots of everything with my phone before moving on to the office.

Black fingerprint powder is more prevalent here, dusting his keyboard and monitor. There was a rectangular impression in the carpet where a PC tower probably sat. Makes sense that the police took it. Probably checking for kiddie porn, or something else that could help stack the charges against him.

In here, Coach's *Star Wars* fetish is on full blast. Framed poster art from the original trilogy occupy three of the walls. Above the desk is an image made to look like an oil painting. Luke Skywalker, both hands over his head, wielding a light saber that's more lightning than the neon glow sticks I've always associated with this franchise. Kneeling at Luke's hip, almost in worship, is the princess, far sexier than I recall her being in the film. In the background, Darth Vader's helmet, large and looming like a black sun. There's a tiny gold plaque in the bottom right corner of the frame that reads:

Star Wars

Released '77

On the next wall, a poster for *The Empire Strikes Back*, released in '80. Then *Return of the Jedi*, released in '83.

Next to the *Jedi* poster, there's a wall calendar featuring a girl that looks my age—though the calendar logo identifies her as a "College Hottie"—in a string bikini mounting a Japanese motorcycle. Bile rises in the back of my throat, and I decide it's best to leave this place before I catch something.

A page from a mini-notepad is taped to the desk, four or five usernames and passwords scribbled on it. They're not much good without the computer, but I photograph them anyway in case Taylor, or maybe Roz, can work some sort of cyber magic with them.

For the rest of the room, I opt for a couple of panoramas that will give me a detailed 360-degree view of everything. When I close the door so I can get the whole room uninterrupted, I discover a fourth movie poster. Something called *THX 1138*.

It looks odd and old. I've never heard of it, unlike *Star Wars*, which everybody knows. Shrugging it off, I move to the center of the room, start the panorama in my camera app, and spin slowly in place to capture everything. I do this a couple of times to make sure I have backup shots. I'm completing the last one when Taylor calls to me.

In the living room, he's leaning behind the DVD shelf, tugging at something.

"What did you find?" I ask.

He emerges, sliding a frame as tall as his hip into the open, flips it so we can see the front.

A poster, featuring a funny little man gripping some sort of magical staff. There's a tiny bronze placard in the lower right corner of the frame reading:

Willow

Released '88

"There are a couple more back here." He drags those out. *Raiders of the Lost Ark* and *Red Tails*. Each with a bronze placard. Released '81 and '12 respectively.

Together, we prop them against the wall side by side, a movie poster lineup.

He says, "I thought they were important because they were hidden."

"You weren't wrong. These are important."

"Him liking movies?"

"There's a pattern here." I bring up *Dante* on my phone. "Look."

I point to the burning framed *American Graffiti* poster in the photo.

Taylor looks at me, then the posters, frowns and says, "I see where you're going, but it's a stretch, right? A lot of people hang posters."

True. Posters in *Dante* and posters in this apartment don't mean the flaming room was in Coach Bottin's house. I suspect there's another connection, though. One that will be harder to write off.

With the internet app on my phone, I enter the following string in Google: *American Graffiti*, *Red Tails*, *Star Wars*.

Almost immediately, a picture of a chubby, salt-and-pepper-haired man in a flannel shirt appears, the top hit.

I turn my phone to Taylor. "Recognize him?"

"George Lucas. He, like, invented *Star Wars*."

Coach Bottin's bumper sticker, *My Other Car Is an X-wing*, bounces lewdly in my thoughts.

Another quick search on *Willow* and *Raiders of the Lost Ark* confirms that George Lucas is affiliated with all the films as a writer, director, or producer. In some cases, as all three.

"Liking framed movie posters might be a coincidence," I say, giddy, "but liking everything one guy does. No. This is Bottin's house in *Dante*. My Admirer torched his place, and Bottin lied to the police about it. It has to be over Keachin. He wouldn't have wanted to explain that."

"I'm glad arson makes you tingly, but I still don't see what you have here, Lauren. We broke into a murder suspect's crib for this? *We* could go to jail."

"Lower your voice. *We're* not going to jail. If we can piece all this together the right way, then we can make everyone see, and they'll believe me." I want to say, *Then I can fix this.*

That's too far. What's happened isn't some broken vase that can be Krazy Glued back together with reason and evidence. Mainly because one huge piece is missing. Keachin.

Taylor stomps across the room. "Believe you about who? You don't have anyone in mind."

"But I'm closer! It's not great, but things are starting to make a kinda-sense."

"Is 'kinda-sense' a word?"

"I'm not the rookie here. I've been doing this for—"

A knock at the door interrupts me.

Taylor and I exchange frightened looks, deer smelling humans on the breeze. If we get caught here . . .

I mouth the words, "Turn on the sink."

"Huh?"

"Just do it," I hiss, and move back toward Bottin's bedroom.

More knocks. Louder and harder. "Hello?" a woman's voice calls. "Who's in there?"

Speeding up, I go to Coach's closet and grab a couple of bath towels off the shelf.

Then, I do what a dead girl probably did here not so long ago.

I strip.

CHAPTER 38

THE WATER IS RUNNING AND TAYLOR is pacing when I return to the kitchen wrapped in a towel, a second towel dangling from my hand. The shock freezes him, but we don't have time for frozen. I yank the spray nozzle next to the faucet, stretching the hose to the limit, motioning for him to take it.

He grabs it. I flip my head forward so my hair dangles into the basin. "Spray me."

The knocker is really persistent now. "I'm about to call the police."

"Hang on! I'm just getting out of the shower!" I shout, praying she's not already dialing 911. "Taylor," I whisper-scream.

He triggers the nozzle and a cold stream douses me. Mussing my hair enough to spread the moisture, I whip the second towel around my dripping locks like a turban. "Hide."

Taylor ducks behind the counter while I move to the door.

Deep breath, I open it a crack. "Yes?"

An elderly brown-skinned lady with eyes so big they seem insectile, like they should be on stalks, examines me. There's a cordless in her hand, as ready as a gunslinger's weapon. "Who are you?"

"I'm your new neighbor," I say. "Moved in yesterday."

"I didn't see any moving trucks yesterday."

Think, Panda. "My furniture hasn't arrived yet. All I've got is an air mattress and some luggage. That's why it took me so long to answer. Got in the shower and realized I didn't unpack my towels. Stupid."

The old lady's lips pinch, making the lower half of her face look like a sad prune. "It's just *you* who moved in?"

Did she hear Taylor talking before? Is she trying to trip me up? I play it neutral. "I have a boyfriend."

More prune puckering. She sighs, becomes more relaxed before my eyes, but with a strange air of sadness. "You're such a pretty girl. I think you can do much better."

"Excuse me?"

"I can't tell you what to do, but if I hear any fighting I will call the police on him. Do you understand?"

My eyes, the bruises. She thinks . . . "Oh, ma'am. No. My boyfriend didn't do this."

She backs off. "I'm sorry to have disturbed you. I don't know if the landlord mentioned your apartment belonged to that nasty teacher who's been in the news."

"I don't watch much news. I need to go. My hair."

She seems put off, but moves away, mumbling, "That's what's wrong with your generation now."

"Good day, ma'am." I close the door, then lean against it because there's very little strength in my legs.

Taylor rises, awed, though I misinterpret what's got his interest piqued. "Are you naked under there?" he asks.

My cheeks blaze. "I've got on underwear, jerk."

I rush back to Bottin's room where I left my clothes. "We're leaving. Take some pictures of those posters first."

He gets to work with the point-and-shoot. "Then what?"

"We show my darling Admirer exactly what we've found."

We're parked at the supermarket where I first met Quinn Beck so we can piggyback the Wi-Fi from the bookstore next door. I upload all the pictures Taylor took to my MacBook, then sync them to my phone so I have everything we shot in hand.

"You sure this is a good idea?" he asks.

"No, but he likes to taunt me. It's how he keeps me off balance. Let's see if it works both ways."

I send snapshots of the Lucas collection with this text: *Any reason you didn't burn these?*

He responds quickly.

> **SecretAdm1r3r:** I notice ur boy toy's not in school today. Was hoping 2 catch him @ the crosswalk, GTA-style.

I show Taylor the message. He gets grim.

"What's 'GTA-style'?" I ask.

"*Grand Theft Auto*, I think." His voice is a little growly, he's flexing his fingers into a fist. "You can run people over for points, or fun."

I'd forgotten about those horrible games. "You like things like that?"

"As of today, no."

What's it like to have your life threatened? Not in some after-school-playground-fight sort of way, but, like, a scary person knows your name. I pat his knee, compounding the weirdness that carried over from last night. After two quick taps, I pull away slowly. "I think we're getting under his skin."

Taylor nods, doesn't seem to grasp the silver lining.

> **Me:** There r benefits 2 being suspended, u know. I have all day
>
> 2 track u down
>
> **Admirer:** I'd be worried if I wasn't smarter/quicker/better than u
>
> **Me:** Can u stay that way?

I silence the phone. He'll keep texting, wanting to keep the jabs going. Let him squirm.

"What now?" Taylor asks.

"We can't sit here all day."

"We could go back to my place."

Now the car seems uncomfortably warm, unusual for fall. "Um."

"I don't mean like"—his voice deepens, faux-smooth—"*come back to my bachelor pad*. I'm saying we can get a better look at those photos. Or watch TV and have a sandwich. Whatever."

"What about pizza?" I've suddenly got a taste for it.

"Pizza's cool. Half peppers and mushrooms." He remembers my preferred toppings.

"Half sausage and those nasty olives you like."

His order. My order. And never the two shall meet.

He plays with a pair of my discarded pizza crusts, forming a *T* on his plate and grinning like he just finished the *Mona Lisa*. Boys.

Without his siblings going Cirque du Soleil on the furniture, the apartment feels vast, and at the same time cramped. Me and him take up a lot of space.

I work around the discomfort by clicking through the photos of Bottin's apartment. The pictures of the coach's passwords are for Taylor. He gets to work on his own rebuilt laptop made from mismatched parts. He notices me noticing the oddity.

"I call it 'the Bride,' as in Frankenstein," he says. "I put this baby together from old throwaways the school was recycling."

"Does lightning need to strike for it to work?"

"Funny. She doesn't look like much, but she's powerful."

When the Bride boots up, the spinning hard drive sounds as loud as a helicopter rotor. My faith in her is not high.

Within minutes, Taylor and the Bride prove me wrong. He says, "The first two accounts were clearly labeled. One is Netflix—I didn't bother to look at his queue. The other is a Patriot Trust bank account log-in. Dude only has twenty-four dollars and seventy-two cents in checking and savings combined, but his credit card debt is crazy. A lot of big purchases in the last six months."

"Like what?" I circle behind him and lean in close to see what the Bride has to offer. Taylor wears cologne now. He didn't used to.

"There's a bunch of different charges, but if you sort it so the highest ones are on top, you get . . ."

A list of high-end clothing stores. Some of the very same stores I photographed Keachin frequenting in the days before I busted her. I thought she was using her daddy's money. Actually, her *sugar* daddy's.

"There are also a few hotel charges. And this." He points to a single charge that's over a thousand dollars. A tuition payment for AGG Technical Institute.

The same tech school I used to gain access to the roof of the Patriot Trust Building.

Coach Bottin had one of their T-shirts in his closet. Of all the assumptions I can make from the charges on his credit card—purchases from a dead girl's favorite stores, random hotel stays—tech school tuition should be the least creepy.

So why is my skin crawling?

"What about the other accounts on that paper?" I ask.

"One's labeled 'PHS'—that's the Portside High faculty portal. I'll take a look at it now. The last one is labeled 'VDMV.' What exactly are we looking for here, Lauren?"

I wish I knew. "Maybe nothing. That bank info might be the best we get, but you're—uh, *the* tech guy. If something looks strange, you're going to know, right?"

He grins, and doesn't seem to notice that I almost called him "*my* tech guy."

"Keep doing your thing," I say, returning to the photos on my Mac-Book. "I'll do mine."

My thing doesn't go so well. What *am* I looking for?

The quick shots, and the panoramas, and the close-ups tell me nothing new. Sleaze and George Lucas.

Also a stunning level of narcissism. There's a cropping of framed photos on the wall in Coach's living room. Selfies showing Coach Bottin on hiking trails, and in a park, and staring at the ocean from a balcony, and posing on his bed with his silk sheets wrapped around him like a centerfold. There are at least a dozen shots showing his appreciation of himself.

Beyond that, nothing.

In the early afternoon, Taylor says, "You're going to want to see this."

I go to the Bride.

"That 'VDMV' log-in, it's for a site the coach has marked as a favorite in his personal faculty portal. The Virginia Department of Motor Vehicles."

He shows me the site with the state seal, and logs in with Coach's credentials. "Coach teaches—*taught*—Driver's Ed. This is how he reported exam scores to the state. It's how they determine if we get to drive."

"Okay."

"Those scores are linked to our driving records," he says, and clicks through a few screens until he gets to a SEARCH field, "which are also linked to the pictures we took for our learning permits. Those pictures eventually end up on our driver's licenses."

He searches his own name, and a picture appears. The same one the Admirer sent me.

"Holy crap," I say.

Taylor repeats the steps and shows me Ocie's picture, then Keachin's. "All three of these photos have been searched for recently. Mine and Mei's were retrieved *after* Coach Bottin was arrested. Your Admirer has access to this account, too."

"Kinda figured."

"Why go through all this?"

Is there a more frustrating question? Arson, murder, elaborate games with pictures, threats, and cars. "It's all such . . ."

"Such what?"

I'm thinking. About what I was going to say. Because I'm not the first person to say it.

She was trying to get away from Bottin's crazy shit.

"Such crazy shit," I say, "she wanted to get away from it. Marcos told me in the hall."

"I thought you said he didn't fit, no tech skills."

"No. He's not *my* Admirer. He knows stuff. More than we do. I was too"—*distracted*—"close to see it. I've been focused on everything after Keachin died, and it's not enough. If Marcos really was Keachin's friend, then she probably told him her side of all this. Stuff that happened *before* she died. That's where we get our answers."

Taylor shakes his head. "Okay, you're better at this part of it than I am. Where do we find him?"

I check the time on my phone. School ended an hour ago. "Monte FISHto"

"Oh, gross. The fried stink of that place gets in your clothes."

"When a twenty-four-piece buffalo popcorn shrimp meal costs five ninety-nine, there are bound to be consequences. Let's go."

CHAPTER 39

THE COUNT OF MONTE FISHTO MASCOT—A giant red cartoon catfish in a waist-coat with a sword and sheath on its hip—leers at us in a way that makes the ocean seem scarier and less appetizing than I'm sure the company intended. We park beneath the grinning sea creature and head inside.

"Fair warning," I say, "he's probably not going to be happy to see me."

"Care to elaborate?" Taylor opens the door and lets out a blast of fish batter aroma that flips my stomach. He winces and brings his shirt collar to his nose like a makeshift gas mask.

I will myself inside and try not to look too closely at big banners advertising Chunky Clam Stew—Here for a Limited Time!

"Last time we talked, we weren't on the friendliest terms," I say.

"Well, me and Marcos are cool. Maybe I can smooth things over."

We approach the counter where an adult in the standard FISHto red button-down shirt and flimsy three-cornered hat greets us. "Welcome to Monte FISHtos! What are you casting your hook for?"

I say, "Is Marcos Dahmer working to—"

"Daniels," Marcos says, stomping from the back, smeared flour on his faded apron, "would you like to try a Depth Charge meal? To go?"

"I want to talk to you."

"We already talked. If you weren't a girl, I would've given you a busted lip to go with those black eyes. Be glad I'm kind of sexist."

"Marcos!" the woman behind the counter says.

"I'm sorry, Ms. Emma. But this is the girl I told you about."

Ms. Emma's distress fades. "Oh, well then."

Is it possible to get used to people instantly despising me? If so, I wish I could get there already.

Taylor says, "Marcos, look—"

"Save it. I thought you had better taste in friends, bro."

"—just listen to her. There's some twisted stuff happening and she's trying to stop it."

"Listen? I thought Gray was all about the pictures. Walk, guys. We're done."

He turns toward the kitchen, blowing us off.

I hoped it wouldn't come to this. I never intended for Marcos—or anyone—to hate me. If he's going to aim that emotion my way, I might as well earn it.

"Talk to us, or I'm going to tell everyone the truth about you and me."

Marcos spins back to us, and Taylor gives me a crooked look.

"There is no 'you and me,' Daniels. What are you trying to pull?"

"The stuff Gray's done, it would be hard to pull off without a partner. If folks don't think that already, it would be really easy to plant the thought."

Marcos comes from behind the counter, gets in my face. "You're crazy!"

"Hey!" Taylor says, shoving him back.

I get between them, trying to calm the situation down before Ms. Emma calls the cops.

"Five minutes," I tell Marcos, and I feel as grimy as the grease-coated tiles I'm standing on. "No one ever has to know about your part in all this."

"My part in—" Marcos's olive complexion gets rosy. He bites his lip and takes a couple of deep breaths. "Fine. Ms. Emma, I'm taking a break. If I'm not back in five minutes, burn this place down with these two in it."

Ms. Emma doesn't respond verbally—what do you say to that?—but her body language speaks volumes. I've earned her hatred as well. And not just hers.

As we make the short walk to the booth in the back of the restaurant, I'm hating myself, too.

Marcos snatches off his apron, scrunches it into a ball, and tosses it in the booth before sitting. I slide in across from him, then Taylor joins me. The padded bench is tiny, so our thighs touch. It's comforting in the wake of Marcos's radiating disgust.

"Ask your questions."

"You said Keachin was confiding in you about Coach Bottin. Why?"

He looks away. "We were friends. I told you that."

"Marcos"—I motion toward a mural of Monte FISHto himself—"don't take this the wrong way, but you work *here*."

"She wasn't what everyone thought. She wasn't shallow. Not for real."

I've got photographic evidence to the contrary. Still: "I don't remember you two being close before. I've never seen you together around school."

"It started over the summer. My dad's landscaping business does her lawn. I was helping out, and she let me come inside for some lemonade. We talked, she told me to text later. I did. It went from there."

It started. *It* went from there. What is "It"? "Are you telling us you and Keachin Myer were *a thing*?"

"We could've been."

He's quieter now, anger replaced by something more raw. Regret?

Him and Keachin, though? He's maybe six inches shorter, thirty pounds lighter, and forty-five IQ points smarter than the typical jock toys Keachin usually wrapped around her finger. Then again, Coach Bottin didn't fit her brand either.

I say, "Did you have sex with her?"

Marcos flinches, and Taylor tactfully rephrases, "Why do you feel like you two could've been more?"

"We used to be friends. Back in the day," he says. "We were in kindergarten together, played together, went to each other's birthday parties. All the way until middle school, then social bullshit got in the way. When we reconnected over the summer, it was like that bad time in the middle never happened. All that stupid stuff when she couldn't speak to me in front of her rich friends and I had to call her names behind her back to feel superior, we got over it."

Did he get over what she did to Nina? Was that water under the bridge?

I don't say it. What would it accomplish? How much deeper do I need to bury a dead girl?

He's watching me, reading my thoughts. "I'm not saying she was perfect, Daniels. I'm saying I could look past her jacked-up public persona."

His moon eyes are off-putting, and I'm not feeling very tactful. "You were in love with her. Weren't you?"

Moon eyes become rage eyes, he leans forward. Taylor's watching us like the referee at a Ping-Pong match.

"It wasn't a one-way thing. We kissed," Marcos says.

"When you were alone? Sneaking around so if it ever came out it would be her word against yours?"

"I don't have to worry about that now. Do I?" He looks at his watch. "One minute."

He's already twisted sideways in his seat, ready to leave when the time is up, his obligation fulfilled.

"In the hall the other day, you said she was going to leave him. Was she doing it for you? Is that what she told you?"

He shakes his head, and I can tell he wishes that were the case. "She was breaking it off because she was tired of all the craziness that came with him."

"Craziness?"

"Bottin's sick. He's like the dude who graduates, but keeps coming back to the high school parties. Only, a thousand times worse. It's like he's sitting in his car down the street from the party waiting to see which chicks are drunk and stumbling home."

"I don't get you."

"He *wants* the vulnerable girls."

"Keachin didn't seem vulnerable to me."

"You don't know her father. That dude could make Wonder Woman have self-esteem issues."

I try not to look surprised, but the implication that Keachin had a problematic home life never occurred to me. Her car was always too shiny, her outfits too pristine.

Camouflage.

"Time's up," Marcos says, rising. Done.

"What craziness, though? What made her want to end it?"

"What aren't you getting?" he says. "The other girl. Keachin wasn't his only one."

He's walking away, and I'm shoving at Taylor to let me out. "Coach was seeing another girl? From Portside?"

Marcos shrugs. What's it matter now?

It matters a lot to me. "Keachin didn't tell you who it was?"

"She didn't know. She said there were clues around his place. An earring between his couch cushions. A bra under the bed. Stuff like that. She said it's like the chick was leaving it on purpose to mess with her. At first, Keachin treated it like some stupid competition. Leaving her own stuff behind. Until a pair of underwear got returned to her doorstep, soaked in lighter fluid."

That makes me back up, like I can smell the combustible fumes. Taylor mumbles, "WTF."

"Yeah," Marcos said. "Two days later, Bottin's crib was charcoal. She got scared. Tried to end things. I wish she'd wised up sooner."

Marcos seems . . . saggy, like his skeleton's too heavy for his muscles. He says, "I don't want to talk about this anymore. You tell whatever lies you're going to tell about me. I'm going back to work."

He does. No good-bye, no "eff off." I know I will never speak to this boy again.

I hope what he gave me was worth it. I think it might be. "Come on."

Taylor follows me to the car. "Would you really have told people he was in on *Gray Scales* if he didn't do what you wanted?" he says.

"No."

"I want to believe you."

So do I.

CHAPTER 40

IT'S LATE AFTERNOON. MY PARENTS WILL be home soon, so I need to be there sooner. But I can't let Marcos's words go.

Keachin wasn't his only one.

Had I been going about this all wrong? I kept thinking this was a Keachin thing, some lovesick boy lashing out because Coach had what he wanted. What if it was the other way around? A vindictive girl tired of sharing?

Someone burned down Coach's house and called it hell.

Hell hath no fury like a woman scorned, as the old saying goes.

We're back at Taylor's place, and I'm on my Mac, clicking to the Gray Beards group on Facebook.

Taylor says, "Do you have any idea what you're looking for?"

"Yes." And I find it. Or her.

Alyssa Burrell.

She's a member of my fan club. I noticed her name and others from my

Digital Photography class the first time I browsed through the group page. I wrote her—and every other girl in the group—off. So stupid.

When I click to Alyssa's profile, on a beeline for her photos—I find all her info is unavailable to me. I've been unfriended. Smart.

"Are you FB friends with Alyssa Burrell?"

"No," Taylor says. "Me and her aren't that cool. You think she's—?"

"We'll know soon enough." Because Alyssa and I have a mutual friend. Roz.

"Fill Roz in on as much as you can, as fast as you can. I want to know if Alyssa Burrell has any particular technical skills that might fit our profile. Also, tell her to copy and send any unusual or spectacular photos from Alyssa's FB albums."

"On it." Taylor steps away to call Roz.

Wow, Gray should've recruited sidekicks a long time ago. It's nice to share the workload.

I hear him running down the details to her. While he does, I cycle through all the various data I've collected on my Admirer. Locations from our game, the dates and times of our chats, an inventory of the photos from Bottin's apartment. All of it in front of me, all overwhelming. Until now. I'm thinking on everything Alyssa's said and done since I blew up the Keachin-Coach affair.

I just shot Coach Pedophile and the football team for the yearbook. Thank God I wasn't alone with him. Who knows what might've happened.

To her, or to him?

Do you mind if I take your picture? It's for my next class project. On grief.

Why say that to me? On that day?

Her photos, always so mediocre in DP class. As were mine. Hiding in plain sight.

A half hour later, Taylor taps me on the shoulder.

Turning toward the Bride, I see the email from THX778083 with a subject line that reads: *This seems important.*

Roz has sent us a picture from Alyssa's FB albums. She's making a pouty, smoochy duck face in a selfie. It's not the overdone pose that catches my eye. I'm stuck on the AGG Tech shirt she's wearing.

It's the one I saw in Coach Bottin's closet.

CHAPTER 41

"FORWARD ME THAT EMAIL FROM ROZ and pack up." I'm at my Mac, saving and closing files, preparing to move.

Taylor says, "Why? What are we doing now?"

"Gray's final exposé."

While he fulfills my request, I dial up Quinn Beck.

On our way to the library Taylor's quiet. As am I.

Alyssa Burrell.

My Admirer. A killer.

I never—*never!*—would've expected her capable of something like this. Apparently, I'm not the only one.

"So, *she's* the other girl Coach Bottin was boning?" Taylor says, the air of disbelief thick in his voice.

The evidence is there, though.

Alyssa's a photographer. She's taking classes at the technical school Bottin dropped a thousand bucks on. The school that's in the same building where *View from Heaven* was taken. A school that could, conceivably, give her the skills to hack my email, and make the world think I exposed my own alter ego.

"I think she is," I say, seeing no solid reason to dispute it.

"She's really different from what he seems to like."

"What do you mean?"

"I mean, I'm a dude. We have types. If your type is Keachin Myer, then your type is not also Alyssa. No disrespect to our potential psycho."

We pull into the library parking lot, me and Beck's favorite meeting spot. "What if his type is *young*? Coach is a predator. Like Marcos said, he looks for vulnerable."

"He also looks for brunettes. Which she isn't."

"How do you know that?"

"Grab your machine, I'll show you."

Inside the library we claim a quiet study room for privacy, and I arrange the Admirer files on my desktop.

"Look," he says, and points to a panorama of Bottin's office, which I enlarge. "Check the calendar."

In the flattened, 360-degree photo the calendar hangs next to the *THX 1138* poster on the door, even though there's a corner between the two in real life. The featured model is indeed brunette.

"Okay, the college hottie of the month has dark hair. That could be coincidence."

Taylor huffs and points again. "Yeah, if the calendar was on the right month. This is November. She's Miss March."

Zooming in, I see he's right. When I saw the calendar initially, I'd been repulsed by the scantily clad girl, so brazenly displayed in an accused murderer's home. Never even glanced at the dates.

"You really do have them Sherlock skills," I say.

"Actually, I sort of stared at that one for a while when you went to the bathroom earlier. She is *special*."

I punch him in the arm for being gross. "Okay, Alyssa doesn't look like a brunette bikini model. What's up with her in the AGG Tech shirt? Combine that with her camera skills, it lines up."

The email he forwarded is in my in-box. I open it to take another look at the photo Roz sent when an odd doubling catches my eye.

The letters *THX* are on my screen twice.

In the *THX 1138* poster on Coach Bottin's office door, and in Roz's THX778083 email address within the forwarded message.

Blinking, I mouse over the paper clip icon to open Alyssa's picture, but can't bring myself to click.

THX

Twice.

"Something wrong?" says Taylor, picking up on my hesitance.

"I don't know."

He starts to say something else; I shush him, afraid of losing this thought, because it's a foggy one. As skittish as a deer in swirling mist, as likely to step forward as to dart away.

I say, "Roz's email address. THX778083 means 'Thanks Gray,' right?"

"Yeah."

Filtering my in-box, I open other emails I've gotten from Roz. I want the one where she confirmed that very thing for me. When I find it, I highlight a line for Taylor.

Us nerds love our Easter eggs and double meanings, and love decoding them even more.

"She says 'double meanings' here. 'Thanks Gray' is just *one* meaning. What's the other?"

He doesn't have an answer. I'm afraid I do.

The corkscrew in my stomach is a spinning blade now. Like the blender you throw a Panda in to get the color Gray.

Back to the panorama. *THX 1138*, a film by George Lucas, released in '71, according to the tiny gold plaque affixed to the frame. Followed by *Star Wars* in '77, *The Empire Strikes Back* in '80, *Return of the Jedi* in '83. All represented by posters arranged in chronological order on Bottin's walls: '77 and '80 and '83.

778083 is a hex code. It's also a combination of the years when George Lucas's most famous films were released. Tack on the three-letter prefix of his first science-fiction film, you get THX778083.

An Easter egg a nerd like Coach Bottin would *love*.

"I know Roz," Taylor says when I float my theory. "She's not a photographer. She can barely defrag a hard drive. No way she did the stuff you're accusing her of."

My head shakes of its own volition. "I know it sounds crazy. I can't wrap my mind around it all the way. But she could've hidden her talents. Easily. You said it yourself. Bottin's got a type. Tall, dark hair, blue eyes. That's Keachin and Roz all the way."

"Roz and Keachin carry those features a lot differently." As if I didn't get it, he turns sideways and cups one hand in front of his chest, while the other hangs by his butt. It's like we're playing charades and he got "Keachin's T&A."

Sigh. "You're thinking of Roz in school. You ever see her when she loses the Nerd Layers?"

Her Facebook page is on my screen in a second, her selfies where her normally conservative looks are set to stun.

"See this shot of her in the canoe? The one with her on the hiking trail? She's gorgeous when she tries." I click to the sexy, bedroom-eyes photo of her. "Check out this one of her rolling in the sheets. It's—"

My head tilts.

"Oh my God."

Through the study room window, I spot Quinn Beck. He slogs over, a "thrill me" look on his face. His timing couldn't be better.

"Let him in," I say to Taylor, while I shrink the browser window for a better view of more pictures from Bottin's place. Specifically the selfies on his living-room wall.

The ones that aren't selfies at all.

When Beck's in the room, he plops his recorder on the table. The power light's glowing red, and the digital timer ticks incrementally. He takes a seat, eyebrows high, expectant. "Well, we gonna have that discussion about cyberbullying now?"

"We could," I say, "but I think you'd like to know about the other young girl Eric Bottin was sleeping with first."

"Lauren . . . ," his voice on scold.

"Look and listen." I point to the photo of Bottin in a canoe; it's lit beautifully. Without another word, I show the Facebook photo of Roz, also in a canoe—the *same* canoe, but the opposite end—overly dark due to the sun's backlighting.

There's a picture of Coach on a hiking trail, with him looking studly, like he'd climbed Everest. There's a picture of Roz. *On the same trail.*

A picture of Coach shirtless, coiled in the silk sheets I'd seen with my own eyes earlier. And Roz, sultry in those same silk sheets, the logo from her AGG Tech T-shirt just in the frame.

All pictures taken in the same place and time. Roz photographing Coach Bottin (with superior skill), and Coach Bottin photographing her. Never together in a shot—because no one could ever know—yet together all the same.

I stop on a picture of Roz, maximizing it. Letting Taylor and Beck see what I missed before. Bottin has a type. Roz fits it perfectly.

She looks like a young Keachin Myer. With some effort.

"This girl killed Keachin. She tried to kill my best friend." I motion to Taylor. "I think she wants to hurt him, too."

For the first time since I told him about the Admirer threat, Taylor looks truly shaken.

"You really think you have enough to prove what you're saying?" Beck asks.

"I do."

"Maybe it's time to show someone," he says.

My phone rings. The only thing that surprises me is how spookily timed it is. I answer and put it on speaker: "Hello."

Roz speaks, her voice wet and phlegm-filled. "Just what is it you think you're going to show?"

CHAPTER 42

HOW?

There are no security cameras in the room. No one beyond the window that I can see. Twisting, searching, I notice the green on light shining next to my Mac's web camera. It shouldn't be.

I shake off the sensation of spiders crawling along my flesh, and mouth to the guys, "She's watching." After a moment of consideration, realizing if she can get the camera, she can get the mic, I say, "And she's listening."

Taylor catches the camera light, too. He leans forward, intending to snap my MacBook shut. I catch his arm and shake my head. There's nothing to hide now. "Let her."

He backs away from the machine, though his jaw is tight. Quinn Beck, on the other hand, seems giddy. He keeps looking at his still-running recorder.

Roz says, "I knew you were close when you made it to Eric's apartment. But this was fast. So fast. I thought that Photoshopping that shirt on

Alyssa would buy me some time. You're good, though."

"Wait until you see how fast I go to the cops, you psycho." Quickly, I drop several damning photos into a folder, and send them to both of her addresses, personal and Admirer. "You'll be receiving some shots from my latest project. I call it *Bye Bye*."

"Big talk considering I could've cracked your skull with a brick any time I felt like it. I've been standing right behind you for weeks, Panda Bear."

The brutal honesty of the statement gives me pause. I start to say something tough.

A sob interrupts me.

"Roz?"

"I guess you won this round," she says, sniffling. "Game's not over, though."

How crazy is she? "It is, Roz."

"It's. Not. I'm going to be in the last place you topped me. One hour. Be there. With your camera."

"You tried to kill my friend. We're supposed to hang now?"

"Bring the cops if you have to. I don't care. Just don't be late."

"Roz. No."

She takes a long time to answer. I wonder if we've lost the connection. The webcam's still on. We're not done yet.

Her next word is softer. "Please."

The webcam winks off, and the call goes dead. My hand's shaking.

"Did that just happen?" Beck asks. Before I answer, he's plugging an earbud into his recorder and reviewing his audio.

Taylor pins me with his gaze. "You know where she's going to be?"

"Yes."

"Now you'll call the cops?"

"I am."

"You're not going to do what she asks? You're not going to her?"

Those questions I don't answer. That's answer enough.

"This is unnecessary, Lauren. Insane," Taylor says from the shotgun seat as we take the highway.

Maybe, but I can't let this go. Not with the way Roz has been playing me. God, that day I got beat up and she met me in the main office, she was texting me as the Admirer from *the same room* while I iced my swollen eyes. She's scary smart, and tricky, and dangerous. And I'm going right to her. I have to.

We hit the bridge, cross the river into downtown Portside. Beck's Jetta trails. Sirens scream faintly in the distance.

"Lauren?"

"I heard you. I don't expect you to understand."

"Okay, I might not understand. Tell me what you're thinking and let me decide if it's over my head. I get that much, right?"

How do I even say it? "I wanted to hurt people, Taylor. Really hurt them. I see that now. I'm not as brave as Roz is about it, though."

He smacks the dashboard. "Brave? You saw what she did to Mei, now you're talking like *you* admire *her*?"

"Don't get it twisted. I could claw that skinny bitch's eyes out for what she did to Mei. I'm saying I tried to play the Gray thing as something different. Like Robin Hood stealing from the rich and pretending he's somehow more than a thief. He wasn't. I'm not."

"You're right. I don't understand."

We're on a street parallel to where Roz wants me, a block away from the Patriot Trust Building and the Cablon Hotel. I swerve into a five-story parking deck and drive in loops until we're at the top level.

We stop and I say, "Maybe I didn't go as far as Roz. That's only because I pushed her ahead of me."

"You didn't kill anybody."

"I killed pieces. What did it feel like when your friends stopped talking to you, when people whispered nasty things? What happened to the you from before my version debuted? Do you get it now? You said I was off the rails. This is how I get back on, Taylor."

He shakes his head, but no longer pretends he's dumbfounded by my motives. "It's a bad move, Lauren."

"It's mine to make."

Beck's beside us, motions for me to lower my window. I do, and he says, "The chatter on my police scanner is crazy. Your girl apparently stole a neighbor's car. Hit the guy over the head with—get this—a tripod. Now she's on an unfinished floor of the Cablon Hotel, just like you said."

Floor forty-two, I'm sure. "What's she doing?"

"Waiting. For her 'Panda.' The cops don't know what to make of it. She's too close to the edge for them to grab her, so the negotiator is exploring the possibility of borrowing a bear from the zoo."

A couple of news choppers buzz the area, and a small contingent of onlookers gather near us, peering over the side of the deck, in the general direction of the chaos Roz is causing. I grab a pair of miniature binoculars from the glove box and go for a look.

Street crowds are bloated. Emergency vehicles block the boulevard where the construction site is located, detouring cars.

The setting sun is behind us. It's the Golden Hour. I doubt the timing is coincidental.

What are you planning, Roz?

Panning with my binoculars, I take in all I can from this angle. No part of the hotel is visible, but the entrance to the Patriot Trust Building is. Gawkers are there, staring skyward, perhaps waiting to see if a girl attempts to fly. Among them, the black-jacketed guard who works the security desk in the PT Building. He's left his post to be part of this circus. Maybe . . .

"Beck? I see a channel nine news van beyond the police barriers. How close can you get us?"

Nodding, pleased, he says, "I've got my badge. That should get us pretty damn close."

"Good." I return to my car and pop the trunk, gathering all kinds of gear and jamming it in a duffel bag.

Taylor says, "You're really going to do this."

When I don't answer, he says, "Okay, we get to the news van. How do you get in the building?"

"Had that covered days ago."

"She's going to try to kill you."

His reasoning isn't faulty, because Roz *has* killed. Yet, I feel this going another way. It hasn't been her pattern to harm those she cares for. She didn't hurt Coach Bottin, not physically. She hasn't made a threat against me.

I'm not any less scared, because a lot of bad things can happen even if you're still breathing.

I hoist my bag as Beck joins us. Taylor says, "I'm going up with you."

"I was hoping you'd be willing to go up"—I press my bag of tricks into his chest—"but you won't be coming with me."

We move and I talk, telling them the plan. Beck's wearing a wide grin the whole time, likely seeing major network appearances in his future. Taylor's shaking his head—a futile gesture—and frowning. Together they resemble the creepy drama masks mounted over the door of the school auditorium.

And me, about to perform for all of Portside. I hope this particular play doesn't end up a tragedy.

I'm probably hoping for too much.

CHAPTER 43

BECK'S BADGE WORKS AS PROMISED, GETTING us through the initial perimeter so we're within a hundred yards of the Cablon Hotel. Further in, sawhorses with Police Line Do Not Cross banners coiled around the crossbeams define the interior perimeter, with a few uniformed officers forming an extra layer of protection beyond the hurdles.

"Please hurry," I say to Taylor and Beck.

Taylor says, "Don't do anything stupid, Lauren."

"I'm probably a few years past that option."

Beck says, "If you make it through this, I get the exclusive?"

"Nice to know you're consistent, Beck. If you help Taylor do what I ask, then it's a deal."

Before we part, Taylor hugs me, rattling the gear in the bag I gave him. I want to tell him be careful with my stuff; instead I hug him back.

We're apart, moving in opposite directions. I hope I see them again.

The cops are crowded around the main entrance to the construction site, ensuring only authorized personnel make it through that funnel. Good. No one notices me slipping into the shadows of the hotel.

A crouch-jog takes me to the portion of fence I cut when I was here before. My plastic zip ties remain intact. I snip them with mini wire cutters and I'm inside the site.

Me and my Admirer will be together soon.

"Perhaps no picture is worth your life. Perhaps," Petra Dobrev says in *Lensing Wild Things.* "To shoot beasts doing what no human eye has seen, and give that image to the world, is its own kind of immortality. Will you chase the prize?"

Her tips, I know them backward and forward. Her words echo in me as I navigate the half shadows of the construction site.

There are cops inside the fence, gathered together, chatting. All that's missing is a water cooler. They're blocking my way to the elevator.

I circle around to an emergency staircase that housekeepers and bell-boys will likely use for sneaking smokes in the future. I make my way up two floors, away from Cop Club, then find the elevator column where I catch my ride.

The floor indicator moves in slow motion, the number winking at me slyly, sharing a grim joke.

Enjoy your trip up, Panda. The trip down's going to be much faster.

My knees feel watery. If the elevator opens on any floor before the forty-second, I might step off, because I'm not this brave. This is stupid. I know it is.

Yet I can't help but go to her any more than iron filings could buck the lure of a magnet. We've come this far together.

The elevator doors part, and a loose grouping of police are yards away, their backs to me. They don't notice me because they're plotting how to reach Roz.

Be bold. Belong.

I step past the cops, my heart striking my sternum like a woodpecker's beak. They go silent, too stunned to stop me before I've crossed whatever invisible line Roz has drawn.

"Who the hell is that?" a cop shouts.

I don't look back.

They won't shoot me. I might get Tasered, but a few more steps convince me that's not happening either.

Roz is dangerously, sickeningly close to the edge of nothing. She catches me from the corner of her eye, wobbles in the wind. My heart lurches for her, but she regains her balance. Her mouth is pinched. This isn't fun for her. It's necessary.

She takes a single step away from the drop. "Where's your camera?"

I hold my phone for her to see.

"You're kidding me," she says, "*that*?"

"I had to travel light."

"Hey!" It's a different cop. "Please come back."

His badge hangs from a lanyard around his neck, but his dress screams Kind Uncle. He's in a sweater with alternating stripes and gray slacks. There's an openness to him. Even his shouts sound measured and assuring. He must be the negotiator Beck talked about. I'm stepping on his toes here.

"It's okay," I call over my shoulder, "I'm the Panda."

Of course, that clears nothing up. Confusion keeps them still.

Roz says, "Come closer."

There's twenty yards between us. I'm willing to cut that distance in half. It's still too far for us to touch.

"What are we doing up here?" I ask, voiced raised to be heard over the wind.

"We're up here so I can beat you. My next photos will be so classic."

Raccoon rings surround her eyes. Tears have spread her makeup, giving the appearance of inkblots rimming her cornea. Even in this low light, there's a stunning quality to it. Knowing what she's capable of, I can't help but wonder if this look is the result of emotion, or is it more meticulous planning on her part? Something staged?

She doesn't look like much, but she's powerful.

Her posture's improved, no slouch. She's almost as tall as Taylor. This is a girl who could be on top of the world in a different way than this. If she wasn't a murdering lunatic.

"Roz, what are we doing here?"

She laughs, turns so I see her in profile. Posing. "Are you getting this? I'm giving you magic right now."

"I've got you." I snap a shot with no flash.

She turns toward the city, yells over her shoulder, "Is this the right floor? The one where you took your picture?"

"Yeah. It is."

"I used a ruler and some string to compare the three tallest buildings in your picture. I triangulated from your vantage point and figured this was very close to the right spot. It's like the navigation techniques sailors used before there were modern instruments to help. Then I calculated my parametric arc. Just so I'd know."

I understand little of what she's saying. "You're very smart, aren't you?"

"I guess so. Doesn't feel that way sometimes. Keachin was an accident, you know."

She's facing me again, and I get another shot, holding the camera at eye level, hoping it conceals my skepticism. "You accidentally ran her over with Bottin's car?"

"I just wanted to talk to her. She was lying, you know, to take blame off her. They didn't start before she was eighteen. Her birthday's on August second. They weren't together then."

There's no smile now. No model-perfect posing. The sun's dipped out of sight, trailing orange and red and a purple that borders black. Shadows lengthen and deepen as if drawn to her.

"How do you know that?" I say.

"Because I was still with him." It's so low I can barely hear. I only catch the words because I've stepped closer. Seven or so yards separate us.

"She didn't know about me and Eric, not for sure. I called her, I told her what we had in common, *I told her* we needed to meet. And I took his clunker just to show her how far back me and him went. Their little *tryst* was nothing. I get to drive the car, she only screws in it, you know?"

No, I don't know. This is sick.

"Why involve me and hurt my friend, though?" I'm going for compassion because I recognize the biggest threat here is the one she poses to herself. I'm not very successful. My voice is not soft, my chest burns. Throwing punches, like those that blacked my eyes, would feel satisfying about now.

"The pictures." She pauses, glances down at her Canon dangling from the canvas and nylon neck strap so that it's suspended at her stomach. It's like she doesn't recognize the device.

There's more stuff here, equipment I didn't notice before, because it's partially hidden in the shadow of a girder. A sleeping laptop with a cell phone resting on it. The tripod that likely cracked her neighbor's skull, a camcorder mounted to it. She shakes her head, as if rattling something loose back into place.

"The photos have such power. I wasn't lying when I thanked you for exposing Randy Sigell. He stole from me so many times. For fun. To see me cry. I got tired and decided I was going to stab him with a knife from my mother's kitchen. Then Gray stepped in."

"Roz . . ."

She was closer to the edge, raising a hand so I'd let her finish. "You got him to stop so I didn't have to hurt him. I liked your way. I taught myself to do what you do.

"That's why I was out there that night. I was going to use my photos to make Eric see how bad Keachin was for him, before someone got hurt. How she could ruin him."

I say, "Particularly if your pictures got out."

The shadows around her eyes darken. "As yours did."

"Is all this payback? I messed up your plan?"

How do you get the color Gray? Throw a Panda in the blender and turn it on.

"No. I *was* mad. In the beginning. But I came around. You and I were in the woods that night for the same thing. That means *we're* the same. I was Gray approved."

"Why the game then? All that cryptic bullshit?"

"I didn't want to disappoint you. Or be disappointed by you. It was easier to admire you from a distance. I challenged you, hacked your computer and phone to track you, monitor your movements. Watched you chase your false leads. It was educational until you lost heart in our cause. You disappointed me after all."

"When did the cause become killing?"

"I told you that was an *accident*! Keachin wanted to drag me into the spotlight after you exposed her. She wanted my story plastered all over the news, and in everyone's mouths like chewed food. She was going to tell her daddy's lawyer about me so everyone would see how Eric manipulated 'us.' She was trying to hurt him *more*, Panda."

"Ocie wasn't going to hurt Coach Bottin."

Now she's not looking at me. Her neck cranes toward the city. "You wouldn't play the game anymore. You were trading me for something better."

"So my best friend became one more of your accidents?" I step closer.

"Young lady," the negotiator yells. I stretch one hand behind my back and show him my palm. *Wait.*

"I did what I know how to do, Panda. I'm not going to let you or anyone put me in a cage for it. You've already told about our game," she says. "Once you give them all you've found, it will be juvie, or jail, or a hospital. I have to use my power first."

"You don't have to do anything. It will be easier if you don't."

Roz ignores me, touches her camera. "I've got an Eye-Fi card in this. A thousand foot range."

An Eye-Fi card connects a camera to a computer via Wi-Fi, sends photos straight to the hard drive for storage and editing. It's great for photography teams, where one person shoots and the other immediately starts touch-ups. It's also good for a photographer who wants their shots saved on a machine that's far away. Roz's machine is only a few feet from her. For now.

Then I calculated my parametric arc. Just so I'd know.

I don't know exactly what a parametric arc is, but I'm certain it's got something to do with falling.

She says, "I'm talking action shots. The city in descent. The sidewalk rushing toward the lens. Very dramatic. I'm going to call it *From Grace.* You're going to need a lot of commitment to top this shoot, Panda." She shows me her back. Faces the drop.

I say, "Please, don't . . ."

"Oh, stop!" she says. "Take my picture so we can get this over with."

CHAPTER 44

"ROZ, WAIT."

"You're stalling!"

"I need a good shot of your face. Let me at least get that."

She spins toward me so fast, I'm afraid the momentum will carry her over. Roz remains on the floor with me and the cops, tears streaming down her cheeks, like she's already grieving for herself. "Hurry."

With stone-still hands, I lift my phone to eye level, and I'm seeing her in duplicate. The real her, visible over the top edge of my phone, and the digital image on my screen. A shutter tap ends this.

Only not the way she thinks.

I scream, "*Drück JETZT ab!*"

Roz's expression shifts. She senses the deception, though she's clueless about *how* she's being deceived. How could she know?

As smart as she is, I'm willing to bet she doesn't speak German.

Before she can be thwarted, Roz faces the ledge and gets a steady grip on her camera. This is the moment when she throws herself from the building.

It's interrupted by the bright flashes going off across the street like lightning in a cloud. I imagine the *SBOOF . . . SBOOF* sound of each explosion.

I didn't bring my phone for its camera abilities, I brought it for its *phone* abilities. It's been on speaker the whole time, connected to Taylor and Beck as they made their way to the top of the Patriot Trust Building with my equipment.

Drück JETZT ab! means "Shoot now!"

My beloved Nikon, a 1200 Lux strobe, and my umbrella-like reflector are with them. Gear meant to generate the brightest possible flash with a shutter click. Enough to distract Roz in the low evening light. Enough for me to close the distance between us.

A camera trap.

For a dangerous animal you can't capture by normal means, just as Petra Dobrev recommends.

I catch Roz by the strap on her Canon, a sturdy piece of canvas and nylon looped over her shoulder. It bites into her neck when I yank, towing her toward me, into my arms, away from her goal.

"No, no!" she shrieks, clawing at any exposed flesh she can reach.

Squeezing her waist, enduring her sharp little nails tearing at my skin, I feel *another* set of arms around me. The Kind Uncle cop.

We're sliding back toward the elevator, the both of us, like two fish on the same hook. At the midway point two officers separate me and Roz.

"You have no right!" She takes pieces of me with her when she's pulled away. "My concept! My shoot!"

She's still swiping at my face when the police pin her to the dusty floor and secure her wrists with plastic ties.

I think they'll do the same for me, but I don't resist, so they allow a set of EMTs to attend to me first. A cop remains nearby, his left hand resting on his Taser.

I'm bleeding from several places, but feel no pain. The adrenaline rushing through me is a welcome anesthetic, though I know it won't last. At the Patriot Trust Building, the flashes continue.

My focus is drawn there, stays there, as I'm swabbed with gauze soaked in stinging liquid. When the paramedics pull them back, they're all sorts of colors from soot black to alarmingly red.

There's blood on my face. And my neck. And on my chest.

The female paramedic assures me I'm going to be okay.

I know.

Because, this time, there is no blood on my hands.

EPILOGUE

LAIR. IN THE DAYS FOLLOWING MY confrontation with Roz in the Cablon Hotel, after the authorities search her house and find what they find, that word keeps popping up in the news reports. Like some supervillain's secret hideout at the bottom of the ocean, or inside a volcano. That's the allusion they are going for. Roz as Lex Luthor, Evil Genius. It's buzzy.

They never show Roz's picture or say her name because of her age. She is "the girl." Meant to be anonymous, though footage of her house, and her bedroom, and her private things hanging loose and silky from tossed drawers become part of the news cycle.

Everyone at school knows, I'm sure. Which means everyone's parents know. Which means all of Portside knows. The effort to "protect her identity" is a joke we're all in on. I would've been offered the same "protection," too, if I hadn't forfeited my unidentified-pronoun status by giving Quinn Beck his exclusive interview in the back of the ambulance that the cops made me take to the hospital. I told the EMTs Beck was my brother. Despite him obviously being a white guy, our complexions were close enough to avoid questioning. Taylor said my looks let me get away with crap like that. If I fought the notion, it was just for posterity. I think I'm aware of what I'm capable of.

I answer Beck's questions—on the record—about everything. Most of it he can't use directly because I'm a minor like Roz. As I said, we're beyond not knowing the culprits here. Channel 9 news finds loopholes, ways to manipulate my quotes without implicating me directly, while, at the same time, pointing a neon arrow directly at my house.

In those weeks before Thanksgiving, when journalists knock on my door daily, wanting a one-on-one like the channel 9 news intern got, at least one of my parents stays home at all times to ensure I don't bring any more pain to our family. I'm barred from electronics, though I manage to sneak some TV when my parents sleep. While watching on mute, with the closed captions on, I notice that word. Over and over.

The next day, I can't shake it. With the electronics lockdown in effect, I break down and pull a dictionary off the shelf. I shouldn't have.

Lair (n): *a wild animal's resting place, especially one that is well hidden.*

The definition gives the corkscrew in my stomach—a near-permanent fixture now—a mighty arm wrestler's heave, to the point where I think my lunch might rise. It doesn't. I put the dictionary away and pick at the healing scratches on my face until Mom yells at me to stop.

Custom PCs. Stolen records. Fake credit cards and identification. The Portside PD discover evidence of "numerous criminal activities" at Roz's residence. Including crime scene and driver's license photos stolen from secure state servers, the driving record of the drunk Roz set up for Ocie's hit-and-run, hours and hours of footage from Coach Bottin being interrogated about Keachin. Also, footage of me at the police station and hospital, thanks to her gaining access to the digital security systems. More unsettling, footage of me sleeping in my bed while she watched through my own webcam. She's been at it a long time.

Detective Vincent explains this all to me and my parents in our living room one afternoon as the coffee Mom made cools without him ever taking a sip.

"The Petrie girl is something new. At least for me," he says, unsettled.

"What's going to happen to her?" I ask.

"A hospital of some sort, most likely. The Myers want her thrown in the deepest hole the state will allow, but she's a minor. Her parents—criminals in their own right: drug charges, petty larceny, fraud—are barely in the picture at all, so social services already have their fingers in this. She'll be comfy until she's eighteen, at least.

"Between you and me," Vincent continues, "her thing with Bottin's going to work in her favor. She doesn't turn sixteen for another three months. We could practically write his name on the sex offender registry right now."

There's apprehension in him, I feel it like trouble on the wind.

Dad picks up on it, too. "You think that's the right call, Detective?"

"For that pervert? Absolutely. But the girl, I think we're lucky to have caught her affinity for violence and manipulation now. She'll get treatment. I only hope whatever she has—whatever she *is*—is something you *can* treat." His eyes are on me when he says this.

I inspired Roz's misdeeds. My site. My crusade. Me.

What do you think I am, Detective?

It's a question I don't ask aloud. I don't think I'd like his answer.

My aunt Victoria is set to arrive two days before Thanksgiving. When she gets here, I know the next time I leave my house will be with a suitcase and boarding pass. So *three* days before Thanksgiving, I break my parents' rules one last time.

It's after midnight and they're sleeping. The lock on Daddy's desk drawer is an easy pick; I retrieve my car keys and phone quickly. The screen got cracked during my fight with Roz, but it still works, evident by the ninety-eight missed texts from Taylor. I don't bother to read them, I simply reply.

> **Me:** If u can, meet me at the playground by your house in 20 mins.
>
> **Taylor:** I'll be there in 15

He's sitting on a graffiti-stained bench when I arrive. Half the streetlamps in the area aren't functional, creating pockets of darkness throughout the neighborhood. In some of those pockets, people lurk. I'm not afraid, though. I've seen scarier.

Taylor sees me, leaves his bench. I climb from my car with a backpack on my shoulder and meet him halfway.

He hugs me hard, then backs away, staring at my healing scars. "Are you all right?"

"Not really."

He opens his mouth, likely to offer words of comfort. I shake my head before he starts. "I don't get to be all right. I'm fine with that. Let's not waste time lying about it."

"Why are we here?"

"To finish." I kneel, open the bag, and illuminate the contents with a tiny flashlight in my palm. Taylor crouches next to me for a better view of the projects I've been working on while in captivity.

The first item is a slim photo album meant for displaying 4 x 6 pictures in a series of cellophane flaps. I push it into his hands. "It's for Mei."

He flips through, viewing select pictures from my and my best friend's better years. Amusement parks. Sleepovers. Good times pulled from a shoe box at the back of my closet.

"Give it to her yourself," he says.

"Now's not the right time. Not while she's still hurt and in the hospital because of what I did."

I feel him tense, but that's all he does. Before he would've assured Mei's injuries weren't on me. He's sticking to my terms, though. No lies.

He says, "Give it to her later."

"I'm not going to be around later." I tell him about my aunt, and Georgia.

He's quiet for a while when I'm done. What's there to say?

When he speaks again, it's about the bag. "Anything else in there for me?"

I zip it up, and kill the light. "No. What I have for you wouldn't fit."

"Are you giving me your car?"

He laughs, but I can't quite manage. "No. An apology. I'm sorry for what I did to you."

Blinking rapidly, like I'd suddenly shined the flashlight in his face, he says, "The jockstrap thing?"

"*Every*thing."

There are ghosts here. The false versions of me and him that I held on to for so long. Too long.

"*Danke*," he says. *Thank you*, in German.

"No thanks necessary." This version—the true version—of Taylor Durham is a good guy. Mei always knew.

"There's something else you can give Mei the next time you see her," I say, "a message. Tell her I said her choices have never been stupid. She's way smarter than I've ever been."

"That's going to make sense to her?"

"Yes. Also, she likes spinach and feta cheese on her half of the pizza."

I trust he'll use that information well.

With that, I turn back toward my car.

"Are you going home now?" he calls after me.

"No. I've got one more stop to make."

"Can I get shotgun?" His concern is thinly veiled.

"Not this time, Taylor."

He doesn't fight it. "Text me when you get home, okay?"

A wave is all I give him.

Good-bye, Taylor Durham.

I'm in my car, on the way to my next destination. My next apology. When I arrive, I'm doused in fear I didn't feel in Taylor's neighborhood, or even up on the forty-second floor.

Graveyards have always had that effect on me.

The Portside Cemetery would be beautiful if you didn't know what it was. It's positioned near the Annabeth River, Portside's skyline visible on the water's black surface. Wavering, wavering, like there's a second sunken city instead of a reflection.

There's no gate to surpass. No fence to climb. It's open and inviting and terrifying. Some childish part of me imagines that there *is* a gate. Some ornate, wrought-iron thing glowing with spectral energy. One that will only be visible once I cross onto the grounds and discover that I will never be allowed to leave.

I shake off the childish spookiness and I follow the asphalt inside.

It takes a few minutes to orient myself to the layout of the grave markers. The map on my phone identifies the row I'm looking for.

My engine remains running as I exit my car and walk a path that's narrower than it has to be. Swatches of grass are wide where I am, but I'm careful not to step on anyone.

There are lampposts along the way; I still cut the dark with my flashlight, glancing at names and dates on the dozens and dozens of tombstones flanking me. There's a tremor in my light beam that's got nothing to do with the cold.

The grave I'm looking for is ahead. I know it before I can read the marble-carved inscription because it's nearly buried in bouquets, both fresh and withered.

When I'm close, I flash my light on it:

KEACHIN JOSEPHINE MYER
DAUGHTER—FRIEND—BEAUTIFUL ANGEL
GONE TOO SOON

Reflexively, I buck against the "Beautiful Angel" part, because I still remember what I felt for her. The Raging Bitch Monster. Change isn't like a shutter click. It's never instant.

Maybe she was the mean girl I knew. But she was other things. Everyone is a bunch of different things, all at once. To her family, her friends, she was a Beautiful Angel. I chose to show the world a different side.

"I'm sorry, Keachin."

There's a bouquet of flowers in my bag, stolen from a vase on the center of our dining-room table. They fit nicely with the others on Keachin's grave.

The only other thing I've brought is my camera. I pull it out, power up, and turn the lens toward the waterfront. It would be such a cool shot. Tempting, but no.

I face the marble tombstone and smash my Nikon on the top edge.

Once, twice, the plastic crunching sounds like a car wreck on repeat. On the third strike, shards sprinkle the grass at my feet. I pick them up by the beam of my flashlight and dump the mangled mess back in my bag.

Doing that hurts, as it should. It's not enough. But I'm not done paying back my wrongs. I may never be done.

That, too, is as it should be.

We're all something we don't know we are.

Or if we know, and we don't like the truth about ourselves, we call it something else that helps us sleep at night.

"Avenger" and "vigilante" and "karma" were the words I chose when I went after people who did despicable things. Really, I should've gone with "just like them." Because I was.

These are my thoughts on my turbulence-free flight to Georgia. My aunt Victoria has the window seat, ignoring the bright-sun view for the latest issue of *Cosmo*. The last two days we've spent together have also been turbulence-free. I'll do my part to keep it that way.

When we land and get the go-ahead to turn on electronic devices, I power on my phone to text my parents, and find I have a message waiting.

It's a picture of me and Mei on a roller coaster. One of the photos in the album I left with Taylor.

Me: That's our black.

Mei responds with a smiley face.

It's a start.

When you know what you are, and it's ugly, it's up to you to be something else. I've got some work to do.

I still love photography. My pandas. *Nat Geo*. I'll return to them soon.

Maybe after some time away from Portside, in a place where people will call me Lauren, and only Lauren. Maybe after my bestie can stand more robust communication than the occasional picture or emoticon. Maybe when I choose to see and show beauty. Without effort.

Life's the picture. But all good photographers know you gotta have the right lens. I'm getting there.

There will be time for my passions—uncorrupted, without malice—again.

For now, I'm going to work on loving people, too.

ACKNOWLEDGMENTS

Here we go again! Writing this page is one of the most awesome parts about the publishing process. Why? Because there's nothing cooler than doing a victory lap with all the people who helped make this possible. Without further adieu . . .

I want to thank God for another opportunity to tell stories for a living. Best. Job. Ever.

Adrienne, you've worn the Writer's Wife badge well. I so appreciate the advice, and encouragement, and sing-alongs on those conference road trips (our vocals are INCREDIBLE when we're alone and encased in a moving bubble). You're a super cheerleader, expert straightener of ties, and a whole bunch of other stuff that could fill a dozen novels. Love you.

Jamie, you're my industry ace. My not-so-secret weapon in the fight for continued employment and uninterrupted utilities. Thank you for entertaining each and every crazy idea that pops into my head. Nobody handles a three-a.m. email like you. I just need you to work on recognizing Brad Pitt. ;)

To my HarperCollins crew: Karen, Jess, and Olivia, thanks for all the hard work you do on my behalf. I must increase your chocolate rations this year. Also, thanks to Phoebe Yeh, the first to see the potential in our vigilante photographer.

To the We Need Diverse Books crew: Ellen, Aisha, Marieke, Ilene, Miranda, and the rest. You rock, and the world agrees.

This book features a number of technical details that exist well outside of my purview. Before I thank those who lent their expertise, the disclaimer: If it's right, it's on them, if it's wrong, it's on me. Got it? Good.

C. S. Ling, you're my favorite wildlife photographer and I was blown away when you agreed to answer my (likely tedious) questions. If Panda ever gets her stuff together, she'd be wise to look you up.

Maika McGlone, thank you for your help on the German. Me and my translation program were set to screw that all up—like we did when Panda was half Italian.

Erin Jade Lange, I really appreciate you schooling me on how television reporters deal with hot button teen issues. I still embellished a bit (forgive me), but I couldn't have done that without the foundation you laid.

James "Brother Jay" Spence, thanks for a peek into the administrative side of schools. The kids are lucky to have you.

Dr. Gary Moss, Dr. Carole Norton, and Dr. John Jane—thank you for telling me a bit about how traumatic head injuries work (if the injured party is as lucky as Ocie).

Now, the lightning round. Special thanks to the extended Giles and Brown families; Mr. and Mrs. Green; Jennifer Bosworth; Meg Medina; Gigi Amateau; Becky Rodgers Boyette; Tara Franzetti, the Hopewell branch of the Appomattox Regional Library System; Patti Parker, Betty Ware, Hopewell High School; Thomas, Melissa, and Amelia Goodwin; Crystal Hunter; Ariane Aramburo and the Hampton Roads Show; Lin Oliver, Sara Rutenberg, and SCBWI; Lisa Hartz, Michael Khandelwal, Alicia Wright Dekker, and the Muse Writers Center; ODU MFA program; Lana Krumwiede and James River Writers; Juanita Giles, Suzy Palmer and Longwood University; NovaTeen; Prince Books, Fountain Books, bbgb Books, Chop Suey books (really, all indie booksellers); the Chesapeake chapter of Sisters in Crime; and, last but not least . . .

You.